THE DEEPFAKE

THE DEEPFAKE

a novel

JOAN COHEN

SHE WRITES PRESS

Published 2024
Printed in the United States of America
Print ISBN: 978-1-64742-606-4
E-ISBN: 978-1-64742-607-1
Library of Congress Control Number: 2023915562

For information, address:
She Writes Press
1569 Solano Ave #546
Berkeley, CA 94707

Interior Design by Tabitha Lahr

She Writes Press is a division of SparkPoint Studio, LLC.

For Heidi, Reuben, Nikki, and Seth

"Our lives are fashioned by our choices. First we make our choices. Then our choices make us."

—ANNE FRANK

CHAPTER 1

I should have known something was wrong as soon as I pulled into the lot at Oak Tree Office Park. Sam never arrived at work before me, yet there was his black BMW in the row closest to the building. It was easy to spot with its glittering hubcaps, like a woman in a black satin gown wearing too much jewelry. As soon as I stepped from my car, I heard my cell phone trilling its heart out in my purse. At that hour, it was unlikely the MacArthur Foundation was calling to award me its genius prize, so I let the message go to voicemail.

Slave to ritual that I was, I never started my workday at AI*future* without stopping first for coffee at Rebecca's Café, the cafeteria in the lobby of my building. I cared little for the Zen of technology creation and experienced no euphoria from the latest Lilliputian wonders etched on a chip of silicon. What I loved was selling artificial intelligence software, which I really believed in, although no matter what the product was, persuading people to buy was the fun part.

The café was stocked with fresh pastries each morning, so I followed the scent of cinnamon, stopping just long enough to fill a large cup with French roast coffee. The cafeteria was nearly empty except for two young temps stuffing envelopes at a front table, the motion of their hands interrupted only by the tossing of their long locks, as though gravity could be intimidated by sheer repetition. Their position afforded them a view of the new BodySculpt gym entrance across the lobby. "Wow, he's hot," I heard one of them comment, and my gaze followed theirs.

Two broad-shouldered physical trainers were greeting clients in the gym's reception area. Sam, a fellow sales rep from AI*future*, appeared at my side.

"What's the attraction?" he asked, his eyes following my gaze to the BodySculpt entrance. "Nice to see you noticing, Sylvie. I thought you'd taken a vow of abstinence after your divorce."

"Not abstinence—selectivity."

"Right." He turned toward the pastry case and stopped. "Can we grab a few minutes together when you come upstairs? I tried to get you on your cell, but you didn't answer." I was not in the frame of mind yet to deal with Sam's problem, for with Sam there was usually a problem. I had learned not to discount his concerns, though, since he sometimes saw trouble coming before I did. I assured him I'd meet with him as soon as I came upstairs.

I paid for my coffee and crossed the lobby slowly enough to allow my eyes to linger on the gym entrance. Maybe I was a candidate for some weight work or cardio. If I felt old at thirty-four, what would I feel like in a decade? In two decades, I'd be a fossil.

I wasn't a total neophyte. I had tried jogging years before when Ashton had decreed I should be fit. His motivation was an insufficient replacement for my own, however, so I gave up on exercise, gave up on the whole marriage while I was at it. *Wouldn't he love to think I was falling apart without him to push me?*

"Are you here for an appointment?"

"Just some information. I've been considering joining a gym." I hadn't planned to start my day talking to people in tracksuits, but a little bit of spontaneity couldn't be bad.

The young man behind the counter extracted a brochure and rate card from a display rack and proffered them ceremoniously, like a Japanese businessman offering his card. "We assign personal trainers to all our clients. Do you have specific physical concerns you'd like to share?"

"Not physical." I hesitated, while he fixed quizzical blue eyes on my face. "To be honest, the only question I have is whether I can stick to an exercise program. I have so little time and such a poor track record with gym memberships. My ex-husband used to say I was the best thing that ever happened to the fitness industry. I'd pay for a year and stop after three months."

"You're hardly unusual." He laughed. "People never think they can make time for exercise. When they have appointments scheduled, though, exercise becomes part of their routine."

"Good pitch," I said. I always had my eye out for clever sales technique.

"Thanks, but my wife tells me I'm not allowed to pitch anything ever again, at least not to her. She had seven-pound twins last month." When he grinned, I realized he was younger than his red beard and mustache made him appear and wondered if that was the purpose they served. His jaw line was rounded, and he seemed too pleasant to hound anyone into a state of fitness. He extended his hand across the desk and introduced himself as Rob Linde.

The gym did look inviting, not like the industrial-strength facilities Ashton had found for me with their rubber floors, heavy metal music, and muscle-bound clientele. The floor was carpeted, the music pleasant, and in the brightly lit room full of weights and equipment, a woman and a man were working out with trainers. The clients wore shorts and T-shirts, not thongs and spandex.

As a dark-haired trainer in a navy tracksuit approached the desk, I noticed his gait, surprisingly graceful for his stocky, powerful frame. His eyes were hazel beneath unruly brows and curly hair, and his square jaw was covered by a fashionable stubble. Rob made introductions, and I shook a meaty hand, which seemed a strange accompaniment to a preppy name like "Fielding Harris" that would have fit one of Ashton's friends from the country club. "Fielding," Rob said, "tell Sylvie how we make sure our clients don't give up on their exercise programs."

"Can't commit to a relationship with a gym? We have ways to change that."

"Try a single session on the house," Rob suggested. "We're running a promotion for ninety days, but I have to tell you, we expect to reach capacity quickly."

"And you don't want to be on our waiting list," Fielding added. "We make people run laps around the parking lot until there's an opening." He had a good deadpan delivery. The two of them looked at me expectantly.

"Do you double-team all your prospective clients?"

Rob smiled. "Only when we think they want to be convinced. Rip and I go back to a time way before I started BodySculpt."

"Rip?" I asked.

"Old baseball nickname. I was a hitter. Rob was the bat boy." Fielding dodged as Rob pulled a punch. "You can call me Rip if you sign up. Otherwise, it's 'Mr. Harris.'"

Maybe it was the prospect of sharing their banter, maybe the influence of the young women in Rebecca's Café who'd made me feel ancient. "Okay," I said. "I'll try it." Rip marked me in the appointment book for 6:00 p.m., Monday. I caught sight of the clock and remembered Sam waiting upstairs.

■ ■ ■

As soon as I'd stowed my purse in a desk drawer and set up my laptop, he appeared in my doorway. He beckoned, so I followed him to the empty conference room between sales and support, where he closed the door behind us and walked to the far end of the polished walnut table before taking a seat.

More often than not, Sam's face wore an appealing gap-toothed smile that made me suspect he charmed his customers into writing purchase orders. Not only had his smile disappeared, but his sleeves had been carelessly rolled, his top button was open, and his tie knot was skewed southwest of his Adam's apple.

"What's with the agita?" I asked.

"I was ringing your cell," he began, "to give you a heads-up. Richard fired Manny last night."

"For what?" I sank back in my chair, deflated by the news. Sam and I both worked for Manny, a talented sales executive I admired. He was my mentor, sharing his knowledge and skill at selling software. Manny reported directly to our CEO. "I can't imagine why Richard would let him go, especially with no warning. It's not as though Manny set the building on fire."

"No, but maybe he stuck his nose in where it didn't belong. Something's going on, something that won't be good for you or me, and maybe not for a lot of other people in this company. Maybe we're getting acquired. I wouldn't be surprised if Richard raised our sales quotas."

Now I was the one with agita. I'd been doing well, but I didn't see myself spinning straw into more gold. "What would make Richard do that in the middle of the year? Isn't that unusual?"

"He could justify it if engineering finished NewAI like Warren promised. There's definitely pent-up demand for it." He sneered. "Fat chance Warren will accomplish that though."

What a cynic Sam was, although he had better instincts than I did about company politics. I'd trusted Richard, thought he was a good CEO. My ex used to warn me that trusting people to do the right thing would bite me in the ass: *In business, politics isn't* part *of your job. It* is *your job.* I could picture his smirk and wagging finger. What a relief to be free of that pedantic coaching. Ashton could play Svengali to someone else or, better yet, go screw himself. I was out of that business.

"You'll never make it without my help," Ashton had said when we signed the divorce papers. "I made you what you are." Just remembering that made me burn. How naive I had been signing that prenup. He told me his dad had made his brothers use prenups too, insisting that after ten years, we'd know if our relationship could go the distance. His dad said he'd be damned if gold-digger chippies were going to abscond with his sons' inherited wealth.

What a crock. I figured that out when Ashton filed for divorce after nine and a half years. I was left with limited means and limited self-esteem, exactly what I'd brought to the marriage.

CHAPTER 2

I hung up my suit and stowed my heels in one of the oak lockers that lined two walls of the BodySculpt women's dressing area. After changing into shorts, a T-shirt, and running shoes, I pulled my hair back into a skimpy ponytail, patting down the wayward wisps escaping the scrunchie.

After surveying the room to check for observers, I assessed myself in the floor-length mirror, breath sucked in and elbows bent in the classic weightlifter's pose. I exhaled with disappointment. No one would mistake me for an Olympian. As I emerged from the locker room, Rip beckoned. "Let's sit in Rob's office for a few minutes and get the paperwork out of the way."

Paperwork? I wasn't sure I wanted to commit myself to paper.

He asked for my address and phone number.

"You need that for a trial session?"

"If you keel over during your workout, which happens all the time, you know, where are we going to dump the body? And while we're on the subject, how old would the body be?"

I groaned and gave him my address and phone number in Needham. "I'm thirty-four going on ninety."

"I'm thirty-four too, but I feel like I've got two-thirds of my life left, so I guess your objectives for your exercise program should include having more energy."

"Objectives? I need a plan for my next fiscal year of exercise?"

"Are you always this cranky? Don't make me pull out my tranquilizer gun."

"I'm sorry. I'm a little on edge. I'll behave."

"You'd better. Don't forget the laps around the parking lot. Okay, objectives?"

"Well, I guess I'd like to be stronger and in better shape." *Lame*, I thought. It wasn't like me to grope for words, but his gaze distracted me. I expected him to take note of my pathetic biceps and triceps. Instead, he sat silent, assessing me, it seemed, from the inside out.

"Drink a lot of caffeine, do you?" He didn't wait for an answer. "What about your diet? Do I need to refer you to our nutritionist?"

"I don't really feel like eating in the morning, just coffee. Are you a trainer or an internist?"

"You seem a little jittery. That's why I asked about the coffee. Do you get enough sleep?"

"Let's not go there."

"Don't need to. I can see the dark circles from here." He stood. "Let's get started. Tonight's session will be part evaluation, part giving you a taste of what the program would be like if you signed up. Most people find it invigorating."

"I'm too tired for 'invigorating.'"

"Well, then, let's just aim for keeping you awake."

He started me on the treadmill and worked his way around the room, explaining the purpose of each exercise and the form to maintain for optimal benefit. I found the gray metal architecture of the exercise stations reassuringly solid. Footrests were right where I needed, hand grips where I instinctively reached to brace myself. He instructed me which muscles to focus on, but the machines isolated the correct ones, keeping me on the physical straight and narrow.

I could have done without the mirrors lining the walls.

I knew they were there so that clients could see if they were doing their exercises correctly, but I couldn't help feeling they were sitting in judgment. Though Rip kept the weights light and the repetitions few, I worried that if I failed to control the weight on the resistance machines, I would be snapped forward, back, up, or down.

"This may sound irrational, but are these machines safe?"

"We haven't crushed any noses or launched anyone butt-first so far. Your muscles will take care of you."

"These? I've got less muscle than a lox."

He laid a mat on the floor and told me to lie down. "There's no such fish as a lox. Lox is smoked salmon. You sound like my father."

"Your father lacks muscle and eats lox?"

He laughed. "I dare you to say that ten times fast." He showed me how to position my hands and bend my legs to begin a set of abdominal crunches. "My father was a rabbi in Brooklyn, lox-and-bagels country. He's gone now."

My words came out in spurts while I worked to finish the set of fifteen. "I'm sorry, Rip. I don't mean to get personal, but the name 'Fielding' doesn't sound like a boy out of Brooklyn."

"As a kid, my dad was a rabid Dodgers fan, at least before the team moved to Los Angeles in 1958."

I hoped he'd let me lie still while he talked. No such luck. He showed me how to work my obliques and motioned me to begin. "How do you talk and count at the same time?" I asked.

He grinned. "Secrets of the trade. C'mon, get started." I began my next set. "Dad particularly admired Pee Wee Reese, who was both a great shortstop and friend to Jackie Robinson. Given that Pee Wee came from a poor white family out of rural Kentucky, you'd expect him to be suspicious of unfamiliar ethnic groups, at least back then. He turned out to be a real mensch. Know what that means?"

Thanks to my friend Eileen, with her penchant for appropriating useful phrases from other languages, I was up on my Yiddish. "Uh-huh," I grunted.

"When I was born, Dad thought about naming me 'Pee Wee' but, mercifully, he decided to go with 'Fielding' instead. Our relatives told him it was a waspy name, but Dad didn't care. He said the Dodgers had great fielding, and he knew for a fact that God was a Dodgers fan." Rip motioned me to stop.

"Finally! So, how did he react when the Dodgers moved to LA?"

"Dad or God?"

"Both." I laughed.

"My father was heartbroken, but he explained that God had given human beings free will, and they didn't always use it to make the best choices."

"No, we don't, do we." I couldn't keep a mournful note out of my voice.

He cocked his head. "We can only schedule discussions of free will for clients' cardio warm-up time on the elliptical trainer. That's policy. You need to sign up for more sessions."

I was tired, as Rip had predicted, but the workout had been satisfying. His snappy comebacks were fun. For a short while, I hadn't thought about my work pressures or how tight for cash I was. "How can I say no to a rabbi's son, one who's no less than the spiritual heir to Pee Wee Reese? I'll go with the six-session package and see where we are at the end of it."

He smiled and gave me a thumbs-up.

Wait till I see Eileen, I thought as I crossed the parking lot. I knew she'd be proud of me, given that her definition of exercise included the physical proximity of attractive single men.

■ ■ ■

Parking in Coolidge Corner was available only to those with infinite time and patience, so instead I left my car at the Riverside

Station in Newton and hopped on the T, changing trains at Cleveland Circle. By the time I'd walked up Beacon Street to the Green Scene, it was 7:30 p.m., and I was fifteen minutes late.

Eileen had taken a table with a clear view of the door and was halfway through her first Cabernet Sauvignon. She lifted her glass to toast me and shook her long brown hair off her shoulders. "L'chaim." Eileen was not Jewish, but toasting in other languages was her hobby. She claimed it enhanced her sense of festivity. "I think it means 'get a life,'" she said.

I sat down across from her. "It means 'to life,' and I have one. I help turn the wheels of commerce."

Eileen grabbed my wrist to take my pulse. "Nope, just as I suspected. You're a zombie."

Reclaiming my wrist, I stuck out my tongue at her. A waiter in a white apron, pad in hand, appeared beside me and took my order for a glass of Pinot Grigio. Eileen sipped her wine with her pinky in the air. She wore a mood ring on her index finger, a necklace of crystals around her neck, and a sweater sewn together from chenille patches. She was as dependably funky in her appearance as I was tailored.

"How does a massage therapist afford the fancy French stuff?" I asked, lifting my water glass and waving my pinky. "Got Bill Gates as a client?"

"As a matter of fact, business has been excellent lately. Must be something to this marketing stuff." Although I had no formal training, I had designed an ad for her and advised a few strategic placements in local publications. "Got any more ideas?" she asked.

The waiter placed a stem glass in front of me, and I sipped gratefully, surveying the trompe l'oeil vegetable garden on the wall beside me. "Hmm, who did you say was paying?" I asked, surveying the menu.

"You'd stick me with the check just because you shared a few marketing pearls? What happened to friendship?"

"People don't value what they get for free, you know. I'm a professional."

Eileen's eyebrow rose.

"Well, maybe I'm not in marketing, but you pick up a lot of that stuff in sales. Besides, you can write off the dinner as a business expense now that you're flush."

"Okay. You win. I'll pick it up, but you're having the children's portion of sprouts, and that's it."

I didn't like sprouts. No matter how they were arranged on the plate, they always appeared out of control, and at the moment, I identified too closely with the haywire greens to enjoy them. I decided on free-range, humanely slaughtered roast chicken, accompanied by organically raised sugar snap peas and brown rice. Eileen ordered some sort of Asian fusion dish with oysters.

"You really should try this," she said, pointing at her plate. "Good for your sex drive. I don't need it, since I handle flesh for a living, but you must miss it."

"Oysters Orientalia?"

She menaced me with her fork. "You know I meant sex. Who does a guy have to be for you to hook up with him?"

"Mr. Perfect, apparently. When Ashton Manhardt and I started dating, that's what my friends called him. He was an MIT graduate who had an in-depth knowledge of artificial intelligence. He'd parlayed that into a consulting business until a venture capital company recruited him, not that he needed their money. He was born to wealth. For my mother, nothing else mattered."

I went on. "Ashton was good-looking in a bland sort of way, pale with watery blue eyes and light brown hair. My mother was ready to throw a net over him. Sometimes you have to live with a person, though, to find out how big an asshole he can be. It never occurred to me that he thought I was close to perfect as well, an idea that destined us for disillusionment. Whatever I lacked, he planned to remediate."

Eileen beckoned to the waiter and ordered two more glasses of wine. "Boy," she said, "I'd like to meet someone who thought I was perfect. The guy I went out with last week told me my eyebrows arched in the wrong place. Remind me never to date a cosmetic surgeon again."

"Don't kid yourself. It's a burden being perceived as flawless, and, in my case, it didn't last. Ashton decided to address whatever required improvement. I could never meet his standards, so my value diminished daily. He got bored with his project." I finished my wine in one swallow, handing my glass to the waiter and picking up the fresh one he placed in front of me.

Eileen cocked her head and extended her arm toward my face, thumb sticking up from her fist at eye level. "I'm trying to find your best angle and determine how you could be improved."

I batted down her hand. "See this skin? Dermabrasion every six months to smooth it." I offered my wrist to be sniffed, and Eileen feigned a swoon. "That sophisticated, heavenly scent akin to some exotic flower is Chanel Grand Extrait. Costs more than I make in a year. Feel my sleeve."

Eileen obliged, running her finger across the downy wool. "Mmm."

"The finest cashmere. I came to the marriage with acrylic and rayon and left with silk and satin."

"I highly recommend hemp if you're in the market for new clothes. It'll give you more of a wholesome earth mother look. He didn't make you have cosmetic surgery, did he?"

"No, but did I mention my blond hair wasn't light enough for him, so off to the hairdresser for platinum with lowlights. Too bad I didn't come with one of those tags warning that irregularities are characteristic of the natural beauty of the weave." I dabbed at my eyes with my napkin.

"Did you ever read Nathaniel Hawthorne in school?"

"You mean like *The Scarlet Letter*?"

"The nuns didn't like that one, because they didn't want us to feel sorry for Hester Prynne. No, I mean his short stories. There's one, 'The Birth-Mark,' that I swear was written about you and Ashton. Seriously, check it out, and while you're at it, give yourself a break. You have such expectations of yourself—at work, at home. You think each day will be better than the last. People's emotions don't recover like that." She wagged her finger at me. "When you push your emotions down, they pop out somewhere else like a hernia." She sipped her drink. "When was Ashton's birthday?

"January 18. Why?"

"I knew it—a Capricorn—status-conscious. You have to learn to pay attention to these things." For the next hour, Eileen admonished me to "find my center" and get in touch with my feelings. She diagnosed me with post-divorce stress syndrome—yes, one could still have it after three years. As usual, her solution was sex, preferably accompanied by romance. From my perspective, it would take both to meet the criteria of necessary and sufficient for cure.

"Remember that accountant from Newton we met at O'Hara's," she asked, "the one who was so shy he didn't have the nerve to ask for your number? Why don't you call him? I bet he's not always that stiff—or maybe he is." She raised an eyebrow, and I threw my napkin at her. "Wait, wait, I know. I have a new client, an interior designer who specializes in Feng Shui. Invite him over for a drink and ask him to look at your bedroom. Maybe he'll rearrange your bedsheets for you." She threw the napkin back at me.

"That's it. I'm leaving."

"Without paying *l'addition*?" She pushed the check toward me, and we agreed to split it.

"Don't expect any more marketing advice."

"Why? My advice is free."

"Free, plentiful, and unsolicited. When I was just your

massage client, I used to leave our sessions with my back relaxed and my ears exhausted."

"Good." She rapped me on the head with her knuckles. "That's where the knots are."

The wind had picked up, blowing hard from the northeast. I turned up the collar of my camel coat, and Eileen tried to wrap her flowing scarf around her neck while the wind blew it the opposite way. Winter was trying to rush fall out the door. Waiting at the T stop promised to be bone-chilling, so she suggested we walk around the corner and pick up a couple of cappuccinos at Starbucks to fortify ourselves.

My coffee came immediately, but we had to wait for Eileen's half-decaf cappuccino with soy milk and two shots of vanilla. I lifted my cup. "Here's an example of marketing for you: 'small' is called 'tall.' Starbucks turns language on its head, and the consumer accepts it. What's a 'venti'? Does anyone outside of Italy know?"

Steam rose from the holes in our dome lids as we walked up to the T stop, where a train soon rumbled to a halt. Once we were settled in our seats, Eileen asked about my plans for Thanksgiving.

"My mother asked me to fly down and join her and Luis, but I haven't committed myself."

"Yeah," Eileen said. "You wouldn't catch me dead on a gorgeous seaside estate beneath swaying palm trees. Who'd want to be around rich Cuban hotties for the holiday."

"Luis's sons and I have nothing in common." My neck muscles tightened in response to the lie. There were things Eileen didn't know about the years before we met, and I wasn't ready to share them.

"Bet you could find something if you worked at it."

"I'll tell you what I'm working at. I joined a gym." Riverside would be the last stop, so I chattered about my exercise program till we reached our destination. We hugged goodbye in the parking lot, laughing at our purple complexions under the halide lights. Once inside my car, I turned on the ignition and closed my eyes, waiting for the heated seat to warm my back. Cuban hotties, accountants—only my pillow would seduce me that night.

CHAPTER 3

Richard Dior was absorbed in something on his laptop. I knocked softly on his open door. While I waited for him to notice me, his inverted reflection on his highly polished mahogany desktop reminded me of Sam's assessment of Richard: a corporate duck, all dapper feathers on the surface with legs paddling like crazy beneath. Early on, I'd found Sam's irreverence surprising, but I was beginning to think I had confused respect for Richard's office with respect for the man.

I had been summoned, unaccountably, at lunchtime, which made my appetite disappear. Richard didn't usually meet with sales reps. The vertical blinds on his windows divided the outside world into manageable slices, and a brown leather couch and two upholstered blue armchairs defined a formal seating area to the left of the door. The mahogany coffee table, standing on a small handmade Oriental rug, held the *Wall Street Journal* and a tray with a china coffee pot and four mugs I was sure had never been used.

"Richard," I began tentatively. "You wanted to talk to me?"

"Indeed. Join me." He motioned toward his oval conference table, where his administrator, Fannette, had placed a plate of sandwich quarters with assorted fillings, two bottled waters, paper plates, and napkins. Once seated at the table,

Richard offered me first pick. I left the roast beef sections for him and took the tuna.

He chewed deliberately, and the creases in his face moved in concert. He was tan and deeply wrinkled, more from sun damage than age, which gave him the weathered aspect of a corporate outdoorsman. Translation: golf addict. He had monogrammed cuffs cinched by monogrammed links to remind others, if not himself, I supposed, who he was. He smoothed the top of his graying hair to keep the bald spot covered and cleared his throat. “I have some good news for you, Sylvie. I’m promoting you, both you and Sam. You’ll become US sales executive, and Sam, European sales executive.”

I was rigid, stunned. I had been worried about the implications of Manny’s firing and whether he was only the first domino to fall. A promotion was not an outcome I’d anticipated, and I wondered if I were worthy of a VP position. Ashton had planted those misgivings in my thoughts. I pushed them away. If Richard thought I should be a sales executive, that was proof enough of my ability.

I couldn’t help worrying, though, what the effect of my battlefield promotion would be on the other sales reps. My former peers would report to me. Could I push them for revenue, or would they resent me? I needed to think this through, but Richard wasn’t finished. “I want you to encourage your reps to go after sales opportunities that can close faster. It’s always nice to land a big fish, but it takes too long. Instead, go for the low-hanging fruit.” I winced at the mixed metaphor.

He went on about how the increasing revenue would make AI*future* larger than life. I could always tell when he was in performance mode. Even his casual conversations were presentations, which made him sound like a Stepford husband. *Great.* I was supposed to make the company look larger than life: venti AI*future*.

"Sylvie, you're a talented sales professional who I have no doubt can get the job done. It's time to take the gloves off." He patted my coupled hands with a paternalism that put my teeth on edge.

"Venture capitalists have no patience," he continued, "with portfolio companies that underperform." Richard rubbed his thumb over an invisible smudge on his cufflink. I knew he was alluding to Tory Partners, Ashton's venture capital firm, which had a seat on our board. If Richard was trying to keep me off balance, it was working. "I have full confidence in you. I'm sure you'll deliver on US revenue." He left off "or else," but the unspoken message hung in the air.

He stood up and carried his plate around to the trash basket behind his desk. The meeting was over, so I cleared my napkin and cup and swiped the crumbs from both our places onto my plate.

"I'd like to pull the executive team together," he added, "at 10:00 a.m., tomorrow."

CHAPTER 4

I surveyed the flock of executives around Richard's conference table. I had positioned myself as far away from Floyd Buckley and his halitosis as I could. His amorphous personality went with his features, as chiseled as yesterday's farina. He was an old-fashioned personnel manager, great at wage curves, medical benefits, and 401(k) issues, but with no clue how to assume his rightful role as an advisor to Richard or trusted confidante of employees.

Kate O'Hara, recently hired to run customer services, sat across from me. She exuded color—blue eyes, pink complexion, tight auburn curls. A tailored navy suit tried without success to impose linearity on her curves, although her cleavage more than peeked out from her V-neck blouse. When I'd met Kate during her interview cycle at AI*future*, her feistiness had appealed to me straight off. Manny, who had been traveling that day, asked me to interview her. I was impressed with her eagerness to take on the challenge. She wasn't the least bit intimidated by the scope of her newly created position.

"Kate, how's the consolidation going?" our CFO Harold Astrove asked, adjusting his wire-rimmed glasses. From the direction of Harold's gaze, I guessed he was more interested in how Kate was put together than her department.

"Persuading the consultation, education, and support teams to work together won't be easy," she replied, "but I think I can whip them into shape."

I felt Harold quiver beside me at the mention of whipping.

First on Richard's agenda was announcing that Sam and I were joining the executive team. After dredging up some worn superlatives to describe our past performances, he went on to surprise us with the unwelcome news that our sales quotas were going up. Sam had been right. My promotion would be short-lived if my reps and I didn't make quota. I wasn't at all sure there was enough "low-hanging fruit."

I hoped Sam wouldn't lose his cool, but he erupted. "Our sales force is selling stuff that's so old, the customer base reads the AARP newsletter instead of *Wired*. When are we going to get NewAI out of engineering? If we had a hot new product to sell, maybe you could justify higher quotas. There's definitely pent-up demand for it." He sneered. "Fat chance Warren will get it done."

Floyd cleared his throat. "Now, Sam, let's not make this adversarial. Management teams have to work together. Think of a pitcher, a catcher, a first baseman . . ." His words hung in the air, a pitch arcing between the mound and the plate. Kate looked at me and rolled her eyes. What on earth had made Floyd choose human resources? He was the weakest conciliator imaginable. At least the interruption defused some of the rancor, or perhaps Sam realized he was out of line. Our engineering VP, Warren Malik, wasn't even in the room. There was no profit in Sam's blowing up in this meeting.

Sam was fidgeting in his chair, so I knew he wasn't finished. "I have another concern. Sales reps have always been able to sell consulting services to their customers who need help implementing our software. Now Kate tells me we can't do that anymore. She's taking that on." He pointed at Kate. "She said sales reps would no longer be paid commissions on selling consulting services." His voice rose along with his indignation. "Higher quotas and less to sell—how's that going to work?"

Richard's demeanor was stern. "I've decided there's no need for the sales force to spend time selling consulting services now that we have Kate."

I could practically see the steam rising from Sam's collar. "That wasn't my understanding when you hired her. What incentive do my sales reps have to bring Kate into their accounts?"

Richard's face contorted with anger. "They'll get to keep their jobs. Is that enough of an incentive?" The conference room was still until Richard continued in a calmer voice. "With Kate beefing up our services offering, the sales reps will have an easier time focusing on product revenue. We have other matters to discuss this morning, folks. Harold, are you ready?"

Harold rolled up his shirtsleeves. The hairs on his arms were as sparse as the pinstripes on his trousers. He handed each executive a set of spreadsheets. "As you can see, we've revised our goals upward."

Richard interrupted. "I have full confidence in the sales organization. Sam and Sylvie just need to take the gloves off."

I wondered if Richard were going to pat Sam's hand, as he had mine, and advise him not to be too nice.

Richard allowed Harold to finish his presentation and ended the meeting. I wanted to talk to Sam, but he was the first one out the door. I figured he wasn't done venting, so marketing or engineering was his logical destination. When sales reps are worried about finding new prospects, they either want sexier technology to sell or marketing campaigns targeting new customers. Getting both is even better.

I went to software engineering first. Though Warren had missed Richard's meeting, I thought he might have returned to the office. Sam stood in Warren's doorway with his back to me and his hands on his hips. I was able to slip by him. Warren was leaning against the metal bookcase under his window, arms crossed. He looked relaxed in jeans, sneakers, and a black T-shirt. His eyes, deep-set under a prominent brow, revealed no emotion. His shadowed jowls completed a near silhouette against the window's steel-framed white sky.

"Sam, I suggest you worry less about how old our products are and more about finding new customers."

"Piece of cake, Warren. You think selling is so easy? I'd like to see your engineers live on a sales rep's base salary just for the chance at a big commission. What's the matter? No risk-takers?"

No longer relaxed, Warren took a step toward Sam. I drew back. Even Floyd Buckley would have been helpful at that moment. "I'd like to see one of your sales reps try creating just one artificial intelligence application, maybe between filing padded expense reports." Warren finished with a nasty laugh, and I pulled Sam out into the hall on the pretext of squeezing in a conversation before my next meeting.

It was a short conversation, since I opened with, "What the fuck?"

"One of these days, I'm going plant my fist in that guy's mouth." He brushed past me to avoid the admonition he knew would follow.

CHAPTER 5

The next day, just before noon, I stopped into the ladies' room where I encountered Kate washing up. Before I could enter a stall, she touched my arm and looked under each of the doors before speaking. "Yesterday's meeting . . . tell me you're not booked for lunch today."

"Tightly scheduled," I said, "but I'm definitely going to eat."

"Let's go across to Legal Seafood. I need to get out of this building."

Half an hour later, Kate and I were seated at a small table at the back of the restaurant. Cobalt blue and ivory tiles and young green plants gave the room a freshness that on any other day would have taken our minds off work. Kate's face brightened as the waitress set down her glass of Kendall Jackson Chardonnay on the white tablecloth.

"Sure you don't want anything?" she asked me.

"No, thanks. I'll just nurse my designer water and lime." Jazz from a speaker overhead mixed with the exclamations of shoppers admiring each other's purchases and the subdued buzz of conferring businesspeople. It was hard not to notice that Kate consumed her wine in two swallows.

"I don't usually drink at lunch," she began. "Is it me, or did the rest of the senior management team work previously on another planet, and how come that evil alien, Warren Malik, wasn't at the meeting?" Kate's blue eyes were wide, her auburn hair looked electric, and as she leaned across the table, I observed once again the serious cleavage on display at the top of her pink sweater.

"Warren's not the warmest guy, you're right, but he really is an asset to the company. Brilliant, 4.0 out of Caltech."

"You're defending him?"

"Warren's technology set this company apart. Does Sam have a point? Sure. Warren let our products age for too long before starting NewAI. On balance, though, I think Warren's worth the pain."

"Not to me, he isn't. I don't deal well with arrogant assholes."

"A bit of advice: you need to be careful what you say in public about Warren. Richard relies on his wisdom for everything related to technology."

Kate crossed her arms. "I'll try, but I grew up in Southie, not Beacon Hill like Richard. I went straight from breast milk to bourbon, and I'm used to telling it like it is. I don't trust Warren. When I first met Sam, I thought he could be my ally, but now he's all pissed off about sales reps losing commissions on selling services. He thinks it's my fault Richard took that away from him."

"It's Richard's call. No reason for anyone to be mad at you."

"It doesn't matter. I have my own ally." She seemed to enjoy my raised eyebrows and leaned across the table. "Please keep this to yourself, but I have something on Richard. He's borrowed money from the company to underwrite his wife's new florist business on Newberry Street."

"And you know that how?"

With a secretive smile, she sat back, made a circle of her thumb and forefinger, and poked her opposite middle finger through. I tried not to cringe, but I liked Kate less at the end of our lunch than at the beginning.

■ ■ ■

I worked into the evening as best I could, distracted by my brain's instant replay of our staff meeting. Sam may have been out of control, but I agreed with him. Given the number of software engineers we employ, it shouldn't be taking this long to get NewAI out the door. Manny might have known why, but he'd been fired. *Oh God, I'm turning into a conspiracy theorist.*

I hated thinking there were secrets at AI*future*. I liked to assume people's motives were pure, although I knew Ashton would have thought me naive. My new title and status were intimidating. I needed to create a sales plan I actually believed would work.

If the key to finding a partner at a singles bar was sex appeal, the key to finding a sales prospect was sexy technology, the veritable thong peeking out from the back of one's corporate jeans. Trouble was, without NewAI, we were buttoned-up and demure.

Frustrated, I pushed my chair back, causing it to travel several feet from my desk. Opening my blinds, I looked out into the darkness, opaque and disturbing with no sign of the perennially moving dots of light from the distant highway. I packed my briefcase and hurried from the building. A heavy haze filled the parking lot, which might as well have been a different country for all I could recognize. Pressing the button on my keyless entry, I found my car by its lights.

Once inside, I peered through the windshield at nothing but inscrutable fog, the kind that belonged in a Brontë novel, provoking the heroine's fear as she hurried across a Yorkshire moor clutching her shawl. America's Technology Highway was usually dominated by the dauntless, but tonight the fog ruled. Working late had been a mistake.

After spending my days and evenings in the corporate land of midnight fluorescence, the dark interior of my car usually soothed my restless senses. I bought it used after our prenuptial agreement separated me from most of what was left of our assets.

Though I tried to relax into the soft upholstery of the bucket seat, the fog demanded my attention. Provoked, I attacked the haze with my high beam, only to be defeated by the counterintuitive: the more light, the less illumination. An army of droplets deflected the assault. No visibility tonight—none.

My eyes burned from locking in on the yellow highway boundaries. They were my only guide through the fog, and I didn't appreciate their coyness about revealing what lay ahead. The exit for Highland Avenue was coming up.

I had lived in Needham only a year, and my landmarks would be enshrouded. I missed the comfort of heading home to a neighborhood where even the shadows were familiar. The Old Mill complex with its cookie-cutter apartments was less than welcoming. At least there were slippers and a fleecy blue robe and steaming lemon tea to look forward to.

When I was this tired, taking off my clothes felt like the start of a vacation. I lost no time climbing into pajama bottoms and a camisole—no more dressing up in the satin and lace confections Ashton purchased. Instead of Ashton, L.L.Bean wrapped me in a fleecy embrace as I secured my robe around me.

My version of brewing tea was microwaving a cup of hot water with a tea bag in it. I watched the carousel make slow circles while I leaned against the kitchen counter, tilted my head back, and practiced neck rolls the way Eileen had instructed. "Wrought iron," she'd observed when she first attempted to knead my rigid neck and shoulders.

"Wrought by my ex," I'd replied. Eileen dug deep to work the knots from my muscles and gave me exercises to do at home. It would take more than neck rolls, though, to relieve the tension Richard had created.

The microwave was still, and I carried my mug of tea to the living room desk. Relaxation was a delicious fantasy, a sliver of time between work and sleep that never satisfied the craving. I retrieved my briefcase, sat down, and before long was absorbed in reworking my sales plan. Hunched over, chin in hand, one leg tucked beneath me, I half-expected Dad to appear and call me "Pretzelita," the pet name he'd used when he found me folded into this pose. At thirteen, I made him swear not to utter the nickname outside our house, but I would have welcomed hearing it then, welcomed hearing the voice I'd never hear again.

An hour later, my eyelids were closing despite the tea, so I pushed away the piles and padded into the bedroom. A worn volume, *Wuthering Heights*, and a paperback on time management lay undisturbed on the nightstand. I slipped into bed and snuggled under the ivory wedding-ring quilt that had once been my mother's, its coziness my last sensation before slumber. I seldom remembered dreaming, but that night I stumbled lost across foggy moors. Where were the yellow lines to guide me? I found them at last, striping my quilt, rays of the sun stealing past the slats of my blinds.

CHAPTER 6

A few minutes before 6:00 p.m., I hitched my gym bag over my shoulder and made my way down to BodySculpt. Rob and Rip were discussing a client's chart when I passed the front desk. Three men were working out in the gym. One, soft and round as a dinner roll, pedaled his stationary bicycle and intently monitored his speed on the control pad. *A fellow neophyte*, I thought. The other two lay on mats finishing their sessions, one grunting his way through abdominal crunches, the other conversing earnestly with his trainer about a hip flexor stretch.

I had the locker room to myself while I changed into navy shorts and a white T-shirt, then sat on a bench to pull on socks and running shoes. Rob Linde's wife had a talent for decorating. In spite of the wall of lockers behind me, the room had the ambience of a spa, a touch of the Southwest in New England. A tray of hand and body lotions gave off the scent of desert flowers.

I stared unseeing at the clay-colored wall until Rip's knock startled me out of my mental fog. "Sylvie, I hope you're not asleep in there. It's past six."

I jumped up and yanked the door handle. "Sorry, it's been a long day. I'm a little out of it." I tugged at a crooked sock.

We started down the hallway toward the gym. "You're sure you want to go ahead with the session? If you're exhausted, we—"

"No, I'll be fine. I had a cup of coffee in the office before I came down."

He arched an eyebrow.

"Don't look at me that way, Dr. Wellness. I remember that quirky eyebrow from our last discussion of caffeine. I had—uh—a cup of chamomile tea. Perked me right up."

"Sure you did." He pointed to the elliptical trainer, so I stepped on and began pushing down on alternating feet as though I were standing up out of a bike seat to climb a hill. I gripped the handrails for balance. After five minutes, Rip's fingers moved across the machine's touch pad.

"Why is this getting harder?" I asked, trying to read the numbers flashing by on the display. My face was damp from the effort of maintaining my pace.

"I'm increasing the resistance to get your heart rate up."

"If my heart rate goes any higher, you'll need to call the paramedics."

"You just told me you felt perky. I'm sure you don't complain like this at work."

"I don't get this much resistance at work."

He paused as he reached for the clipboard that held my chart. "Pretty quick on your feet, aren't you? Should have started you on the treadmill." He handed me a towel and pointed to a heavy mat in the corner. "Since I'm seeing some attitude, you must be warmed up. We'll begin with stretches, same as last time."

I lay down, and he kneeled so he could push my right knee gently toward my chest. He was detached and professional, and I wondered if he were always able to focus on the biomechanics of women's bodies when he had his hands on them. No man had touched me since my divorce, unless, of course, you counted Richard's patting my hand and telling me I was too nice.

Rip let up the pressure. "Now the left knee."

Not that men hadn't tried. Eileen had set me up with a bearded yoga instructor who turned out to have a side interest in erotic poses. I was supposed to do the posing. He liked to watch. Sam had introduced me to an old college buddy whose ideas about sex were vintage fraternity party. Maybe I was just comparing them to my stepbrother. No way they could measure up, but then Carlos was a wild boy, a whole different story.

Rip put his hand on my right shin. "Now both."

Didn't I miss sex, Eileen had asked. Truth was, I missed hugs. It had been longer since I'd had one of those from a man who cared.

"Good," he said. "Stand up and stretch your quads."

I scrambled to my feet, put my left hand on the wall, and bent my right knee so I could reach back and grab my foot.

"You know this stretch?" he asked.

"I used to run."

"Oh yeah? What kind of distance?"

Great, I thought, *he's probably a marathoner*. "Not much, really, but I've been thinking about getting back into it. Took what I thought was a hiatus after my divorce, only the hiatus hasn't ended."

He smiled. "I'd like to work with you on your fitness program if you're serious about it. You've got a lot of potential. I would recommend you run four times a week and come to the gym twice." He motioned me over to the leg press, where he directed me to recline on the angled bench and position my feet up on the tilted metal plate supporting the machine's carriage. I pushed the carriage up and down slowly, following his instructions on pace and position. He nodded, warning me not to lock my knees when I straightened them. As he watched my quads, I watched him. He had a dimple in his chin enhanced by the chiaroscuro effect of his stubble. I focused on it to take my mind off my shaking muscles.

After we completed leg extensions, we moved on to hamstrings. He adjusted the weights on the machine, and I bent my knee behind me, raising the padded bar that lay on my lower calf. I was situated in front of the mirror and had ample time to observe my awkward position and pained expression. Rip's face was a study in concentration. The interplay of my muscles, tendons, and ligaments was an engineering problem for him.

I remembered what Eileen had said. She didn't need to enhance her sex drive because she worked with flesh all day. Why did Rip seemed so detached? He placed his fingers on my lower spine. "Don't let your back steal the exercise from your hamstrings." After I set down the weight and changed legs, he touched me again, riveting my attention on the point beneath his fingertips, hamstrings far from my thoughts.

I climbed off the machine quickly after the last repetition. "So, you're telling me compensating for one's weaknesses isn't positive?"

"Maybe upstairs in your office," he replied, laughing. "No cheating allowed down here. Let's see how you do with free weights."

I liked sitting sideways on the bench with my left hand on one knee and my right elbow braced as the pivot on the other. I watched my bicep rise and fall with each curl and imagined myself as Wonder Woman. The exercise was more difficult with my left arm. By the twelfth repetition, both Wonder Woman and I were faltering. Rip showed me how to lie on my back and work my triceps, but my arms shook after only a few reps.

"You're fading, aren't you?" he asked. "We just have abs left. Told you, caffeine is no substitute for sleep."

I groaned. "Dr. Wellness is back."

"I studied health and wellness in college, so I really can't help it," he said. "You don't seem to take care of yourself."

I sat up and straddled the bench. "I'm over the limit on guys who know what's good for me. My ex was relentless. Give it a rest, okay?" I felt guilty about bristling. He didn't mean to touch a nerve.

Rip looked as though he wanted to respond but thought better of it, subjecting me instead to one of his searching looks. "Why don't we just do some stretching, maybe even deep breathing exercises. We can skip your abs for now."

He gestured toward a corner where the floor was covered with black mats. Stepping onto one, I sank down and stretched out. The ceiling was an orderly checkerboard of acoustic tiles and fluorescent fixtures. Above it, I knew naked ducts, sweating pipes, and snaking wires writhed unseen—unseen like Ashton's inner thoughts. Why couldn't he have been more like the Pompidou museum in Paris, where the infrastructure shows on the outside of the building? I'd never have married him.

I tried to relax, breathing as Rip directed. Why had I exposed my pain to him like some neurotic housewife venting to her hairdresser?

"That's right, deep breaths. Let your body relax and feel heavy. Sink into the mat." After a couple of minutes of what seemed like sleep to me, although Eileen would have called it meditation, Rip spoke my name softly. When I opened my eyes, he extended his hand and pulled me up. "Still want to schedule more appointments?"

I was embarrassed about my earlier attack and nodded sheepishly as I followed him to the front desk. "Maybe you should consider a running session, Sylvie. Some of the trainers run outdoors with their clients for a cardio warmup. Given that you're considering running again, I think I could help you: monitor your stance, foot plant, arm motion, and pace, and I could advise you on how to set up the best program for your goals. Interested?"

"More of those pesky goals—let me think about it, okay?"

"Don't think about it for too long, or we'll miss out on the beautiful autumn weather."

"And I can't enjoy it without you?"

He grinned. "It won't be the same. Trust me."

CHAPTER 7

As I pushed open the glass doors into AI*future*'s reception area, Rona, who sat behind the front desk, greeted me with her usual nasal *good morning*. It had taken me a while to get past that intonation, more New York than Boston, and the pencil-lined, iridescent lips and midnight-black hair that projected a dance-club image I would not have chosen for our front office. Floyd Buckley knew a fox when he saw one, tawdry or not, but I had discovered Rona was pretty sharp and likely overqualified for her job.

The reception desk sat on a raised platform covered with gray tweed commercial-grade carpet. A metal AI*future* logo was mounted on the wall behind it. Creativity was lacking in our lobby decor. The walls were gray and a close match for the two vinyl-covered chairs that sat on either side of a gray laminate table displaying a *Boston Globe*—yesterday's. The two abstract prints on facing walls were standard motel room issue. Maybe Rona was just what the lobby needed.

"Sylvie, Rona." Sam acknowledged us as he entered the reception area. He had brought the outdoors in with him, cold air trapped in the folds of his trench coat. I thought heat was lost to cold and not the other way around, but Sam was impervious to the laws of nature. "Couldn't you hear me when

I called from my car?" Sam asked. "My cell connection kept breaking up. I wanted to know if you had open time today."

"Was that you? I thought the Chinese restaurant was confirming my lunch order."

Rona, always an obliging audience, laughed and covered her mouth with her hand. I was liking her more all the time.

"Don't encourage her, Rona."

"But I like Sylvie's sense of humor."

Sam wrinkled his nose, which made him look like an overgrown pug. I agreed to have coffee with him downstairs in the café at 10:30, which seemed to satisfy him. I wondered if I might have better luck than Sam at getting Warren to provide an update on NewAI. I didn't think Warren suspected my antipathy toward him and felt we had a more cordial relationship than he had with Sam.

Accounting and engineering shared the second floor, but traveling through the former on the way to the latter was like having lunch with bankers in Geneva and dinner on the Parisian Left Bank. My grandmother would have called software developers "Bohemian," but "crunchy granola," "geek," "propeller head," or just "out there" were more current. The engineers of Silicon Valley were reputed to work barefoot, but those who commuted through New England winters could ill afford that symbol of eccentricity. Despite that, I'd seen more than a few mismatched socks.

Technical people might not be any stranger than the rest of us, but I knew from my own experience the subtle pressure one feels in any department to conform, even to nonconformity. When I went into sales, acquaintances who had never doubted my integrity teased me about selling snake oil. I was proud, though, of "carrying a bag," "pounding the pavement," and "beating the bushes for orders."

Sales clichés were a shorthand for communicating with other reps, letting them know we shared one another's challenges. We were the ones who convinced customers our product provided value equal to the dollars they exchanged for it. Sometimes we even educated them. I couldn't understand why those who knew me failed to see my profession in that positive light.

Though salespeople were always on the move, leaving their cubicles empty on any given day, engineers could pass for mannequins, two to an office, transfixed by their monitors. The easy communication provided by the abbreviated walls of cubicles was an anathema to engineers, who needed quiet to maintain their concentration.

I heard footsteps behind me and watched Manfred Schmidt pass, turning his head to acknowledge me. He had pointed ears, and his hair was pulled into a man-bun like a wiry cottontail. He nodded at me with a jerk of his chin and pushed his glasses up on the bridge of his pink nose as he scurried ahead. If there were assertive engineers in Warren's department, I couldn't think of one. Threats to his authority were mysteriously "excessed" in the name of controlling expenses.

I knocked on Warren's open door to announce myself, then entered and sat in one of the guest chairs that faced him across his desk. He sat at a right angle to me, peering at the monitor on his turnaround, and quickly moved to minimize the page on his screen before returning my gaze.

Sitting close to Warren always made me wish I were further away. His scowling eyebrows pulled down to meet just above his beaklike nose. If there was any truth to the theory of reincarnation, Warren had been a hawk in his last life. I could well imagine his swooping down and carrying away a tabby cat to devour. I couldn't help glancing at his nails, but, no, he didn't have talons.

"I hope Sam hasn't been in your face since that unfortunate blowup." I wasn't sure my effort to distance myself from Sam would work. Warren knew we were friends.

"He's a hothead. I don't let people like that get to me," he responded with disdain.

I was offended on Sam's behalf, although Warren wasn't entirely wrong. Sam's temperament was combustible. "I know you think Sam's out of his lane pressuring you on the status of NewAI, but I'm here only to enlist your help. Richard's asking for faster sales cycles and increased revenue."

The hawk swooped down, and I could've sworn I heard the beating of wings. "Not a chance."

I tried again. "Warren, please. I'm a new executive, managing people who were my peers a day ago. I think I could get them to work with me if they knew it was a sprint, not a marathon, till they had NewAI. Can't you tell me anything at all I can use as an incentive?"

Warren's tone softened. "I can't help you, even though I can appreciate the difficulty of your position. Let's be honest here—you lack the experience to be a sales executive. Richard thought you were a promising novice, and he needed a replacement for Manny . . . someone more malleable."

Stung, I straightened my back. "'Malleable' as in flexible?"

He didn't answer, but with the faintest of smiles, he swiveled back to his screen.

■ ■ ■

Sam was already in the cafeteria sitting by the window when I came downstairs. I could see the autumn colors through the windows and felt a sudden desire to take Rip up on his offer to run together. Business offered few opportunities for spontaneity, however, so I headed toward Sam's table. I could still hear the starlings engaged in their ceaseless chirping and tried not to think of the hawk upstairs. The birds seemed a prescient Greek chorus. Tragedy was in the offing.

I looked at Sam's worried face and wondered if I could say or do anything to raise his spirits. I hoped his concerns were overblown. Since he had been my first friend at AI*future*, reaching out to me when I joined the company, numb from my divorce, I was fond of him. He had been through divorce himself and knew that even when a relationship is dreadful, its end feels like a profound loss.

I related my conversation with Warren. "Thought I might get further than you had with a tad more collegial approach, but instead he unloaded on me. There's no point in pressuring him."

Sam snorted. "Save your breath. I just found out NewAI's a wet dream. Got that from one of Warren's most loyal lieutenants, a guy who wants to get it right and knows it will take more resources. There's a side project no one knows about, and Warren has recruited my informant to work with him on this mystery software instead of NewAI. The engineer who confided in me was hoping someone outside engineering would lean on his boss." Sam ran his fingers through his gray-streaked hair. "Warren would put a dagger through the guy's heart if he knew." He sat back and sighed. "The problem with telling Richard, though, is that I don't think he wants to know. He'd have to take Warren on, and he doesn't have the balls. He doesn't know how to tie his shoes without Warren's help."

"Don't you think Richard knows? Maybe he's given Warren's side project his blessing."

Sam's neck was growing flushed above his shirt collar. "Doubt it. He's probably going to sell the company and leave us behind like flattened roadkill."

I noticed disturbed glances coming our way from a nearby table where two women with tablets next to their mugs were having a working coffee break. "We won't be roadkill," I whispered. "We have stock options that vest if there's a change of control."

He leaned across the table. "That's how it's supposed to work, but it all depends on the deal cut between the acquiring company and AI*future*. We might have to wait some period of time before we can sell, or we might be limited to selling a certain amount of stock at a time—all depends—and what if the stock tanks?"

Was I naive or was Sam just Chicken Little? I looked out at the starlings, wondering if they worried about the sky falling.

Maybe I didn't even belong in this business. Wasn't it just the selling part I enjoyed? I could be happy hawking bedsheets or barbells. New software products might dazzle more often than the sun shines, and the bouquet of stock options intoxicate, but I was amazed anyone could find inspiration in the 1.0 release of a software product to rival that of an autumn morning like this one.

■ ■ ■

That night, I couldn't stop thinking about Warren's words. He'd called me "malleable." Was that the trait that had attracted Ashton to me? Eileen had advised me to look up Hawthorne's story. I googled "The Birth-Mark" and found a summary.

Professor Aylmer, a scientist like Ashton, loved and married Georgiana. When he became obsessed with her singular flaw, a tiny red hand-shaped birthmark on her face, he devoted himself to removing it. After numerous experiments, he finally found a potion he was sure would work. Georgiana drank it, and as the birthmark faded, she died.

So much for chasing perfection, I thought, *without considering unintended consequences*. I didn't know if Eileen saw only the parallel of Aylmer's behavior to Ashton's, but I was struck instead by Georgiana's to mine. She had misgivings and only drank the potion because of how much it meant to Aylmer.

CHAPTER 8

Warren and Richard were fighting, their raised voices audible down the hall. Richard's administrator, Fannette, sat at her desk outside his office with her head cocked in their direction. She straightened up when she saw me approach.

Sam had dubbed her Little Annie Fannie after a *Mad Magazine* cartoon character from decades ago. Fannette lacked the curves of the cartoon Fannie, having a body that was all angles and a complexion pale as chalk, but that was the point. The nickname was unkind, not to mention sexist, but like many an unkind nickname, it stuck. Fannette jumped as Richard's office door slammed shut.

"Wow. What was that about?" I asked.

Fannette's eyes shifted like a squirrel's. Warren and Richard didn't argue, so this dispute was about something important to the company.

"I didn't mean to make you uncomfortable, but if you heard something that alarmed you, I'm happy to help. I can be a confidential sounding board."

Fannette nodded ever so slightly, her eyes downcast.

I walked down the hallway, wondering if there was really reason for worry or if I was just letting Sam spook me. *Nobody likes change*, Ashton had said. *You have to learn how to roll with it, Sylvie.* If only I could get his preaching out of my head.

Kate was new to the company, yet she seemed to know more than I did. I wondered who her ally could be. By her own admission, she used sex as a bargaining chip, so it had to be Harold, who trembled in her presence.

* * *

The next morning, I decided to confront Harold. I had no plans to seduce him, but my powers of persuasion might work. Warren's words still rankled. They were so reminiscent of Ashton's. *Malleable, my ass*, I said to myself as I approached Harold's office.

I found him staring at his monitor, his bony fingers wrapped around a mug of coffee. I didn't wait for an invitation but closed his door and pulled up a chair beside his desk. "I heard something disturbing about Richard, and I have to know if it's true. Please don't put me off. Did he borrow money from the company?"

His watery eyes widened. "How did you . . . ?"

"Don't ask. I just know, okay?"

He got up from his desk and walked to the window, leaving me to stare at his narrow back. When he turned, he seemed to have regained his composure. "Don't concern yourself, Sylvie. I'll try to explain it, but I ask that you trust me." If he was trying to dispel my concerns, his words had the opposite effect.

"Money owed to the company would normally be considered an asset, the way accounts receivable is. We're not a public company, though, and hence are not answerable to the SEC, so we can be a bit more flexible. I'm sure you understand, Sylvie, that Richard wanted to be discreet. There's nothing here that's not legitimate, because the loan's not really material to our financial condition. We've been planning to pursue incremental business in Asia, perhaps by investing in a joint venture, so we've chosen to account for the loan under that heading. Richard claims he has a friend in Japan, so I'm just exercising a little creativity." He forced a laugh.

Had his head swiveled three hundred sixty degrees, I wouldn't have been surprised. He appeared to be speaking in tongues. "Rest assured," Harold said, "the loan is on the books."

■ ■ ■

Kate and I had a lunch date, but I begged off. I was upset about what I'd heard from Harold, and I had too much pressing work to leave the building. On my way to pick up a sandwich from the café, I arrived at the elevator at the same time as Kate. "Sorry to cancel on you," I said.

"Oh, that's okay," she replied airily. "I'm buried too."

Her tone struck me as odd, and she didn't look right either. Her usually rosy complexion was coated with makeup. Her under-eye concealer looked as though she had applied it with a palette knife. She had the kind of washed-out look that made a poor substrate for blush—painted before she'd been primed. Leaning her head back against the wall of the empty elevator, she closed her eyes and exhaled the merest suggestion of bourbon.

"Are you all right?" I asked.

"Oh, sure."

We entered the café together, walked in different directions, and arrived at the cashier's line at the same time. She had nothing on her tray but consommé, quivering in its bowl as she withdrew a five-dollar bill from her wallet with shaking hands. I wanted to talk further, but she turned and strode toward a table. Clear enough message there. My Styrofoam-encased salad squeaked as my grip tightened.

After my father's death, Mother's hands had shaken too. Every time I'd visited the house, I'd found her cleaning. First, she cleaned out the beer, because pushing a vacuum was such hot work. Next, she dusted off the whiskey for no reason in particular. Soon the liquor cabinet was immaculate, and her hands shook too badly for housework. The more I considered Kate's odd behavior, the more parallels to Mother's came to mind.

Something had happened, but Kate obviously didn't want to talk about it, and I'd had enough intrigue over the last few days to last me till New Year's. I'd decided to act on Eileen's advice and spend Thanksgiving in Miami, but the bourbon on Kate's breath was an unwelcome reminder of a sad time. Mother had recovered quickly from her bereavement, in spite of—or perhaps because of—her drinking. She had always chafed under the spending limits of a pharmacist's wife, so she made financial security her priority.

Just as she had urged me years before to grab Ashton, she followed her own advice when Luis proposed an end to her two-year widowhood. Unlike Ashton, he didn't insist on a prenup. He was a widower, a sweet man who was smitten with Mother. Married and installed in Luis's oceanfront home in Miami in time to host a lavish Christmas bash, she had adapted so well that, on my last visit, I'd found her blond, tan, bejeweled, and fresh from her latest Botox party.

After lunch, I called Eileen from my office. I knew I'd be conversing with her voicemail while she oiled a client's sacroiliac to the tinkling notes of New Age dulcimer music. "Pack up your flip-flops," I commanded after her recorded voice. "You pushed me to jump on my mother's invitation, so you're coming too."

Although I was due at BodySculpt at six, I arrived five minutes early. Rip was poring over the appointment book with a phone to his ear, so I changed and began my warm-up on the elliptical. Rob Linde stopped to greet me and ask how I was enjoying my workouts so far. As I saw Rip approaching, clipboard in hand, I replied in a stage whisper, "Marquis de Sade reborn—the man has no mercy."

"My most abusive client," Rip insisted, arriving in time to defend himself.

Rob smiled. "Then I guess you two are well paired."

Rip checked the settings on the machine's digital panel and increased the steepness of the incline.

"You see," I called after Rob, who had started toward the front desk. "I told you—no sooner than you turn your back . . ."

"Here's what I think the problem is, Sylvie," Rip said. "As your strength increases, your attitude regresses. Too bad I don't remember how to do regression analysis."

"You think you're pretty clever, don't you? Look at that smug face."

He touched his chest with his fingers. "Me? I'm just a trainer trying to keep up with a corporate gunslinger." He pointed to the leg extension machine, and we began our circuit, starting with lower-body exercises and moving to upper. As I strained to complete my repetitions on the seated row, perspiration turned to trickles, working their way down my face with maddening slowness. I stuck the tip of my tongue out the side of my mouth to catch a salty drop, prompting Rip to fetch a towel.

"Keep counting," he called over his shoulder.

"No trust," I muttered. As soon as he returned, I said "twenty" emphatically and let go of the handles so they banged against the footrest. His eyes narrowed as I rose from the machine. "Are you going to give me that towel or use it yourself?" I asked. He looped the towel around my neck, and his hands seemed to linger on the two ends. Had Eileen been a fly on the wall, surely her identity in a previous life, she would have pronounced his reluctance to release me a certainty. I looked down at his hands, and he dropped them to his sides. Nonplussed, I dabbed at my face. "You know what this gym reminds me of? Stations of the cross."

"Come again?"

"You know, the crucifixion? Never mind. Forgot you're a rabbi's son." I stopped dabbing and pressed the whole towel against my face.

"Very focused on torture and torment tonight, aren't you?" he asked, guiding me to a mat for abdominal crunches.

"You know, I'm not one."

"One what?" he asked.

"A corporate gunslinger."

"Did I say you were?"

"You said you were trying to keep up . . ."

"All I meant . . ."

"I've worked with people who are, and believe me, I'm nothing like them." Warren's words stuck in my mind: "novice," "malleable." There was no way Rip could understand. He worked for a living as a trainer, a smart one who knew about regression analysis, but he didn't have to survive in the corporate world.

Even though I had little interest in the virtual cogs inside a software product, Ashton had convinced me technology, especially artificial intelligence, could enhance people's lives. He'd pushed me to get into AI, so of course I had. He believed the best salespeople cut corners to make their numbers, but now that I had some experience, I disagreed. Customers buy from people they trust, so I tried to be that kind of sales rep. "Naïve," said Ashton, shaking his head. Could some temptation pull me away from the straight and narrow? I didn't think so, but Ashton's advice always swayed me.

If I were a CEO, I certainly wouldn't borrow money on the sly from my company, at least I don't think I would. Maybe it's just a slippery slope. You start stealing pens from the supply room, you lie on your expense report, you book an order that isn't quite real to make your year-end quota, and before you know it, you're stealing from the company.

Rip was silent as he guided me through my stretches,

which made me feel guilty about snapping at him. I wondered how I could make amends. "I'd like to try running with you, if the offer is still open."

"Done." He smiled.

■ ■ ■

That evening, I tried to work my way through my email backlog at home. I looked down at my fingertips resting lightly on the keyboard. My hands were twins of Mother's without the frosted nail polish and gold bracelets encircling each wrist. Her hands looked sophisticated, mine serviceable.

Hands were telling—Rip's hands holding my towel, Kate's hands shaking. I wondered if Mother's hands still shook. A screenful of messages went unanswered as my mind drifted. I must have dozed, because Rip, Kate, and my mother were all arguing with me in my living room when the phone woke me up. Sleeping in my desk chair gave me a stiff neck.

Caller ID told me it was Eileen. While rubbing my neck, I denied I'd been sleeping.

"You sound exhausted," she said, "and down. You know what? I'm coming right over. Whatever it is, we'll talk it out. I'm a therapist."

"You're a massage therapist."

"So?" Eileen's logic was inductive when everyone else's was deductive and vice versa. Arguing with her was an exercise that could raise the blood pressure of a slug.

"It's late, so I'm tired, but I'm fine . . . honest. Let's just talk about Miami."

"Okay, then—Miami. Sylvie, unlike you, I have dependents. I can't possibly leave my cat or my poinsettias. I'm keeping my plants in the closet so they'll bloom for the holidays, and they'll be lonely if I go away. Anyway, I was planning to clean my refrigerator Thanksgiving weekend. Something's growing under the produce drawer."

"Trust me, it will still be there when you get back. Need I remind you that you've been talking about meeting my stepbrothers for a while now?"

"I know, but—"

"But the shelf life of handsome single men is short, and the trip is for only a few days. Imagine yourself prone on a chaise in the warm sun, the music of the surf in your ears. A strong hand—not mine—rubs oil on your back."

She sighed. "Okay already. I'll go. You're a pit bull."

"I think of myself as persuasive, but I'll take that as a compliment. We're leaving the Tuesday night before Thanksgiving and returning Saturday to beat the crush. Mother and Luis will be delighted to have you as our guest."

"You've got the whole thing figured out. 'No' was never an option, was it?"

"I just don't want you to miss out." I couldn't tell her the truth. I needed a buffer between Mother and me . . . and Carlos.

* * *

Saturday morning, berating myself for my vanity, I applied blush and lip gloss to my pale face before going out the door. Autumn, my favorite season, had begun its departure all too soon. Golden leaves, shooed from the treetops by November gusts, scuttled along the pavement. The springiness of my gel-cushioned shoes provided an illusory sense of fitness, and I felt clean and new, as though I had been turned inside out for a good airing. I was a subsistence breather as a rule, my lungs working on puffs of air the way my car ran on fumes. I was too preoccupied with work to fill either one properly.

My garden apartment was at the front of a faux colonial complex, so it faced the street rather than the scenic path that wound though the property. Because of its lack of view, my unit was less expensive than the others. I looked out at a street lined with modest homes. Rip's car was already parked out front, and

I could see his black-and-white-clad figure stretching gracefully, so I hustled down my walk to meet him.

"I was afraid I was going to have to tour your neighborhood on my own."

"Sorry, guess I'm a few minutes late."

"Ready to do some stretching?"

I joined him, and when we were ready to run, he urged me to start slowly. We jogged up the street and turned onto Bittersweet Lane. He matched his pace to mine. "Take it easy, Sylvie. It's more important to go the distance than run quickly. Speed comes on its own from conditioning."

I was grateful for permission to slow down. I hadn't intended to run fast, but I wanted to impress him with my athleticism and didn't have the wind for it. Ashton had run with me occasionally, but he had an annoying habit of planting his feet with a thud to keep time with my steps. His exaggerated trot seemed a rebuke for my inadequate speed.

Where did jogging leave off and running begin? Jogging meant landing with an audible thud. Running was the taut, springy gait I was after. Would a ten-minute mile be running? If I lengthened my stride, raised my heart rate a little higher, looked a little more athletic . . . ? I was getting ahead of myself. This was work.

"You okay with this pace?" he asked.

"I'm sorry if I'm too slow. I must be torturing you."

He raised a bushy eyebrow. "No more than in the gym."

"Guess I teed that one up for you." We ran in silence for a few minutes, our feet striking the pavement in comfortable synchronicity.

He took a deep breath. "I love being outdoors. Sometimes I wish I could deliver the mail for a living."

"And you can't?"

"I was supposed to become a Talmudic scholar and a rabbi like my father and his before him. He loved being a spiritual leader and counseling his congregants. He even had a PhD in psychology. His temple was four blocks from our apartment building in Bay Ridge. It was old-fashioned by today's standards, all dark wood and worn velvet pews, but as a rabbi, he was a new thinker, an early endorser of Reform Judaism. His sermons were legend, and he put more emphasis on ethics than ritual. I left home so I could become a trainer. Loving baseball my father understood, and we could bond over batting practice. Becoming a trainer, though? I might just as well have joined a circus. I returned home a year later, but our relationship never recovered." He squinted into the distance.

"Was it unthinkable to him that you would follow your interests?"

"Those are the right words, but he drew a distinction between vocation and avocation. To him, working in a gym was a hobby, not a career. His attitude wouldn't have been so hurtful if he hadn't been a hypocrite, counseling parents in his congregation to make peace with whatever career choices their kids made. For me, a descendant of distinguished rabbis, nothing but the rabbinate would do." He sighed. "When parents say, 'I just want you to be happy,' the next word is 'but.'"

"Or 'I just want what's best for you,'" I added. "That one's a trap too. My mother started lobbying me to marry Ashton right after I met him."

"Guess he didn't work in a circus, huh?"

"Software developer turned venture capitalist. He was an expert on artificial intelligence."

He laughed. "Not that it mattered, right? As easy to love a rich man as a poor one."

I bit my lip. I didn't like the implication, although everyone I knew thought Ashton was a catch, especially Mother. I'd been letting her run my life for a long time. I didn't even notice after a while. "Maybe it's as easy to marry one, but to love one—I'm not sure. Looking back on it, I think he just impressed the hell out of me. In those days, I was impressed with everyone, especially VCs. I hadn't yet heard the phrase 'vulture capitalists.' I thought they were swashbuckling risk-takers."

"So, you met Ashton on a pirate ship?"

"Close, on a party cruise, a charity fundraiser sponsored by Tory Partners. I was invited because I worked for the firm's public relations agency."

"Well, he obviously flipped over you."

"Ashton's desire for me more closely resembled his need for an Armani suit than love. I was one more acquisition for his collected assets."

"I think you're wrong. I bet he really fell for you."

Rip looked straight at me, and I felt myself blushing, or maybe I just noticed how warm the sun was. I wiped the perspiration from my forehead with my sleeve. "Do you mind if we circle back?"

He agreed. When we turned down Endicott Lane, a gardener started up his leaf blower. Anyone still sleeping would have been awakened by the machine's whining reveille as it chased whorls of leaves from grass to street, restoring the geometry of the neighborhood's lawns and asphalt drives. The homeowner's ritual assertion of control over nature was not so different from a corporation's control over its workforce. We had our own means of pruning, yanking like weeds those who failed to conform.

"So, your investment didn't pan out?" Rip asked, slowing the pace.

I winced, although his description was apt. "Not saying it wasn't my fault, but my mother pushed me to marry Ashton. I learned that reducing people to their credentials doesn't tell you much. I bought shares based on the prospectus and suffered the consequences. He was a real Svengali. I fell under his spell, changing my hair color, makeup, and clothes to please him. I left my firm, where I was happy, because Ashton thought I would climb faster and earn more in technology sales. I waited to have children, because he would be ready in a year, or two, or five."

"Sylvie, I hope I didn't offend you. I mean I don't even know your ex. I wasn't trying to make you seem like a gold digger or anything."

"Forget it." I mustered my brightest smile. "What I really want to know is whether you think I have potential as an Olympic runner."

"I think you have all kinds of potential, but don't let it go to your head. You're hard enough to deal with already."

My legs were tired, and the crisp air had turned hot in my throat. We could see the entrance to Old Mill and slowed to a walk to cool down. I peeked over at Rip, who'd become quiet. I wondered if he were still thinking about his father. Did the rabbi's disapproval motivate Rip to prove himself? I remembered Mother telling me I was just like my father. Eventually I came to understand she didn't mean it as a compliment.

"Good work," Rip said, patting my shoulder.

"Maybe you were right. Having a running coach is a good idea—at least for a while."

We agreed to compare calendars after my next session at the gym. I shook off the voice in my head reminding me of the limitations on my free time and discretionary funds. Surely, we weren't meant to spend this glorious season in an office.

CHAPTER 9

We encountered the tropical humidity as soon as we stepped from the plane into the jetway, a welcome relief from endlessly circulated but never refreshed dryness. Our fellow passengers marched resolutely into the gate area with their duffels shouldered, luggage wheeled, and children prodded. Eileen had insisted we check the luggage we could easily have carried on—bad for our shoulder muscles, she had warned.

When it was our turn to emerge into the gate area, we were greeted by a changed palette—darker skins and brighter clothes—than we had left behind at Logan Airport in Boston. The rust and hunter green of Yankee autumn had become Florida's flamingo pink and beach-ball turquoise. The scene brought me up short as though elevator doors had opened on an unexpected floor. Now the preponderance of faces looked Cuban, black-haired men and a handful of redheaded women. Mothers scolded their children, but the chatter had changed to Spanish in the space of four airborne hours.

Although the terminal was thoroughly air-conditioned, that breath of the jetway's humid air had altered our expectations, flipped a switch, and I was anxious to shed my brown barn jacket and feel the sun on my shoulders. We followed the signs to baggage claim, where Eileen decided we'd need a cart and left me to shoulder my way forward toward the moving belt.

"Coming through. On your left." Eileen maneuvered her cart through the pressing crowd.

"Why can't everyone just stand back a little, so we can each step forward to claim our bag?" I knew I sounded cranky, but the pleasant prospect of seeing palm trees had been fleeting. I had a tight feeling in my chest in anticipation of seeing Mother and Carlos. Nowhere does nature abhor a vacuum so much as in our thoughts.

Once our bags were situated on the cart, Eileen wheeled it out the automatic doors. The sidewalk was crowded, but I heard someone shout my name and recognized Miguel standing next to a silver Mercedes convertible parked at the island across from the taxi stand. Eileen spotted him, too, and ditched the cart, grabbing her suitcase and tote and lurching in his direction.

Her bag teetered back and forth from one wheel to the other as she dodged piles of luggage in her path. I couldn't help laughing. The Miami Dolphins could probably use a broken-field runner of her caliber. Although she held no pigskin under her arm, the tote suspended from her shoulder could have accommodated one. It looked like a cross between a striped awning and a horse's feed bag, and each time she altered course, one of its straps slid down her arm, causing her to hitch up her shoulder to hold it.

I did my best to follow her syncopated progress in the direction of Miguel, who never stopped grinning. We must have appeared the ultimate gringos. He apologized for not crossing the road to help, but with a security officer telling him to move his car, he was afraid he'd be towed if he left it.

He gave me a quick hug and smiled expectantly at Eileen. The gleam of his straight white teeth gave serious competition to the iridescent Mercedes. Eileen had left any coyness in Boston. As I introduced the two, she extended her hand, which he grasped in both of his own until I cleared my throat.

One of us had to sit up front so Miguel wouldn't feel he was chauffeuring. Eileen settled quickly into the passenger seat. I sat in back watching her long dark hair bob up and down with each coquettish tilt of her head. She and Miguel discussed the sights as though their attention weren't engaged by points of interest a bucket seat away. I decided not to worry about her. Perhaps Miguel was the one in need of a warning. Eileen had hands of steel.

Once we crossed the causeway to Miami Beach, I could see the yachts anchored along Indian Creek, their whiteness as intense as the afternoon sun. My neck was still damp from our sprint to Miguel's car, so I pulled my hair back with the scrunchie Eileen had bought me at Logan Airport. "Bright green frogs," she'd said, "just the touch of whimsy you so desperately need." It was the kind of accessory she could carry off better than I, but I took perverse pleasure in the thought that Mother would find it déclassé. If only she and I could limit our disagreements to the superficial.

Fifteen minutes later, we pulled up the circular drive. Miguel stopped before the broad white steps leading to the veranda, ringed by a wealth of azaleas and blue daze.

"Nice digs," Eileen whispered before Miguel opened her door and extended his hand to help her out. I didn't wait for him to open mine, and as soon as I alighted from the car, Mother swept out the front door.

She wore capris covered with purple orchids and a white tube top, which set off her honey-colored shoulders, tanner than I'd ever seen them. Her hair was a color that suited only South Florida or Scandinavia. When she hugged me, the fragrance of her pricey Clive Christian perfume surrounded both of us.

Mother appeared sober but possessed the means to banish external evidence of her libations. Money could buy the best in cosmetic surgery, not to mention regular Botox injections. Mother's skin was now smooth as a girl's. I remembered how worn Kate looked before I left, though she was so many years Mother's junior. Of course, Kate had been pickled.

She pulled away from me, the better to survey my appearance, her face expressionless until she spotted the frog-covered scrunchie. "Maybe we can fit in some shopping, dear." She turned. "Ah, this must be your friend Eileen." Mother embraced her, kissing the air beside Eileen's cheek. It jolted me to realize Mother might be as relieved as I was to have Eileen between us.

"Margaret, thank you so much for welcoming me into your home for the holiday."

"I'm delighted you're here." Mother took her arm and pulled her into the house. "I understand you're a massage therapist . . ."

The housekeeper, whom Mother referred to as "the incomparable Celia," had prepared a platter of crabmeat rolls and fresh fruit salad, along with a pitcher of iced tea, and laid them out on the living room coffee table. I crossed the polished expanse of terra cotta tile and installed myself on the peach silk sofa nearest the sliding glass doors.

Miguel and Mother had already guided Eileen out to the pool, so I poured myself an iced tea and opened one of the large books of illustrations lying beside the tray. *Antiques of South America* seemed unlikely reading for Mother, but then her previous existence as the wife of a pharmacist seemed as remote as life on Mars. She had transformed herself, and I couldn't help feeling that in doing so, she had obliterated some of my past along with her own.

The sliding door opened and closed, and I looked up to find her slipping into the white club chair opposite me. "Isn't that a marvelous book?" she asked, tilting the pitcher into a tall glass.

"A little out of my line, I'm afraid." I turned back to the cover.

"The Spanish style, yes, but you and Ashton had a beautifully decorated house. Have you lost interest?"

"I spend too many hours in the office to make the decor of my apartment a priority."

"But it's your home," she said reproachfully.

"So, it should feel homey like yours?" I gestured at our palatial surroundings. "Ashton made sure I no longer have the money for this."

She sighed. "Are you going to make a career out of being angry at me?"

"For what?" We both knew the question was as disingenuous as it was rhetorical. Where would I begin, anyway? With her pushing me to marry Ashton? Drinking herself into oblivion?

"Don't be flip, Sylvie."

I bit my lip as she rose from her chair and walked to the bar, pausing and then turning empty-handed toward the glass doors, clasping and unclasping her fingers, twisting her rings. Wringing hands and ringing bracelets—what were those? Homonyms? Antonyms? No, antonyms were opposites. Mother and I were look-alike opposites. I knew no name for that.

"Not an ounce of charity in your heart, is there? It's not as though you grew up with an alcoholic mother. You were already an adult. I wish you could understand what it's like . . ." She faltered. "Losing the love of your life."

She sounded like a soap opera character, and I noted the tacit admission of what my marriage hadn't been. I was hurt by her proprietary attitude toward my father's memory. "I lost Dad, too, you know." She looked at me with wet, distressed eyes, which no doubt mirrored my own. Here we were, just as I had feared, mired in misunderstanding. "Hope you don't mind, but I could really use a nap. Work has been brutal, and flying wears me out." I made my way up the stairs and lay down on the bed.

When I awakened, the light coming through my window had dulled to the color of old aluminum, and for a moment I thought I was back in Needham. It was late, about to rain, or both. I heard deep-voiced laughter from downstairs. Luis must be home. I wondered if Mother had told him about our conversation.

I couldn't imagine anyone disliking Luis. He beamed at me as I descended the stairs and embraced me in his substantial arms. If he knew about my scene with Mother, his face didn't betray it. "Miguel." He spoke in the gravelly voice of a heavy smoker. "A glass of Champagne for my favorite daughter." As the father of sons, Luis had been delighted to inherit a stepdaughter when he married Mother. He had a generous spirit I discovered. His affection for me was unexpected and welcome.

Miguel brought me a glass, and Luis raised his for a toast. I half-expected Eileen to pop out some newly acquired Spanish version of "to life," but she seemed content to remain in her place, especially with Miguel returning to her side. She fairly purred. Luis gave his toast in English for our benefit, proposing that we drink to family reunions. The crystal stemware pinged as we touched glasses. I was spared reaching out to Mother when Luis put his arm around her, squeezed affectionately, and kissed her cheek.

"Sylvie, what about me?" Carlos had entered silently, and as I turned and looked up into his face, he brushed his fingers past mine, clinking glasses. "I'm sorry I couldn't come to the airport with Miguel to meet you and Eileen. We've missed you."

Current flowed from the backs of his fingers to my own. His magnetic field was as riveting as the night he first seduced me, willing though I had been. Carlos didn't know that my sighs of ecstasy had as much to do with the intense pleasure of finding my powers of attraction intact as his expert caresses. We'd agreed our affair was over when I left Miami, at least I thought we had.

How powerful are touch and texture. In college, I read a study showing that baby monkeys removed from their mothers preferred a cloth surrogate to a wire look-alike or simulated beating heart. My own mother was no doubt staring at Carlos and me. Her cloth was silk, her wire, platinum. Sometimes I thought her heart was a simulation as well.

I turned to face the group, my mind a blank. "L'chaim," I said, tossing back my Champagne like a shot of tequila. Eileen raised an eyebrow as she lifted her glass to her lips.

At dinner, I sat at the end of the table closest to Luis, but even at a distance, I could feel the heat in Carlos's glance. He and Miguel left after dinner, promising to return the next evening to take Eileen and me on an excursion to South Beach. The next night and Thanksgiving, they would be able to stay at the house, "which will be much more convenient," Carlos added, with a meaningful look in my direction.

There was no shortage of innuendo with Carlos. As the first son of a wealthy, indifferent mother, Rosa Carmelina, he was displayed and encouraged to perform for the guests who attended his parents' galas. Carlos was rewarded for his precociousness and flowery recitations until Miguel was born. Miguel's sweet disposition won his mother's heart, displacing Carlos.

I could easily imagine Carlos spending his childhood trying to win back his mother's approbation with charm, his greatest asset. Rosa Carmelina died of ovarian cancer when Carlos was a teenager, but he never gave up his courtly style. He grew up blessed with good looks, including heavy-lidded dark eyes and sensuous lips. No telling how many of us had fallen for his soulful gaze. Propinquity was the only aphrodisiac Carlos required.

I said my good nights early and returned to my room to check my cell phone. Nothing that couldn't wait. Concentrating was impossible with Carlos in the house. I had hoped to greet him as a friend, but my body was not cooperating.

There was a whiff of danger about Carlos. Somehow you just knew he was a "bad boy," and I was embarrassed to admit to myself that it was part of what made him so hot. Any fantasies about Rip were a plane ride away.

I needed to come up with a strategy for handling Carlos, but what did I want? As I sat on the bed pushing off the heel straps of my sandals, I wondered how I could possibly contemplate a night in his bed. It seemed risky, yet I had taken a bigger chance when Ashton and I were still married. Hadn't worked out so well, although Ashton cheated first. I was hurt and angry.

Eileen rapped on the door. Without waiting for an invitation to enter, she crossed the room and flung herself onto the frond-patterned cushions of my rattan settee. Flexing her fingers, she warned, "Don't make me practice deep tissue massage on your windpipe. Tell me everything now. If I had a brother who looked at me that way, I'd call in family services."

"Step. He's my stepbrother."

"There was more heat and history between you and Carlos than between Bogart and Bergman in *Casablanca*."

"We had a . . . thing," I admitted.

"A thing? That's crazy. Your mother must have been furious, unless—she doesn't know, does she? Why didn't you tell me?"

"That's what you're mad about, isn't it? It wasn't an affair, more like serial hookups."

Eileen's words came out in a rush. "I know you think I'm excessively interested in your sex life—sex as therapy and all that—but I hope you know I'm only half serious. I've just been stymied by your lack of enthusiasm. All your energies go into work." She paused for breath and rested her forehead in her hand. "When did your non-affair happen? Didn't you wonder what Margaret and Luis would think?"

"Look, it's not like I planned it. After Mother and Luis had made a couple of visits to Boston, they insisted I come down to Miami, see the house, and get to know Carlos and Miguel. I had met them only briefly at Mother's wedding. Carlos and I hit it off." I lay back on the bed with my hands behind my head.

"It was my first day down here, and Mother and Luis were out. You know how on clear days, the shadows get really long in the late afternoon, and the light is beautiful? I took a glass of Cabernet out to the veranda to watch the sunset. No one was around, just me and the perfume of hibiscus blossoms. The sky was deep blue, the clouds turning from white to gray to pink and . . ."

"And then," said Eileen, determined to keep me on point.

"Carlos came out to join me. He sat down in the wicker rocker next to mine. 'The departing sun is like a diva,' he said. 'Her boa has all the colors of a conch shell, and she trails it behind her as she makes her exit.'"

Eileen snorted. "A 'diva'? More like a fan dancer."

"Oh, I know. Under normal circumstances, I would have thought what a crock, but at that moment, I was vulnerable. So, shoot me—I put poetry before pragmatism."

"That's a cop-out," she said. "What happened to 'look but don't touch'? It never occurred to you or Carlos that what you regarded as poetry your parents would see as adultery."

"How about poetic license?" I asked, trying to lighten the mood. "Licentiousness? Not every choice is black or white. There are shades of gray."

"Yeah, but not fifty."

I threw a pillow at her.

After the merest hint of a smile, she turned thoughtful again, braiding and unbraiding the dark strands of hair beside her face. The crease between her brows deepened. "You weren't separated yet, right? And this was before Ashton started seeing what's-her-name, Gwen?"

I stared at her, uncomprehending. "You think it's inappropriate to sleep with a guy who became my stepbrother five minutes ago, and now you're going to pull your parochial school morality out of mothballs, you of all people?"

She shifted in her seat. "That's why I'm single. Marriage vows are a serious commitment. You're supposed to resist temptations, and not just the little ones. I have no illusions about my ability to do that."

"How about your church's prohibition against premarital sex? You just pick and choose which rules you follow?"

"Doesn't everyone? You included?" She sighed and put her feet down on the floor. One side of her hair was still braided. All she needed was a pleated skirt and green knee socks to be the nuns' nemesis again. "Look, I know Ashton could be a prick, and you were going through a tough stretch when you met Carlos. There's just something creepy about that guy. I'm not saying I don't understand—he's hot. I'm just disappointed. You caught me by surprise, okay? Let's forget it." She stood up. "I'm beat."

Four years ago, when Carlos seduced me, the sex was welcome and wonderful. I was grateful for the respite from Ashton's pedantry, his tutoring and manuals on boosting orgasm. There may be women who would relish such a man, but Ashton had reduced our sex life to a mechanistic operation to be analyzed and optimized for higher return on investment.

Who could sleep? Perhaps it was my long nap, but the day's conversations, first with Mother, then Eileen, replayed themselves in my mind. The windows of my room were shut tight, so I had no chanting cicadas or surging surf to lull me, only the mechanical hum of central air—conditioned air—forced air. How totalitarian that sounded. "Free as air" must have gone the way of the free lunch. Didn't Mother used to talk about "free sex"? Now there was a quaint expression.

CHAPTER 10

Eileen was cheerful at breakfast. Either she had decided to drop the issue of my infidelity to Ashton, or she had indulged in a mimosa before I came down. More likely, she was consumed with excitement at the prospect of an evening with the South Beach jet set, Miguel in particular. We spent the morning at the pool, and after two hours in a chaise-induced drowse, I was startled by her pronouncement: "Shit. I didn't bring anything to wear tonight."

"Of course you did." I yawned and sat up. "I told you we'd probably go out."

"But we were still in Boston then. I wasn't feeling like . . ."

"Like there was a fire in your furnace?" I replied, prompting her to frisbee her straw sunhat in my direction.

"Go ahead and make fun, but I'm not partying with the beautiful people in an outfit I wore to a contra dance. You can look like a New England matron if you want, but I'm going to find Margaret. I'm sure she can direct me to the nearest boutique."

Mother insisted on taking us herself. I was sure that meant she planned to pay. Not much point in arguing since our destination was certain to be pricey.

After we had selected our outfits, Eileen tried to prevent Mother from pulling her platinum card out of her Gucci wallet. The salesclerk waited patiently at the register while

Mother wore Eileen down, claiming Luis would go loco if she didn't treat us. I shook my head at Eileen to signal the futility of her protest.

In the end, she persuaded Mother to accept a complimentary ninety-minute massage: Swedish, shiatsu, trigger point, the best of Eileen's repertoire. No question in my mind Eileen had given better than she'd gotten. Mother must have thought so, too, because she gave Eileen a hug and told her how lucky I was to have such a friend. Eileen's eyes were moist when they pulled apart.

By the time we returned to the house, the wind was blowing damp and hard, slapping the leaves of the Areca palms against each other like a family feud. Gray clouds obliterated the sun. Eileen was worried that rain might ruin our evening, but Mother assured her the squall would pass quickly.

"Nothing mars our perfect days for long."

I had the sense she was reassuring herself.

I love dramatic weather changes. All-day rains are dreary, but thunderstorms arouse a primitive excitement in me. While Eileen fretted over the prospect of jumping puddles in her new high-heeled sandals, my own sense of anticipation rose in direct proportion to the fall in barometric pressure. Wind was heard but not seen. Like the invisible man who became partially corporeal in clothing, wind wore whatever bent or blew before it.

Did it matter if I slept with Carlos now that I was single? As wrong as I thought Eileen was about the whiff of incest associated with my affair, I knew Mother and Luis would be upset if they knew. To be fair, I understood Eileen's disapproval. Had my brief affair with Carlos complicated my relationship with Ashton? No, certainly not. It had brought clarity—at least until Ashton appeared unannounced.

There was no lack of clarity in the brothers' appreciative expressions when Eileen and I descended the stairs that evening. V-neck halter tops could be relied on to show off a woman's softness and tight dressy jeans her curves. Eileen had chosen lime-green high heels, and her long brown hair shone in the lamplight. My hair was swept up on top of my head, and my sparkly silver sandals had the highest heels I'd ever worn, but I told myself they didn't qualify as stilettos. Eileen, who had a history of wearing Birkenstocks, had been practicing walking in her heels all afternoon. I wondered how we would manage salsa dancing in those shoes.

Both of us wore sultry shades of eye makeup and chandelier-style earrings borrowed from Mother. Mine were silver, although Mother, insulted, informed me they were white gold. For the first time, I jingled softly, as she did, when I turned my head. I felt as though I were headed out for the older-but-wiser version of prom night.

Luis came into the foyer to greet his sons. "Take care of these gorgeous women," he warned, placing his arm around me protectively. "It's easy to lose track of people in those crowded dance clubs." Officially, Carlos and Miguel were hosts, not dates, and Eileen and I were dressed like the natives, not man-hunters.

Costumes have a way of altering one's identity. Eileen seemed to be enjoying her transformation as much as any little girl dressed for Halloween as a fairy princess, feeling as glamorous and liberated as I felt constrained. In a sixth-grade holiday pageant, I had played the role of the Grinch that stole Christmas, and having to pretend I was mean-spirited made me feel cranky and disagreeable.

I told myself I was just playing the part of Eileen's wingman. If she wanted Miguel, even for one night, I would do my best to keep the atmosphere fully charged. Taking on the role of a South Beach swinger without giving Carlos the wrong idea, however, turned out to be as tall an order as our bottomless tequila glasses.

The drinks and the ambiguity of our respective roles kept me off balance. First Carlos pulled his chair closer, then rested his arm on the back of my chair. He pointed out a couple on the dance floor. Both the man and woman were bald and heavily tattooed. Carlos leaned his head toward mine. "You know, at the start of the evening they both had hair." I giggled and let my cheek graze his. He squeezed my knee, and his hand slid well up my thigh before I laughed and pushed it away.

Eileen lured me to the ladies' room. "What are you doing? This is how you cool a guy down?"

I promised to end the evening early and get Carlos to take me back, so she and Miguel could be alone. Somehow that didn't happen, and by our third dance club, I was in an altered state, my senses in overdrive, my common sense in neutral. "Park" would have served me better as the musical tempo changed.

The perfume of bodies seemed to have been atomized through the air, an earthy combination of sweat, cologne, and pheromones. Carlos pulled me close. "My favorite slow dance," he said, his breath in my ear. We danced without moving our feet, both his arms around me, while Miguel and Eileen glided past.

"Hey, you two," Miguel called out, "get a room." Eileen glared at me over his shoulder. The sound of Miguel's laughter faded quickly as they were engulfed by the crowd. I felt myself dissolving into Carlos as his hands moved down my back. When he looked at me to ask the inevitable question, he held my hips locked to his. Yes, of course, it was time to go.

Miguel had the car keys, so Carlos and I took a taxi back to the house. The wind had diminished, but the night air was still laden with moisture. Once inside, he pulled me into the dark shadows of the dining room and untied the halter straps behind my neck, his fingertips tracing their path as they slid down my chest. My breath caught in my throat, and I closed my eyes.

No, no . . . "No." I clutched at my halter and pushed him away.

"What's wrong?" He slid his arm around my waist as I tried to retie my halter straps.

"I'm sorry, Carlos." I broke free of his embrace. "Sorry for the mixed signals—bush league, I know—the drinks . . . We talked about this four years ago. Let's not have an instant replay."

"But it was wonderful. Don't you remember?" His hands were on my shoulders.

"For us, yes, but not for the family. It would be too complicated to have you as more than my—my brother."

His eyes narrowed as surprise became anger. I didn't wait for a reply but turned and ran up the stairs. Carlos was right behind me. He grabbed me around the waist and then scooped me up like a bride, carrying me across the threshold of my bedroom and closing the door with his foot. I beat his chest with my fists, but he threw me on the bed and covered my mouth with his hand. "Shh," he whispered. You'll wake up Margaret and my father. They won't understand."

I tried to bite him, but that only seemed to arouse him further. He opened my jeans with one hand and tugged them down along with my underwear, while his other hand moved to imprison my wrists over my head. With my mouth uncovered, I turned my head to yell but couldn't bring myself to raise an alarm. I kept imagining Mother and Luis running in, horrified by my screams.

Carlos was an expert at undressing women and was strong enough to withstand my attempts at writhing out from under him. He seemed to enjoy my struggling, and in moments, he was hard inside me. His need was urgent and quickly satisfied. "See," he said, his face close to mine, "just as wonderful as last time. Don't pretend you want me to be your brother."

"You raped me, you shit," I hissed, pushing his weight off me, tears of rage filling my eyes.

"You loved it."

I pushed him toward the door. "Nobody loves being raped."

He wedged his arm into the door and looked back at me, menace in his narrowed eyes. "Don't bother crying 'rape.' Miguel and Eileen saw how you behaved tonight, so no one will believe you. Did I mention we have a security system in the house with cameras in all the downstairs rooms?"

"Your camera will show me stopping you."

"I think it will show you racing upstairs to your bedroom with me following your lead."

I locked my bedroom door behind him. Ripping out Mother's earrings, I threw them on the tile floor where they landed together with a soft jangle. This screwup was all mine, though, and couldn't be blamed on her. Eileen and I were eager participants in the South Beach swinger outing. It worked out well for Eileen, but I should have known better than to a dress up like a sex kitten. I had assumed the identity of my costume, and Carlos ate it up.

CHAPTER 11

When I woke, the sun was high and so bright, the previous day's storm seemed unreal. Surely it was Halloween, not Thanksgiving, because my head had become as heavy and unwieldy as a pumpkin. The mirror reflected back eyes hollowed out like a jack-o'-lantern's, but where a grotesque grin should have been, backlit by flame, a mouth winced with each throb of my temples. The smell of Carlos was in my nostrils, making me sick.

It didn't take long for Mother to figure out what was going on between Eileen and Miguel, since their locked gazes were not at all those of a house guest and host. She seemed pleased by their holiday romance. Carlos and I avoided each other, which prevented me from scratching his eyes out. If Mother observed our behavior, she made no mention of it.

I made a private vow never to set foot in a South Beach club again. It was Thanksgiving, and the end of our visit was in sight. If I had to chant one of Eileen's mantras to divert my thoughts from Carlos, then "ohm" it would be till the pumpkin pie was served.

Eileen wanted to talk with me alone, but I wasn't ready to admit how poorly I had handled the previous night's outing and how disastrously it had ended. I begged off, telling her I needed to see Luis, who'd promised to provide me with his secret hangover remedy. That excuse elicited a raised eyebrow, though it was absolutely true. Luis's brew was magical. It smelled foul but was worthy of a patent to judge from my headache's hasty retreat.

Eileen and Miguel were in T-shirts and shorts, reading by the pool, so I walked down the steps to the beach instead. Perhaps I could store in my memory the glitter of the ocean and the radiance of the sun. The night before, I had tried to avoid the undertow of my emotions, deluding myself into thinking I could safely splash in the shallow waters of my tequila glass and keep my relationship with Carlos platonic.

The trouble was he hadn't shared my delusion. *Yes, he'd raped me, his actions criminal, but did I bear some guilt for my role? Had I been a shameless cock tease?* Maybe Warren was right when he said I was malleable.

When I returned to the patio, I found Eileen and Miguel stretched out on adjacent lounges, asleep on their stomachs. Eileen's straw hat was askew, covering her profile. Miguel's arms hung down on either side of his chaise. Luis sat at the glass-topped wrought iron table reading the *Miami Herald* and smoking a cigarette.

Carlos emerged from the house but, seeing me, reached for the sliding door to return. Luis had already spotted him, though, and using his reading glasses pointed at the slumbering pair. "When I asked you and Miguel to show Sylvie and Eileen around town, I meant for the evening, not until the roosters crow."

Carlos gave me a stony look, ignoring his father's remark. Miguel flipped over, sat up, and smiled at Luis. "These northern women are a bad influence. You wouldn't believe the places they made us take them."

"You're right," Luis replied in his sandpaper voice. "I wouldn't believe it."

Eileen pushed the hat off her face, yawned, and turned

over. She looked around. "We're all here except Margaret. Don't tell me she's still teaching Celia about the Pilgrims and the Indians."

"Native Americans," Miguel corrected her.

"Indigenous peoples," she replied, "and you have terry cloth ridges embossed on your cheek."

"Margaret's not instructing," Luis said. "She's cooking. She wants Thanksgiving dinner to bear her personal touch."

Eileen stood and pushed her feet into her flip-flops. "Maybe we should go see if she needs some help. Sylvie?" She looked at me over the top of her sunglasses. I had no desire to join Mother, but with Carlos installing himself opposite Luis at the table and commandeering the business section of the paper, the kitchen was likely to be the friendlier locale. As we closed the glass doors behind us, she said, "I can't believe your mother. She's been so sweet, and now she's going to spend the day in the kitchen when she could just as easily let Celia cook the meal."

"And not apply her fabled personal touch? Hope she can find it. It's been a while."

"It's been a while since you cut her some slack, Syl."

The activity in the kitchen put an end to further conversation. Mother, to my surprise, was wearing a red and green plaid apron I recognized from our kitchen back in Reading. She was peering into a wall oven. A cookbook lay open on the black granite counter. She smiled when she saw us and brushed her hair off her forehead with a hand enveloped in a checkered oven mitt.

"I'd forgotten what hot work this is." She turned to look at the cook. "Celia, you're a marvel."

Celia beamed back at her. "My pleasure, Señora."

"I know what you need," Eileen said, dashing out of the kitchen. When she returned moments later, she held up the green frog scrunchie she'd bought me at the airport. "Voilà!"

she said to Mother. "You'll be cooler if you tie your hair back. Sylvie isn't going to use this again."

I was sure if I had suggested it, Mother would have disdained having her coiffure restrained in such a fashion. How differently she related to Eileen, as though Eileen were the daughter and I, the houseguest. Eileen kept everyone at precisely arm's distance in her work but never in her personal life.

"You wish to help?" Celia asked as she handed me a bowl of fruit and pointed to the knife rack and cutting board. "Fruit salad, please." She set Eileen up beside me with two loaves of French bread to cube for stuffing. Celia, as it turned out, was remarkably voluble. Despite her formal appearance, with black hair pinned in a tight bun and starched white apron overlaying a black uniform, she wore tangerine lipstick, and her mouth moved constantly as she described, in her own colorful variant of English, her family, both here and in Cuba. Her hands moved like an overheated metronome, chopping, whipping, molding, and garnishing.

As the aroma of roasting turkey permeated the air, chatter turned to clatter. Celia removed stacks of fine china from the mahogany hutch in the dining room and positioned them on the damask tablecloth. I watched her through the door as she opened the silver chest with reverence and began removing the flatware. She was so obviously loyal and committed to Luis's family—and to Mother.

We'd been working for half an hour when I realized Mother had been frowning over her cookbook for ten minutes. Celia moved to her side, blocking my view. She said something to Mother I couldn't hear, closed the book, and shooed her upstairs for a nap. *Guess it takes longer*, I thought, *for one of Mother's age and station, to accrue the requisite beauty sleep*. I could have used a nap myself, but Eileen chose that moment to quiz me on what had happened after Carlos and I left the club.

"Syl, I'd like to think you and Carlos were letting Miguel

and me end the evening together, but the last time I saw the two of you, you were close enough to share a pair of panties. How come he looks so pissed off today?"

"I gave him the wrong idea even though it seemed like the right idea until we got home. It didn't end well." Mercifully, Celia's exits and entrances prevented all but fragmented conversation. Eileen didn't berate me. She didn't need to. I had the job covered.

When Celia dismissed us from our kitchen duties, Eileen returned to the patio. Luis was just coming in and asked me to join him in the garden. Even before we were out of earshot of the house, I was transported by the scent. Once I could see the profusion of blossoms, the colors were brilliant. I recognized only the roses, so Luis proudly identified his flame of Jamaica, Ceylon senna, plumeria, fringed hibiscus, and weeping blue ginger.

Luis stooped to inspect a leaf, rubbing it gently between his thumb and forefinger, as one would admire the texture of a supple suede. "A garden plant is like a child," he said. "No matter how much you water, fertilize, and prune, you can never create perfection. You just hope it will stand tall and healthy, its flowers massing harmoniously with others." He straightened up. "Does that sound corny?"

"No, but I can see where Carlos gets his gift for flowery prose."

"When Rosa Carmelina was alive, she judged the garden by the number of blossoms. She never had the patience for tending each plant and didn't understand why, with a staff of gardeners, I needed to get my hands dirty. What's that expression? 'As exciting as watching grass grow.' Now you know the secret of what excites me."

For a moment, I felt as one with Mother. It was impossible not to love Luis. We continued down the path until we reached the rose bushes. Luis removed a pair of clippers from his pocket and snipped off a yellow one. He presented it to me with a flourish. "Señorita," he said, bowing low. I didn't correct him, though given my previous marriage, I was now Señora.

I curtsied and placed the rose in my hair.

"Bella," he said. "You are beautiful like your mother. I'm not surprised Carlos has noticed. I saw how warmly he greeted you Tuesday evening."

I felt my chest tighten.

"And then I saw him ignore you this morning. You must have rebuffed him last night. I know my son."

"It was nothing, honest. No big deal." The lie brought a flush to my face. I couldn't breathe.

"I'm not asking why. That's between the two of you. I think of you as my daughter, and I want you to know why he expects so much from the women in his life. His mother, I hate to say it, favored Miguel, the sweeter and easier child. Carlos is needy and impulsive, quick to anger, and he expects the rose to have no thorns, at least not for him. Do you see that shrub with the yellow flowers? It's lantana, a lovely plant with toxic leaves. Carlos must learn to be cautious in the presence of beauty." He shook his head mournfully and turned back toward the house.

I prayed Luis meant it when he said he would not look into the changed relationship between Carlos and me. If he did, Carlos would justify his behavior based on our brief affair. Luis might believe Carlos had seduced me once, but multiple times? I was heartsick at the thought he would find out I had been—at first—a willing partner. But how could he believe his own son raped me? Telling him was pointless.

Dinner was elegant. Celia had filled the vases with fresh flowers, and everything shone, from the silver water pitcher and serving platters to the elaborate cut crystal decanter. Luis continually filled our glasses with his finest Beaujolais. I drank judiciously, but from my first swallow, I felt suffused with warmth.

Mother looked rested and happy, and though Carlos avoided eye contact with me, comfort and discomfort had agreed to lodge amiably within me, at least for Thanksgiving. That's what families are, oil and vinegar, shaken into a pleasing emulsion that gets us through childhood or, at least, the salad course, before it inevitably separates.

* * *

Carlos and Miguel had arranged to leave Friday afternoon. Carlos's departure would provide relief for me, but the timing was unfortunate for Eileen and Miguel. I watched them head out for a last stroll on the beach, his arm around her shoulders and hers around his waist. I wondered what he would say, how they would leave things, although I assumed this was a fun-while-it-lasted conversation.

When they returned, I walked with them to the veranda and remained there as they continued down the steps, hands joined and swinging. Carlos stowed their bags in the trunk of the Mercedes, while Miguel took Eileen's face in his hands and kissed her with a tenderness that surprised me. Then he hopped over the door into the driver's seat and grinned as he revved the powerful engine. Carlos climbed in beside him, and the car exploded forward, spewing gravel behind its tires.

Mother was waiting in the living room with a pitcher of iced tea, and Eileen asked if she minded her taking a glass out to the patio where she'd left her book. "Of course not, dear. Sylvie, could you stay a moment?"

There was no escape. I sat down across from her.

"Is this your idea of getting back at me?" she asked icily.

"What do you mean?" I stalled, feeling panic rise from my chest to my throat the way it had when, as a child, I'd broken some sacred rule of the house.

"Because I believe that's your priority, paying me back for my supposed sins against you." She sputtered before coming up with "sins," and her long gold earrings tinkled as her head shook.

How could she know when Luis had not yet spoken with Carlos?

"Something happened Wednesday night between you and Carlos, and now you're not on speaking terms. Do you think I'm blind?"

She didn't know about the earlier affair. That was a relief. She assumed, though, that whatever happened between Carlos and me was my fault. I was trapped. I couldn't speak about our night in South Beach without explaining why Carlos expected to find a willing partner in me, why there was "heat and history" between us, as Eileen had observed. For some reason, Mother was taking whatever had happened the night before last personally. "You think this is payback for Ashton?" I asked.

"Let's talk about what *you* think—that I forced you to marry Ashton for his money. Even if I had, would that have been so awful? It's not as though he were some sort of"—she spied the scrunchie on the end table and picked it up—"frog prince. Sometimes, when it's the right match, a mother has to give a little push. You were young and needed direction."

"I certainly got that," I shot back.

"If I didn't know you'd ridicule me, I'd say, 'Wait till you're a mother.' You think parenting is easy?" She twisted the scrunchie around her fingers. "Little Pretzelita," she mocked, "full of nostalgia for Daddy's drugstore. I have news for you. Your father may have been Mr. Congeniality, but he was no businessman. I put in long hours helping him make a go of it. I was the one, not him." She tapped her forefinger against her chest. "I was the one who kept our creditors from the door and figured out how to pay for your ice skates and prom dresses. Those big box stores, the supermarkets, the pharmacies, they killed him, but he made it easy." Her words became choked.

I'd heard it all before, how Dad hadn't been up to the rigors of making a business successful, although he was the one who got credit for it. He was a pharmacist, but he inspired so much trust, everyone in town called him "Doc." I loved working in the store as a kid. When I was nine, Dad gave me the job of counting stacks of pennies, nickels, dimes, and quarters from the register. He said I was his banker. As a teenager, I graduated to arranging stock on the shelves and decorating for the holidays.

I remembered standing in the drugstore window, more tinsel in my hair than on the Christmas tree, while Dad leaned on the counter in his white jacket. His laugh was irresistible, and I listened to our customers share his mirth as I inhaled the scent of peppermint candy canes all around me. Mother had a tiny office behind the pharmacy and a metal desk covered with ledgers.

I could see a sliver of her face frowning, always frowning. I could hear her pressing harder with her mechanical pencil and clicking to force a new lead into the point. The more he laughed with the customers, the more she clicked. I lived for his warm smiles. I needed his approval, and the desire for approval stuck with me into adulthood when Ashton used it to destroy whatever self I had left.

Why did Mother have to tear Dad down? She and I became like her bangle bracelets, destined to circle and collide. "Let's not talk about Dad. He has nothing to do with Carlos or Luis."

"Luis is a kind, sweet man."

"Yes, he is, but let's not pretend that's the only reason you married him."

"I know, you hold his money against him—or me. Whatever has happened between you and Carlos is hurting Luis, and he doesn't deserve that. Family, not money, is everything to him. He dotes on you, so much that he thinks Carlos is to blame, and—"

"And you think it's me." Fury overcame me. "He raped me!"

Mother ceased sputtering. Her face blanched, and I could see her chest rising and falling. Tears, blackened by mascara, began to run down her cheeks. She turned away, pushing her face into the crook of her elbow, seeking comfort in the upholstered arm of her loveseat. She was sobbing now, frightening me.

"Mother . . ." I moved to her side, offering a cocktail napkin. Inadequate. Pathetic. I should have hugged her, but my arms wouldn't move. I was still smarting from her scorn. She wiped her face with the back of her hand and used the napkin to blot the tear stains on the loveseat. I placed my hand on hers to stop the futile dabbing. "It's okay. I'll take care of it."

She turned her streaked and puffy face toward me, and I reached out to brush away the strands of hair stuck to her skin. Gone was the illusion of youthfulness. "Nothing lasts," she said. "Everything falls apart."

"Your life isn't falling apart. Carlos is gone. I'll be leaving tomorrow, and your life will return to normal."

"Life isn't like an elastic band that snaps back to its original shape. One change affects everything." She clasped her hands together. "I have to tell you something important, Sylvie, so please don't quarrel with my every word. We don't have much time." She looked around the room furtively, as though someone might be lurking behind the drapes, and lowered her voice. "I'm not well, and Luis doesn't know."

My heart began to beat faster, my thoughts flashing back to Celia fussing over her in the kitchen and sending her upstairs for a nap. Steadying her voice, she continued, "I asked for a second opinion, but the doctors say it's esophageal cancer, usually terminal."

I was too shocked to respond. I'd been playing tug-of-war, and now there was no one pulling on the other end. The object of my resentment was gone, replaced by a weak, sick, aging woman. Botox or perhaps a recent face lift had disguised the facial signs of her failing health. I wondered how long this had been going on.

"Luis has a serious heart condition. I'll find the right time to reveal the news to him in a comforting way. Some people do survive this." She put her hand on my arm. Her pleading eyes sought mine. "You're my daughter, Sylvie. Besides Luis, I have no one else. If Luis dies first, who'll take care of me?" I tried to absorb all she was telling me, this sea change. I covered her hand with mine.

"Margaret?" Eileen stood at the entrance to the living room. When Mother turned her red eyes in Eileen's direction, Eileen looked to me for a cue. All I could do was grimace and shrug. Eileen began to back away. "I'm so sorry for interrupting. Since Sylvie and I are leaving tomorrow, I thought we should try to fit in your massage this afternoon. It can certainly wait."

"There won't be a better time, dear. A massage is just what I need." She looked back at me. "We'll talk later."

I listened to them climb the stairs and sank back into the loveseat's cushions. Its tear-stained arm was an affront to the elegant room. I had imagined Mother's life of wealth impervious to disaster. How naive I'd been, or perhaps that was a choice I'd made. I abandoned the loveseat and slid open the glass doors, hoping the thrashing surf would drown out my guilt.

In Boston, when the wind blew from the east, one could catch a pleasant whiff of the ocean that was nothing at all like the heavy pungency of that afternoon's sea air as I ran across the beach, kicked off my sandals, and waded in. I stood knee-deep in water, feeling the pull of the receding tide. My dug-in toes tried to resist.

CHAPTER 12

I pulled the two zipper tabs of my swollen bag in opposite directions, and my compressed clothes exhaled with relief like an overfed diner loosening his belt. After unpacking my toiletries and returning my sandals to the back of my closet, where the rest of my out-of-season footwear had a head start on its coating of winter dust, I dumped the contents of my luggage into the laundry basket at my feet and padded off to start the washer.

As long as I didn't look in the mirror, I wouldn't have to confront any visible reminders of my holiday in Miami. I knew my face looked medium-rare—pink cheeks, forehead, nose, and chin, but I hoped ample basting with moisturizer would tone it down to a more uniformly cooked shade.

Eileen's natural complexion was darker than mine, tawny after four days in the sun. Add to that the glow of love . . . well, maybe it wasn't love, but she and Miguel seemed equally smitten. On our return flight, she had rhapsodized over him—how sweet, how down-to-earth he was, how jaded with the South Beach party scene. She'd met him at just the right moment, and did I know he collected geodes? He had a lighted curio cabinet, where he displayed them, and on her next trip down . . . yes, she would be going down for New Year's, staying in his condo.

I loved seeing her so happy but wondered where Miguel was leading her. He seemed sincere to me, but he was Carlos's brother. Eileen was swept up in a romance worthy of a Harlequin novel: folk music–loving massage therapist from New England on tropical vacation falls for Cuban American businessman and aficionado of salsa dancing. My own storybook romance with Ashton had left me cynical about the genre.

I consolidated my pillows and lay down with my tablet to check out the latest news on industry websites. It would be tough to get excited about a technology blog tonight, but I had to get my head back in the game.

■ ■ ■

Eileen had tried to get me to talk about Mother on the flight home after her description of shepherding Margaret upstairs for a massage. In spite of Mother's red eyes, she had appeared composed, but her back was tense and tight under Eileen's hands. "Let it go, Margaret, just breathe," Eileen had murmured. Mother had loosened up all right, resuming her weeping as though Eileen had opened a sluice.

She had offered Eileen no explanation, nor had I, but I ached at this retelling and looked out the window, searching the thin clouds between wing and ocean, as though a suitable response hovered there. I knew Eileen was challenging me to acknowledge the effects of my cold war with Mother.

"She was stressed out from the holiday dinner and house full of guests," I said.

Eileen looked unconvinced but didn't pursue the issue. Telling her the truth would have put an unfair burden on her, a secret she'd need to keep from Miguel. I had to conceal not only Mother's cancer but Luis's heart condition.

There was an empty seat between us. I laid my book on it, planning to end the conversation with a nap, but Eileen hadn't covered all the questions on her agenda.

"So, tell me what happened between you and Carlos after you left the club. You said it didn't end well, and I noticed the two of you avoiding each other the rest of the trip."

"We just came back to the house." The lie was hard to tell with my wrists still sore from Carlos's grip.

"Bullshit."

"I don't want to ruin your good mood."

Eileen raised an eyebrow. "My moods aren't that fragile. You're stalling." She must have seen my glassy eyes, so close to spilling over. "My God, Sylvie." She shoved my book to the floor, raised the arm rest and pulled me into the middle seat.

My face wet against her shoulder, my whisper muffled, I forced out the words, "Carlos raped me."

She wrapped her arm around me. "That shit! I'm so sorry, Syl. If I'd had any idea, I wouldn't have given you a hard time about not telling me. I thought you were being evasive. Instead, you were traumatized." She grabbed a cocktail napkin and dabbed at my tears.

"I was embarrassed."

"Embarrassed that you were raped?"

"You saw how much encouragement I gave him, how I couldn't hold myself back."

"Yes, I saw all that, but so what? You were the victim. He forced himself on you. How could his attack be your fault? You know that, don't you?"

"I know, but it doesn't change how I feel. What's important, though"—I pulled away from her arm—"is that you don't tell Miguel. I don't mean to put you in the middle, but if Miguel tells his father, Luis will be livid and call Carlos on the carpet. Carlos will tell Luis I slept with him willingly in the past."

"I don't think Luis will believe Carlos. When I gave Margaret her massage, she told me Carlos couldn't be trusted. He raped some teenager in Cuba, although he claimed it was consensual. She refused to have an abortion, so he's been supporting the child ever since. He didn't think the Cuban family would come after him legally, but Luis didn't care. He insisted Carlos support his child."

Would it have mattered if I'd known earlier? What's the difference—the cards are played. Mother was right. Everything falls apart.

■ ■ ■

I was accomplishing nothing staring unseeing at my tablet. I couldn't banish my thoughts as easily as I had disposed of the contents of my suitcase. Visiting Mother had made me miss Dad. I used to seek him out after my fights with her. He didn't often take my side, but he was comforting. Going to him was as natural as pulling a cozy chair under the warm light of a favorite lamp.

On impulse, I retrieved a stepladder from my kitchen and stood it in the bedroom closet. Once I had climbed high enough to reach the top shelf, I could see the stored cartons from the home Ashton and I had owned in Weston. I tried without success to maneuver one of the boxes into my arms, but it slipped from my grip and spilled its contents.

I stepped down from the ladder and sat cross-legged on the floor. On top of the pile was the smiling Manhardt couple in front of a vintage New England colonial. Our house with its narrow white clapboards and black shutters was quaint in style but imposing in scale. A generous portico sheltered the entrance, and brass lamps flanked the doorway.

Sitting at the top of a rise on winding Glendale Road, the house made the impression Ashton desired: a prosperous couple resided within. It wasn't so much the house I missed as its surroundings. Beyond our circular drive, sap cans clung to maples, and chunky boulders lay about, their cragginess softened by the wealth of feathery evergreens.

I got on my knees and dug through the photos until I found a manila envelope. Inside were several shots of Dad smiling broadly in front of his store, Hometown Pharmacy. I'd never noticed Mother before, her face wraithlike behind the glass.

Sitting back on my heels, I recalled her bitter words, "*I* was the one, not him." How scornfully she had dubbed him "Mr. Congeniality," as though his likeability counted for nothing. While it may not have shown up on the store's balance sheet, it counted with me. I shuffled through the other photos in the envelope until I found one with no enigmatic face in the window. After piling the spilled photos back in the box, I leaned Dad's photo against my mirror. Seeing his face alongside my reflection made me feel as though he were still beside me.

■ ■ ■

The next morning at ten, I was still lounging under the covers when the phone rang. Eileen, I assumed.

"Hi, it's Rip. Thought I'd give you a chance to catch up on your sleep before I called."

"Thanks, but I've been up for quite a while." Did twenty minutes qualify?

"Want to run off some of that turkey stuffing?"

I wanted to hide under my quilt indefinitely, especially from anyone possessing a Y chromosome. I'd been working hard to keep my thoughts away from the Carlos debacle. *Would a run help?* I agreed.

The temperature was forty degrees and the air quiet. I hated boring gray days when the sun never quite committed to appearing. I much preferred serious darkening that impelled me to turn on the lights and check the weather report. Rip pulled up to Old Mill precisely at noon. I wondered if trainers were like shrinks, incapable of beginning any activity other than on the hour. Having a breakthrough? Sorry, time's up. Next session, we'll start where we left off, with your latissimus dorsi.

"Nice nose," Rip said, grinning, as I climbed into his Jeep. "Does that thing glow in the dark?"

"Go ahead. Get it out of your system." As I pulled the door shut, a dog's head appeared beside my face and commenced licking me. "And who is this?"

"Dinger, cut it out."

"Dinger?"

"In baseball it means a home run."

I turned to the beautiful golden retriever whose tongue was washing my cheek. "Dinger, not on a first date."

"Sorry, we're still working on manners. Dinger is a rescue, abandoned on church steps with his mom and littermates."

"What happened to them?"

"Someone found them and delivered them to a shelter."

"Oh, Dinger, that's a sad story. I'm glad it ended happily, at least for you." Dinger concurred, which he demonstrated by thumping his tail against the back seat and returning his wet tongue to my face.

We'd agreed to run in Newton where an exercise trail wound through sixty acres of fields and woods at Cold Spring Park. I could see why the place appealed to Rip, even on a dull November day. Woods screened out the backs of the colonials and Victorians on the surrounding streets, and squirrels' nests sat exposed like knots among the twiggy tresses of oaks and maples. Dinger was ecstatic and, unlike us, felt no need to stick to the path. He ran full out and inspired me to do the same, but Rip held me back to a more human speed.

"I can see you had plenty of sun in Miami Beach. How was your trip otherwise?"

"Uh . . . very nice, thanks." *Outside of Carlos's rape and Mother's news.* "Thanksgiving was, you know, festive."

We had to watch our footing, since a layer of leaves had blown across the path, obscuring rocks and tree roots. "Did you enjoy spending time with your family?"

Truth was there had been moments of connection and warmth: gathering around the table for our holiday dinner, walking in the garden with Luis, even shopping with Mother and Eileen like a trio of overaged teens. If only . . .

"I'm sorry. Was my question too personal?"

"Expectations, you know, they're always so high, and then something unpleasant happens or something pleasant doesn't, and you end the holiday with an unsettled feeling."

"Ah, yes, shpilkes," he said with a knowing smile. "Literally means sitting on pins, but people use it to describe nerves, agita, the feeling that keeps you up at night."

"Sounds like a neighboring nation to Brobdingnag. Do you get shpilkes after seeing your family?"

"Before and during too."

I wondered if his mother was on his case for choosing a career as a physical trainer or if that conflict had died with the rabbi. It was appalling that his family would disapprove of a legitimate career as though he stuck up liquor stores to pay his bills. If I were in the market for a husband, would I have any reservations about marrying a trainer? What if he were an AI expert and venture capitalist like Ashton?

I sneaked a look at his profile, trying to imagine that stubbly chin over a starched white collar and Armani tie. Impossible. Why would I care about such credentials anyway—because I still held Ashton in such high esteem? Only Mother would be appalled by my marrying a trainer. Eileen would be appalled if anyone raised the issue. She'd point out that Madonna had married her trainer.

Mother thought I'd been naive. She'd made it clear she was happier married to Luis than to my father, even though Dad was the "love of her life." Money and status represented happiness to her. Could I honestly say they didn't matter to me? Money had been tight while I was growing up, and now, without Ashton, it was tight again, but at least I have a career and can pay most of my bills. I don't need a guy to rescue me.

"Relationships," I said. "You can't be too careful." I immediately regretted the non sequitur.

His bushy eyebrows rose. "Do you mean family or other kinds of relationships?"

I wondered what he'd say if I told him I'd combined the two. "Family . . . no, both."

"Maybe you're too cautious. Do you downhill ski, Sylvie?"

I nodded.

"When a novice finds his skis headed straight down the mountain, he hangs back against the hill for security because leaning back seems like best way to control speed. Except it isn't—it just makes you go faster."

"Aha," I said. "The counterintuitive gets you every time."

"Same with relationships. Caution doesn't always bring control. If you're not going to commit to the mountain, don't get on the lift."

He had a point there. I definitely shouldn't have gotten on the "lift" with Carlos. There were so many contradictions about Rip. For one, delivering life guidance made him sound more like a rabbi than a trainer. We turned onto a less traveled path through the woods with only enough width to run single file. He gestured for me to take the lead and whistled for Dinger.

Rip's skiing metaphor notwithstanding, I'd gotten into serious trouble before my divorce throwing caution to the ocean winds of Miami Beach. During the visit when Carlos and I first hooked up, Ashton flew to Miami and showed up at the house unannounced. Said he wanted to surprise me. I wasn't surprised. I was horrified. Mother and Luis were out at a friend's garden party. I showed Ashton to my room so he could unpack. Unfortunately, Carlos, who'd made love to me with abandon before dawn, had abandoned his abbreviated black briefs on the far side of the bed.

Ashton never found out whose briefs those were but was so pissed he left before anyone even knew he'd been there, before

I could feign surprise and ask, "Where did those come from?" He filed for divorce as soon as he returned home. We had a ten-year prenup, and the clock was on the field. Game over.

"Look out!" Rip's warning came too late.

I found myself on my hands and knees with a sharp shooting pain in my right knee. I sat down and brushed the dirt off my palms. The large rock I had tripped over was partially hidden by leaves. My running pants were ripped and blood was beginning to seep through.

"Sylvie, I'm so sorry. I should have reminded you to watch the ground." Dinger charged over and tried to insert himself between Rip and me. "Dr. Dinger, you're not needed here." He gently pushed the dog aside.

Manipulating my knee, Rip proclaimed it not seriously injured but in need of ice. He pulled me to my feet and, supporting my arm, led me out of the park to his Jeep. I didn't really need his assistance to walk, but despite the pain, I was enjoying his closeness too much to tell him.

"I don't know where my mind was to make me miss that rock. Sorry you have to cut short your run."

"Oh, forget it. Women have gone to much greater lengths to get away from me."

Women, I thought, *not clients*.

CHAPTER 13

Sam was back in town and called me Monday morning to see if we could get together. I had finished most of my coffee by the time he joined me in the festively decorated but nearly empty cafeteria. The weeks between Thanksgiving and Christmas were quiet in many businesses, although sales reps were often pushing for orders so they could make quota by year-end. Sam's customers were in Europe, probably the reason for his showing up in jeans and a golf shirt.

"You're peeling," he said, pointing to my nose. "I thought Warren was the only one around here that molted."

"Birds lose their feathers, not their skin, and while we're on the subject of ruffled feathers, did your family recognize you on Thanksgiving? You've been away a lot."

His hands made finger waves in his salt-and-pepper hair. "I've been taking heat for that, but what choice do I have? It's only going to get worse. I'll be spending even more time overseas."

"Is it possible that's what Warren wanted?" I asked. "I don't know if he influenced Richard's decision, but Richard could just as easily have made me the international sales exec and given you the US." I remembered Warren's implication: Richard wanted to send the pain-in-the-ass guy to Europe and keep the malleable woman around, the one who wouldn't press.

Sam drummed his fingers on the table, putting me in mind of Rip's shpilkes. "You might be right. They could pursue getting us acquired without dealing with my demands for NewAI. Bastards. I wish I knew who Richard was talking to. That would at least tell me whether the potential buyer wanted us for our technology, our customer base, or even our cash in the bank, and whether we'd be likely to keep our jobs after the acquisition."

I wondered how much cash we actually had in the bank after providing Richard with his loan. My knee ached and I craved Advil, but I couldn't leave Sam there stewing. "Why did you want to get together?"

"Oh, right. I just wanted to know if you got the same deal I did. I'm not asking what they're paying you, but Richard said it was so late in the fiscal year, he couldn't do much for me in the way of a salary bump until January 1. He gave me more stock options. I'm not saying I need it to buy off my wife, but it wouldn't hurt if she could see there might be advantages to my new job."

I nodded. "Same deal, except I don't have to convince anyone I've made a beneficial tradeoff. Actually, the less I'm around, the happier it makes the mice living under my dishwasher." I couldn't even get a smile out of Sam. I felt like Christopher Robin trying to have a conversation with Eeyore. There must be something I could say to cheer him up. "Maybe we can find a leaker to tell us what's going on behind closed doors."

Sam looked up hopefully. "You really think so? Your soft touch didn't work on Warren."

"I won't make that mistake again. I'm thinking of Fannette."

"Little Annie Fannie?"

"I'll only talk to her if you promise to drop that sexist nickname."

Sam made a face but didn't protest. "I'm leaving for Paris on Friday, so email me if you find out anything from Little—I mean Fannette. Use my Gmail address, not my company account, and don't send it from the office."

By lunchtime, I was buried. I had a conference call at three with the US sales force and prep work to do before that. I ran down to the café to get a sandwich, and while at the register I caught sight of Rona and Fannette at a corner table. My imagination might have been in overdrive, but they seemed to be leaning toward each other with a conspiratorial air. Rona glanced up and saw me watching them. I hadn't even realized they were friends.

■ ■ ■

The next morning in the reception area, Rona beckoned me over to the reception desk. "Can I come talk to you when I'm on break?"

I agreed, curious.

When she arrived, she pulled her chair close to me. "Thank you for meeting with me. Fannette was afraid to come talk to you. She's a worrier, but maybe that comes with the job of executive assistant to the CEO. I wouldn't want it."

Whether or not Fannette was strung high and taut as a circus wire, I had no doubt she could be a reliable source of information, at least via Rona, but the thought of encouraging the two women to become corporate snitches made me squirm. Even though I had suggested to Sam that we find a leaker, I felt guilty.

"Rona, as a rule I would never try to persuade Fannette to part with confidential information, but I had the feeling she was upset at hearing Richard and Warren so angry with one another. Now that I'm on the executive staff, maybe I can put her mind at ease or help in some way."

Rona looked over her shoulder. "Warren was mad at Richard. He started yelling about Richard's messing up a deal. That's when the door slammed. Is Richard allowed to borrow money from the company?"

I didn't see that coming. The loan was supposed to be a secret. "Yes, I believe he is, assuming it's accounted for. Fannette may have misunderstood." I doubted Richard's loan was kosher, but I didn't want Rona and Fannette obsessing over it. I wondered if Manny had objected to Richard's loan and gotten himself fired over it. "What deal? Were they discussing a customer?"

Rona shook her head. "Fannette didn't think so. Maybe somebody buying us?"

"There's no reason at this point to think we're being acquired, but thank Fannette for the information." If I wasn't sure I was lying, why did I feel guilty?

* * *

My knee was improving, but I felt some trepidation about keeping my appointment at BodySculpt. Rip's idea of going easy on me was delivering ten lashes instead of twenty. As it turned out, he was planning upper-body exercises and core work. My cardio was on a stationary hand bike. I pushed myself to make my arms stronger, propelled by the memory of Carlos pinning me to the bed. *Never again*, I told myself at each revolution.

Rip returned to my side and looked at the digital readout. "Boy, you're an animal tonight. I wish all my clients were this motivated."

"Managing sales in the software business is a tough job. I'm working out my aggressions in the gym. Isn't that supposed to be healthy?"

"Maybe you just feel guilty about selling a product people think will save them, when it's actually going to lead to the end of the human race. You're selling a golem."

I was about to protest his implication, but he caught me up short with his golem reference. "What the hell is that?"

"A creature artificially brought to life. In sixteenth-century

Prague, a rabbi created a golem, a humanoid of sorts, out of clay. It was supposed to protect the community, but it became dangerous, so he got rid of it. There have been other golems too, but according to the stories, they were brought to life and then became evil monsters. The moral dilemma is how do you improve on creation without the risk of doing harm?" He handed me a towel.

"You think I'm selling a monster?"

He led me over to the free weights and handed me two. "Bicep curls. Two sets of fifteen. Don't you ever consider the logical extension of artificial intelligence, the potential for harm? Newspapers and magazines are full of articles on AI. Everyone's learning about it."

I was hot, tired, weary of bicep curls, and starting to get pissed off. "Maybe you've just learned enough to be dangerous."

Rip took the weights from me and gestured toward the chest press. I waited for him to adjust the seat height and set the weights before I sat down and commenced yanking on the handles as hard as I could.

"Easy," he said. "Smooth motion. Look, I'm not trying to make you angry, but these robots don't necessarily limit themselves to what they're first programmed to do. They learn from experience and data, tons of it, and then act on what they've learned or extrapolated. Machine ethics is an oxymoron. Who knows what your golem could do next?"

For someone not trying to make me angry, Rip was doing a crappy job. "Next time you're on an operating room table and some golem is saving your life, or if you're hopelessly lost and the golem in your GPS keeps you from freezing to death overnight in your car, you might change your mind."

Rip made a face.

I couldn't stop myself, nor could I keep testiness out of my voice. "The neural networks of artificial intelligence are inspired by the design of the human brain. They can find cures for diseases, detect problems in radiology reports, translate languages, make predictions, find patterns . . . They're going to keep helping humans in ways we can't even predict."

"Okay, point taken." He gave in, but if he was a sore loser, I was a sore winner.

CHAPTER 14

Thanksgiving to Christmas seemed to last only fifteen minutes. The pressure of booking deals by year's end was exponentially greater because of my new management responsibilities and Richard's micromanaging. I missed working for Manny. No one knew whether he'd gone to another company or taken an extended vacation. He'd just disappeared.

Rona deserved credit for making all of us who labored heads down mindful of the holidays. When we arrived and departed through the reception area, tiny snowmen, candy canes, and iridescent ornaments bobbed on the plastic limbs of the company's Christmas tree in the artificial breeze of our swinging glass doors. An electric menorah burned brightly for more than the obligatory eight days, demanding equal time from those admiring the tinseled competition in the opposite corner.

As I loosened my scarf and unbuttoned my coat, Rona asked if I were coming to the Christmas party. I'd been dimly aware of the preparations, and though I'd forgotten the party was only two days away, I assured Rona I would be there.

I would, of course, be going solo. Better that way. Romance was the favored grist for the company gossip mill, and the sex lives of executives was premium grade. I had nothing to wear and no time to shop, but I needed to get out of the office and decided to spend lunchtime at Nordstrom.

The task would be simpler than shopping for a night out in South Beach. Mother wouldn't be steering me to the priciest garments nor Eileen surprising me by advocating for skimpy coverage. I knew the men on the AI*future* management team would wear tuxedos to the party. Kate, who had continued her distancing behavior in the days since my return from Florida, had not encouraged any what-are-you-wearing female bonding.

I walked briskly through the store, ignoring the tempting displays along the way, dodging young mothers with strollers and slow-moving octogenarians. The eveningwear department glittered with holiday gowns, a Christmas spectacle all on its own with racks of luscious velvets and sequins.

Pleasure turned to anxiety as precious minutes passed. There were too many possibilities. Nothing seemed right. I tried on a blue silk skirt with a short-sleeved beaded top—too matronly. A low-cut, curve-hugging black jersey was too provocative, at least for an executive. Feeling like the Goldilocks of haberdashery, I didn't even zip up two dresses that were all wrong the moment I pulled them past my hips.

When I slipped into a fitted satin camisole and black pants, softened with the addition of a sheer black jacket, I knew I'd found "just right," or at least the "just right" derived by a process of elimination. My appearance was not too sexy, modest, festive, or formal. Who said blondes weren't smart? Goldilocks and I were soul sisters.

■ ■ ■

Saturday night was frigid. An ice-white moon reminded me of the round fluorescent fixture in our Reading kitchen. As a young girl flipping through the *Mademoiselle* and *Glamour* issues Mother brought home from Dad's drugstore, I never envisioned myself stepping out for the evening sans man. *This is part of the job*, I reminded myself. A company gala is a command performance. When I'm credited with AI*future*'s huge success, the adoration of the masses will more than make up for the absence of a man to drink Champagne from my size 8 evening shoe.

I followed the sound of laughter through the Marriott's festooned hallways to the AI*future* cocktail party. Our CEO was the first person I saw. Richard's red bow tie and dated-looking cummerbund made him appear an accessory to his wife's crimson gown. She was an imposing woman, straight-backed with swept-up chestnut hair and a demeanor of studied graciousness well-suited to the proprietress of a Newbury Street florist shop—our shop, that is, paid for with company funds.

She gestured expansively, her diamond bracelets winking in the light, to an audience consisting of the Astroves and Buckleys. They listened politely as she raved about a protégé's design skills. The young woman had just created the centerpieces for a wedding at the Ritz-Carlton, and the client was blown away. She couldn't divulge the customer's name, but the wedding was very chichi, "a Boston Brahmin family you'd know," she boasted.

I excused myself from the fan club as quickly as possible and headed straight for the bar, where I grabbed a white wine off the corner. Warren was socializing with his engineers, most of whom were unrecognizable in suits. This annual event was at its heart a masquerade. None of us looked like our workaday selves, and the presence of spouses altered the dynamics of our interactions. The sweet-faced Asian woman beside Warren didn't look like she belonged anywhere near those dark jowls.

Sam had not yet arrived, nor did I see Kate, whose red hair usually drew attention like a traffic flare. Our local sales reps pulled me into their group and began introductions. Nobody's spouse looked like what I expected. Our rep for downtown Boston, dressed in a brilliant turquoise sheath, was the peacock of her pair, since her quiet round-faced husband was as expressionless as a dinnerplate. The salesman who worked out of Washington, DC, looked like Paul Bunyan without the plaid shirt. His wife, a birdlike woman with a pointy nose and shrewd black eyes, was a third the size of him.

Husbands and wives had no outlet for frustrations with their spouses' employers. Part of the tension of the company's family gatherings was the undercurrent created when spouses met the executives they'd been hearing about during dinner diatribes and had to greet them politely, any sense of outrage checked at the coat room. I doubted Warren felt guilty about shading the truth to his people. Maybe that was the job—every manager a marketer managing the perceptions of subordinates. Was that more or less legitimate than managing perceptions outside the company?

I was commenting to "Paul Bunyan's" wife how valuable his contribution had been to our sales revenue, when I noticed her husband looking past me. Kate was making her way toward us in a low-cut purple satin dress and silver spike heels. Every head turned except those of people pretending they weren't looking, but the pang of envy I felt had less to do with her appearance than her escort, whom she introduced to all of us as Fielding Harris. Rip's stubble was gone, and he wore a well-tailored navy-blue suit, pale blue shirt, and maroon silk tie.

"I didn't know . . . how did you . . . ?" I tried to frame a question that would convey my surprise but not my dismay.

"He's not your *private* personal trainer," said Kate. Her teasing tone bore no hint of her previous standoffishness, which I was beginning to understand, but she no doubt meant the comment as a competitive poke. She went on to explain she had begun training at BodySculpt before Thanksgiving. She hadn't hit it off with her first trainer, so Rob Linde had obligingly substituted Rip. "He's helped me in so many ways already," she said, taking his arm, a clear signal of ownership. Rip demurred, insisting she had done all the work, and smiled broadly at me as though the three of us had pulled something off together. A cheerleading pyramid flashed into my mind—a positively nauseating thought—so I excused myself and retreated to the ladies' room.

Fuck, fuck, fuck. I was afraid to show any sign that I was upset lest I become the subject of company gossip, so I smiled into the mirror as two older administrators from Kate's department leaned in to restore the candy-apple luster to their faded lips. Despite my studied reapplication of blush, my eyes were on my just-right ensemble, which now seemed understated enough for a run to the supermarket.

While I'd been wondering how to look professional in evening clothes, Kate was playing the game from both sides, buttoned down by day and undone by night. She set the bar high at work and draped herself over it after hours. I reminded myself that I had no evidence of that. Perhaps she was discreet, a closet drinker.

How ironic that Rip should look every bit the corporate executive in a Savile Row suit. I'd relegated him to a compartment, as though his only incarnation was trainer-in-tracksuit. Was it the light over the mirror that made my eyes look greener than usual? I couldn't blame Rip for finding Kate attractive. I'd given him less reason to think I was interested than a Victorian maiden dropping her hankie a moment too late. *I have to remember to add to my resume "expertise in giving mixed signals."* Bet I could count on Carlos to be a reference.

You're at a business function, I lectured myself, *not a high school prom.* Returning to the party, I saw Rip place his hand on Kate's bare back. Some professional I was. I wanted to rip her face off.

The crowd had begun drifting into the ballroom where people were queuing up at two buffet stations. Fannette and Rona were in line together, and they greeted me warmly as I approached. Fannette wore a brown knit sheath, an unfortunate choice that emphasized her small breasts. Rona, by contrast, was resplendent in gold taffeta, her convexity as complementary to Fannette's concavity as that of neighboring pieces in a jigsaw puzzle.

I was about to ask Fannette and Rona to join me at one of the sales reps' tables, when Sam interrupted to tell me Richard was rounding up the executive team to sit with him. Elitism, of course, but I had no choice.

I've never liked long rectangular tables, by nature an impediment to conversation, but I was grateful to be at the other end from Kate and Rip. Sam and his wife, Susan, sat down across from them, and after a quick round of musical chairs, I found myself opposite Warren and the lovely Maya, with Richard at the head of the table and his wife, Etta, beside him. I caught a glimpse of Rip looking my way and absorbed myself in arranging my napkin on my lap. Seeing him here on my turf, or rather my artificial turf, was making my stomach do flip-flops.

I turned my attention to Maya, who was massaging her prominent belly like my Uncle Max used to do after his second slice of pumpkin pie. It was too early in the evening for either satiety or indigestion, so I wasn't surprised when Maya announced, "We're pregnant." Warren's face wore an unrecognizable expression—adulation.

Maya had to be younger by fifteen years, lithe-bodied and golden-skinned, with long glossy hair and lips that celebrity actresses possessed only by virtue of their collagen injections. Her eyes met Warren's, and she lowered her lids demurely. Hadn't that gone out with the geishas?

I didn't know if she were subservient or if I was projecting my stereotype of what Warren's wife would need to be to survive. Maya chose that moment to offer up her conviction that her kind and brilliant husband would be father of the year. Poor deluded darling. It frightened me to think of Warren spawning.

The deejay was playing a number with a Latin beat, which

I was sure I had danced to in South Beach. Kate and Rip were among the first to take the floor. *Tell me he can't dance*, I silently implored the gods, but, of course, he was a lynx, confidently guiding Kate, who laughed with delight, her head tilted back as she looked up at him. Warren's eyes followed mine.

"Nice couple," he commented. "Your trainer, isn't he?"

"I should get a commission from BodySculpt. Guess there's more than one type of personal training."

"Meow," said Sam in a stage whisper from the other end of the table.

"Rabbit ears," I shot back.

From Warren's throat emerged an unfamiliar sound, laughter. He nodded toward the throng of dancers. "Harold seems to have deep concerns, too." The Astroves were on the dance floor, and Harold was endeavoring to look down Kate's dress over his wife's shoulder. Who could blame him? Kate looked as voluptuous as a fertility goddess.

Between the main course and dessert, when Harold's wife went to the ladies' room, Harold asked Kate to dance. She hesitated before rising unsteadily from the table. She could hardly refuse, though she looked as though she'd been asked to plunge her hand into the cold water of a toilet tank to reconnect the flusher chain. Connect they did, however, with Harold wrapping his arm tightly around her waist. I thought for sure he was about to tango and wondered if I were the only one who knew she had slept with him.

Rip stood behind my chair. "Sylvie?" He pulled me up without waiting for a response. "Are you mad at me?" he asked, as we began to dance.

Who, me? I thought. "Of course not, I'm just a little off my game tonight."

"Well, it doesn't show. You look beautiful."

"Thanks." I avoided his eyes. "I didn't know you were working with Kate." Rip was silent, and I was sorry I had raised the issue at the party. How could he not find my question accusatory? I looked around the dance floor and observed Mrs. Astrove's return from the ladies' room. She took up a post at the edge of the crowd, plum-colored lips pursed and freshly outlined with purple pencil. If she wanted to appear a casual and amused observer, it wasn't working. Her narrowed eyes were focused on her husband's tentacled clutch on Kate.

I whispered in Rip's ear, "A P&L statement in the making."

"Huh?"

"Harold's profit is his wife's loss, and I think she's about to launch a one-woman stockholder revolt."

"I do love your sense of humor," he said, "but every so often, something underneath jumps out to bite me."

"Under? I didn't know your personal training extended to my subconscious. Do you provide the same service to Kate?" I bit my tongue.

"Yeah, jumps out like that."

Mrs. Astrove chose that moment to cut in on Harold and Kate. Her lips formed the word "bastard" as clearly as if she had spoken aloud. She grabbed the arm of her flyweight husband as he was in the middle of swooping Kate into a dip. Kate was too lubricated with bourbon to coordinate a backbend and, without Harold's support, landed on the floor. "And there goes the balance sheet," I quipped softly to myself, since Rip had left my side to collect Kate in his arms. She was unhurt but pale and rushed off to the ladies' room. I doubted she was on a mission to freshen her lip liner.

The dancing resumed, albeit with clusters of smirking observers among those with front-row seats. The show was over. Now it was time for the critics to perform. Etta and Richard had been on the dance floor when Kate fell, and the lines in Richard's forehead remained after her flight. Etta's under-eye cover-up had taken a powder, and a reddish glow from her gown reflected off the swollen bags beneath her eyes.

One strap had slipped off Maya's perfect golden shoulder, and Sam's shirt appeared soaked with perspiration as he removed his tuxedo jacket. The evening was fraying around the edges and needed to be retired from service. I skipped the goodbyes and withdrew as unobtrusively as I could from the ballroom. Out in the foyer, Rip was speaking earnestly to Kate. I couldn't hear what he was saying, but he held her hand and didn't see my retreat.

Before I reached the front door, I heard my name. Sam's wife, Susan, had followed me to the lobby. "Can I talk to you for a sec before you go?" She was an attractive but worn-looking fortysomething in a dark blue cocktail dress.

She looked over her shoulder and then back at me. "Sam would kill me if he knew I was talking to you, but I have to know if something's going on that he isn't telling me. I'm really worried." Her fingers kept working the clasp on her gold beaded evening bag. "He's traveling all the time, of course, but when he's home, he's testy and yells at me and the kids. His mood has always correlated with how well his sales are going, but this feels different."

"We've all been pretty stressed out—lots of year-end changes. I'm sure he's fatigued from his international travel, but Sam's a pro. He'll get through it." Susan's eyes were wet, so I hugged her. "I'll keep an eye on him, okay? Maybe I can get him home to you in time for dinner, at least the nights he's in town."

"Thank you. Anything you can do." She turned and hurried down the corridor, the rustling of her cocktail dress fading as she turned the corner. I was more worried about Sam's state of mind than I'd acknowledged to Susan. I knew it had to do with his suspicions about what Warren was hiding and concerns about our acquisition.

The hotel parking lot was cold and the light from the lampposts thin. The evening had not conformed to my expectations. Company parties were supposed to provide a pleasant gloss, a festive veneer, on normal interaction. Nothing substantive was supposed to change during those interludes. Rip and Kate, Kate and Harold . . . I shivered and folded my arms tight against my chest.

Back at Old Mill, I undressed quickly and filled my bathtub. When I had last taken a bath I couldn't recall, but Eileen had given me bath salts as part of a gift basket on our return from Miami. I poured the purple powder into the water surging from the faucet and inhaled the lavendered atmosphere. After climbing over the tub's faux porcelain rim, I immersed myself in welcoming warmth, trying to clear my mind of all but the soothing scent.

The folded wet washcloth I placed over my eyes blocked the light, but not my thoughts, as the evening replayed itself behind my lids. I could never admit to Eileen that I found myself seeking the meditative peace she touted. I silently repeated the mantra "ohm," which seemed to morph into "home" and carried me back to our yard in Reading where Mother tended the garden. I had forgotten that uncharacteristic bit of nurturing, but I could see her perfectly. I must have been small because she'd picked me up so I could smell the lilacs.

I'd been trying to keep thoughts of Mother out of my head, but that was beginning to take more effort than letting them in. I'd called a few times, but she'd been noncommittal about her condition. Miami was like a window on my computer that I kept forgetting was open. Whenever I closed down a task, it would be there, reminding me of Mother's failure to be honest and of my inadequate attention.

CHAPTER 15

As I described the party to Eileen on Sunday afternoon, I did my best to turn it into the story of an amusing soiree. We were lunching at the Green Scene, fast becoming Eileen's favorite restaurant, and she ate one forkful after another of her kale and mushroom salad with eyes fastened on my face. I described the entrance of Rip and Kate, with special emphasis on Kate's breasts, bursting forth like two overripe eggplants from their purple satin skins. The coup de grace, of course, was the sprawl brawl on the dance floor that, though comical in the retelling, had surely caused strife in the Astrove bedroom that night.

"And how was your BodySculpted bod adorned?"

"Hey, I put a lot of time and effort into finding the perfectly appropriate outfit."

"Why the obsession with 'perfect'? It's not like there was a prize for best costume. I think you may still be trying to conform to Ashton's standard."

The server brought Eileen her tea and topped off my glass of sparkling water from a blue bottle. When she returned with a basket of warm rolls, she deposited one in the exact center of each bread plate. I wondered if she practiced with tongs at home. I could have used a pair to keep my problems at arm's length.

"Look, I have to maintain professional distance at all times. You know the things Ashton tells people about me."

"That asshole. Why isn't he afraid you'll do the same?"

"He warned me not to, because he was the injured party. He's a powerful guy. Everyone knows him. I don't know what I expected—maybe just some snide remarks about me. Did I really deserve his telling everyone he'd stoically preserved a marriage riven by disputes, that I was an emotionally unstable wife, that out of loyalty he had concealed from the world my irrational behavior, that I—"

"You're a lot of things, Syl, but irrational isn't one of them. Who'd believe him?"

"You're forgetting how credible he is." Tears rolled toward my chin till I stopped them with my napkin. After I composed myself, I explained the stature of Tory Partners and how easy it was for Ashton to start a rumor that would permeate the industry like the smell of rotten eggs. "He considers my career to be something he gave me that he can take away, like the assets he protected under our prenup. That's why I have to be so careful. I never know who's heard stories about me. It's not the kind of thing you can ask."

"So much for Mr. Perfect." She sighed. "Syl, you have a way bigger problem than dressing too conservatively for the company Christmas party. There must be a way to get him to stop."

I shook my head and blew my nose while Eileen contemplated her chai, stirring slowly. Steam rose from the dark mug, carrying the scent of cloves and cinnamon to my nostrils, the smell of childhood Christmases when Mother would open the oven door, allowing mingled fragrances to escape and meander from room to room.

No hidden agendas had spoiled the day—at least none that I could remember. The news media hadn't begun publishing the worrisome side of celebrating: we didn't suspect salmonella lurked within the stuffing or excessive carbs within the gingerbread. It never occurred to us that our local department store Santa might be a pedophile. If I had imagined myself married one day, it was to Cinderella's prince, and neither of us would suffer from the Goldilocks compulsion to try out bed after bed.

Eileen sat back and gave me a half-hearted smile. "One thing I can tell you, I'll never see another eggplant without thinking about Kate flaunting hers at your man."

"He's not my man."

"Oh, admit it. You want him to be."

"Give me a break. He's a personal trainer."

Eileen sat up straight, indignant. "And you think Ashton's a snob? Have you forgotten that I'm just a massage therapist?"

"Eileen! That's not what I meant."

"Yes, it is. That's why you were so pissed off that Kate saw the prince within the frog."

I felt a tightening in my gut, a pang of guilt that was visceral. She was right. It was time to lay off fairy tales.

CHAPTER 16

The static cling of my shirts and skirts wasn't the most frustrating aspect of winter, but it was the appropriate manifestation of the electric current running beneath the surface at AI*future*. Richard's door was often closed, especially when Warren was in there. Rona was my confidential informant, but she had little to reveal at the moment. I still worried about the effect of letting her fill that role.

In TV police dramas, confidential informants were recruited from the underworld. I hoped I wasn't corrupting her. A more realistic concern was that she and Fannette might get in trouble for leaking secrets to me. If only Sam had told me which engineer confided in him, I could try to find out more.

Miguel reached me on my cell as I sat in my office attempting to rework my sales forecast. I didn't recognize the number, but I picked up because it was a Miami area code. He'd never called before, so I was surprised to hear his voice.

"Sylvie, I'm calling about your mother. Her cancer is very bad. She's asking for you. The doctor said if you're planning to come, you'd better hurry. Luis was too distraught to phone, and Carlos thought you wouldn't take a call from him."

"How could this happen so fast? I was just there."

"The doctor said it's a very aggressive cancer that she'd had for months before she saw a doctor."

I was stricken and promised to leave immediately. I called the airline from my car and was relieved to be spared endless repeats of "your call is important to us" before a reservationist answered. He found me a seat on the next flight, leaving me with no travel worries besides navigating my way down Interstate 93 in heavy traffic, cursing any driver who failed to move out of my way.

My mind careened back and forth between fear my mother was slipping away and anger that whenever I'd called, she'd lied to me about her worsening condition. When had she told Luis about her cancer? Was his heart condition really that bad? Keeping a secret means appropriating the other person's right to react. Although it's rationalized as sparing them, it means making their decisions for them.

I couldn't eat anything on the flight. My guts were churning. I'd been blaming Mother for so many years I'd walled off my feelings for her. If I couldn't get to Miami in time—if I couldn't forgive her and tell her I love her—I'd be forever shadowboxing with her memory.

As soon as we landed, Miguel called my cell. I spotted his luminous Mercedes at the curb outside the baggage area, but instead of the broad smile that had enchanted Eileen at Thanksgiving, a face creased with consternation watched for me. He jumped out and came to me with open arms, his hug releasing my tears.

"When did you know?" I asked.

"She was so worried about my father, she wanted it to be a secret. Celia tried to shield her, but it was obvious she was going downhill fast. If the chemo was helping, we couldn't see it. It made her even more miserable. Luis hovered over her like a bird protecting its nest. He wanted to call you, but your mother was stubborn."

Maybe she wanted to spare me the worry, or maybe she anticipated how I was feeling right now: guilty about shutting her out of my life. Cancer makes a grudge pointless.

Would Carlos be at the house? I hoped not. He'd been through this already with his own mother. I thought about Rosa Carmelina, lying ill in the very same bed as Margaret. Given how much she favored Miguel, I wondered if Carlos had felt guilty about resenting his mother and whether he had forgiven her before her death.

The day was unusually raw for Miami. The flowers in front of the estate seemed less profuse than on my last visit, and no scent greeted me when I opened the car door. Celia stood on the veranda, but her apron was missing, and a lock of black hair that had worked its way loose from her bun hung down behind her ear. She hugged me.

"Your mother will be so happy. You're the reason she's been holding on."

Holding on for me? I could no longer hang back on the periphery of her life. "Where's Luis?"

"Out on the beach, just standing and staring at the breaking waves. He hasn't slept in I don't know how long. He lost Rosa Carmelina a long time ago, but Margaret brought him back to life." She shook her head. I could picture Luis out there in the wind, oblivious to the sand in his shoes. The tide was going out for both of them, and he knew it.

I climbed the stairs to the master bedroom. I'd never seen someone with terminal cancer, although I'd known people who had it. Doesn't everyone? Some had died and others had survived, but the news always came in a phone conversation, an email message, or an obituary. I didn't read obituaries. Only old people like my grandmother did. I had to be directed to one. I couldn't imagine an obituary for my mother, the stunning Margaret, mistress of an elegant Miami manse.

I stood in the doorway of the darkened room, where shadows cast by the shuttered windows tinted the rose walls magenta. When I saw her in the bed, I reached for the doorframe in shock. Beneath the satin quilt lay a skeletal being with unnaturally prominent cheekbones and sunken eyes that opened to meet my gaze. I couldn't imagine how she could have lost so much weight that fast. Her gnarled hand reached out to me with nails half polished, the pink ceding ground to the bare surface as the robust Margaret gave in to her disease. I couldn't catch my breath, couldn't stop the vibrations in my chest, until Miguel came up beside me and took my elbow. He had pulled up a chair for me close to Margaret's bedside.

I tried to compose my face, but she saw my dismay. "Ironic, isn't it," she said, in a quavering voice, "ending my days looking like this." She reached up to touch the gray wisps on her nearly bald head. "If my hairdresser could see me, he'd kill me." She tried to laugh at her own gallows humor but could only manage a coughing fit.

I heard the bedroom door close as Miguel departed, and I took a deep breath to steady myself. The room smelled medicinal, and something else was in the air—impending death. Perhaps Miguel recognized it. He was a teenager when his mother died. I wondered whether Miguel had understood the reason for his brother's distant behavior toward her. Maybe Miguel felt guilty about being the favored child, felt he owed something to Carlos. Was Rosa Carmelina responsible for turning Carlos into a rapist? That was nuts. I wasn't going to waste time feeling sympathy for Carlos.

Mother's fingers were cold as she tried to lean over and grasp mine. "I need to tell you something about Luis," she whispered hoarsely. "I told him Carlos raped you."

I pulled my hand away. "Why would you do that? Didn't you tell me Luis has a weak heart?"

"I want Luis to leave you money, more than just the money he would have left me, and I don't want Carlos telling lies about you to screw up my plan. With an inheritance from Luis, you'll never need to depend on a man like Ashton again."

She was trying to make up for pushing me into Ashton's arms for money. We could finally talk about that chapter in our lives without acrimony, or so I thought, until she fell back against the pillows, spent by the effort to impress on me what needed to happen—what she would make happen even if it required reaching out from the grave. I couldn't protest her strategy. She looked as though a reprimand would end her tenuous hold on life. I walked to the window and raised a slat of the shutter. Even the palm fronds had ceased their waving, in deference to Mother's condition.

I was running out of time to tell her how sorry I was for shutting her out. Why were the words so hard? "Mom . . ." I turned and looked into her lifeless eyes. Too late. Her hand hung over the edge of the bed. Gone was my resistance to all things touched by Margaret, pointless now. I collapsed in the chair, stunned. I felt nothing.

When I was a little girl, she had loved me fiercely. I remembered her hugs, could practically feel them. At first, I couldn't cry, then suddenly I was sobbing. Miguel must have heard me, because I felt his arm around me, guiding me from the room.

I sat at the kitchen table watching Celia make tea. Surely, we would hear Mother tapping her way downstairs in high-heeled sandals, see her breezing into the kitchen in a hot pink tube top and white slacks, layered gold necklaces encircling her tanned neck. All I heard was the whistling kettle. All I saw was steam rising from the spout as Celia poured hot water into my cup.

"She's gone now, isn't she, Sylvie?"

I nodded, and she crossed herself. I blotted my eyes with a napkin while she went to get Luis. I heard his muffled crying as he ascended the stairs to the bedroom.

I'd left Boston without going home to pack, so staying for the funeral meant borrowing from my mother's dresser and closet. Wearing her clothes, even her underwear, felt wrong, inappropriate, creepy. I was taking on her mantle, which I didn't want, and though we looked alike, we were so different inside. I had trouble finding a dress I felt comfortable wearing to a funeral.

■ ■ ■

Miguel had his arm around his father, but Carlos was scarcely present except at the graveside service, where he stood beside Luis. Celia stood behind him, sniffling into her black shawl as the priest recited his prayers.

Both my parents were gone now. I had a brief moment of fear, the sense that I was unmoored in the world with no refuge of last resort and no one to blame, fairly or not, for my choices. I had told Rip I felt old at the start of my first session at the gym. How one's perspective can change. My mother's death left me frightened as a child.

When we returned to the house, Luis asked me to join him on the patio. His eyes were swollen from crying, and he looked as though he'd aged ten years since Thanksgiving. He set a large polished wooden box on the glass table. "Although I wish you could stay, I know you need to return to work. Will you come back to see me?"

I nodded and stretched across to hug him.

"Before you go, your mother wanted you to have her jewelry. I removed all of it from the safe. She left an antique gold pendant, bracelet, and earrings to Celia. I've already given them to her."

He slid the box over to me. "Open it." If Luis's love for Margaret could be measured in carats, it was immense. One of the velvet cases held an elaborate diamond necklace, the kind one would wear . . . where? I had seen evening gowns in her closet for charity balls, perfect occasions for these gems. I frequented no venue where this spectacular array of jewelry would be appropriate.

"Luis, how generous you are."

His eyes moist, he turned away. "You are my daughter."

CHAPTER 17

The evening after I returned from Miami, Eileen swept into my apartment in a fringed poncho and plunked herself down on my sofa. The white box she pulled from her bag filled the air with the taste bud–teasing aroma of bakery cookies. "I wasn't sure if I was supposed to bring food or flowers to a shiva call, so I opted for something you could eat."

"Thank you, but I'm not sitting shiva for my mother, since I'm not Jewish, which of course you know. Not only that, but there's got to be a pound of cookies in that box, and there's no one here but me. If you don't share them with me, I'll eat all of them. How about some tea?"

She followed me into the kitchen. "I'm sorry I couldn't be there to support you. In spite of my flu shot, I came down with the flu. It didn't last as long as I expected, a fact my doctor thought I should rejoice over, but I wish I'd been able to come for the funeral." Frowning, she sat down at the table, licked her forefinger, and began rubbing a coffee stain on the surface. "I've talked with Miguel several times about his father. Poor Luis just sits on the beach watching the waves. Celia has to remind him to eat."

"I wanted to stay and comfort him, but work . . . shit. The truth is I just had to get out of there."

"Don't feel guilty, Syl. He has his sons. I know you'll go back to see him as soon as you can get away, maybe when I visit Miguel."

We carried our mugs of green tea into the living room, and I pointed out that I'd purchased that variety just for her.

"Well, the tea is healthy but the cookies aren't. Do you think they cancel each other out?" she asked.

"I'm afraid it's not a zero-sum game." I put out of mind any worries about my next visit to the gym and pawed through the box looking for anything with chocolate on top or in the middle. When I'd eaten so many I felt as green as the tea, I pushed the cookies to Eileen's end of my coffee table and curled my feet up behind me on the couch. Crumbs on my sweater dispersed themselves on the maroon faux oriental below, but I didn't have the energy to pick them up.

I debated whether I should tell Eileen about my mother's dying words. It was unseemly, even if true to form, that Mother was thinking about Luis's money on her deathbed. I was embarrassed, although feeling the need to apologize for my dead mother was probably irrational.

I wished Mother had taken the secret of my rape to her grave. Deep down, I was even sorry I had asked Eileen to travel with me on Thanksgiving. Now that she was involved with Miguel, I couldn't hit a backspace key and delete Miami and its inhabitants from my life. Couldn't anyway, I suppose, in light of my promise to Luis. I'd have to go back.

"Syl, do you think I'm nuts letting this thing with Miguel go into high gear? I mean, I know he feels the same way, but we're so different from each other, and it's happened so fast."

I wanted to tell Eileen to stay away, that hers was a romance with no future, but I was hardly a disinterested observer. "I don't think you're nuts, but I also don't want to see you get hurt. Yeah, I'm guessing geography will put the brakes on for now."

She sighed and brushed the remaining crumbs from the coffee table into the depleted collection in the cookie box. "Guess I just have to let things play out. By the way, if you weigh five pounds more the next time you go to the gym, you can tell your trainer it's my fault."

As she rose to go, I reached for her arm. "Don't leave, please. There's one more thing I need to tell you even though I hate talking about it."

Puzzled, she listened to my description of mother's plan for me to inherit, presumably at Carlos's expense.

"She told Luis that Carlos raped me."

Eileen thought for a moment. "She did it for you, Syl. Don't be too hard on her."

"But, if Luis unloads on Carlos, the story about our earlier consensual sex will come out. Why would Luis believe me instead of his son?"

Eileen had no answer. She just shook her head.

CHAPTER 18

The lobby of my building still sparkled with Christmas decorations my first day back at work. Even in the BodySculpt entrance, a tree covered with tinsel sat beside the reception desk. As the bleakest months of winter approached, people were reluctant to dismantle the cheerful remnants of the holiday.

I would have been happy to see the decorations go since they reminded me of AI*future's* Christmas party and the disturbing sight of Rip's hand on Kate's bare back. I wondered if he'd given as much thought as I had to her drunken humiliation. I managed a wave for Rob Linde, who greeted me as I passed him on my way to the locker room.

When I emerged for my session, Rip was wiping down a floor mat. "Ready to warm up?" he asked. "Treadmill? Elliptical?"

A heavy snowfall two days prior had put a temporary halt to outdoor running, so I chose the treadmill. "Can I run away from my problems?" I asked.

"If you can, you'll be the first." He smiled, which made me feel less anxious about getting through the next hour. I knew Rip wouldn't consider my work pressure an excuse to slack off, rather the opposite. As for Kate, I'd promised myself I wouldn't mention her. Unfortunately, Rip had made no such commitment. "I haven't seen you since the debacle at your company's Christmas party."

Out of my mouth came a crack I instantly regretted about Kate's being dressed to kill but with Harold Astrove not her intended victim. Rip raised an eyebrow and was silent for a moment before defending her. I hadn't given him much choice.

"If you're saying she looked sexy and a little flamboyant, I agree, but that's who she is. I give people credit for being authentic."

I didn't reply, my mind flashing back to my similar choice of attire in Miami before Thanksgiving, aiming for a sexy South Beach look.

Chastened, I crossed the room and stepped on a free treadmill. Rip followed me and adjusted the settings. "Did you know about her drinking problem?" he asked. "She wants me to help her with it."

I could just imagine the kind of help Kate wanted from Rip, but I shook my head. Better not to mention what I'd observed of her recent appearance at work.

There were more people in the gym than usual, which made me feel agreeably inconspicuous as I cranked up my speed and began to run. The men on either side of me looked out of shape, one in his sixties with a paunch, and the other, a redhead in his twenties. We were in this together, running but never getting anywhere. Rip was running in place too, but he always seemed to be going faster.

After my warmup, Rip was quiet as he led me through each element of my workout. He'd increased the weight on the machines and the repetitions on the free weights. "Are you out to get me today?" I asked, breathing hard.

"You said you wanted to be strong."

"Yes, but I wasn't planning on getting there in one day." Despite my resistance, I wondered if I would have been able to force Carlos off me if I'd been more diligent at the gym.

"How are things at work?" he asked. "Weren't you worried about the stretch leading up to the end of the year? Sell enough robots?"

"We don't sell robots, just software."

"Same thing," he answered, placing a large inflated ball on a mat. I was supposed to sit on it, lean back, and roll forward till I was in position to do abdominal crunches. I couldn't talk when I was tightening my abs, and Rip took advantage of my wordless gasps to tell me about the latest article he had seen on artificial intelligence.

"What will happen when a robot kills someone? Can you execute a robot? You can't indict the software developer because he just programmed it at the beginning. The robot learns by going through tons of data, faster than any human could. Its behavior is based on its learning, which is exactly how its human masters designed it. Maybe the robot thinks the person it kills needs to be eliminated. Maybe it thinks there are extenuating circumstances. Maybe it thinks it's killing to serve the greater good."

"Maybe, maybe, maybe!" I sat up on the ball. "Do you spend your time thinking about all the wonderful technology humans have invented that can be misused: computers, the internet, social media, cell phones . . . ?"

"The atomic bomb." He glared at me. My sweating compatriots were looking our way from the hamstring machine and leg press respectively.

"My abs and I are both done."

He didn't object but pushed the ball away and told me to lie down so we could finish with stretches. I complied, calling him a Luddite under my breath. Whenever Rip started in on artificial intelligence, I wanted to grab a resistance band and choke him to death, but when I was on a mat with Rip hovering near to stretch my leg muscles, my anger drained away. I fought the urge to pull him toward me. It was so strong, I worried he could sense it. I turned my head away.

* * *

The next night, Rip called me to apologize. "I didn't mean to go off on you about AI. It's just my nature to worry about things that seem to be happening too fast. That's why I like training people. Working out is slow, purposeful. No shortcuts."

"It's okay. I'm starting to understand the way you think. Anyway, I should apologize too. I was on edge for lots of reasons but mostly because my mother just died."

There was silence on the other end.

"Rip?"

"I'm here. It's just . . . I'm really sorry."

CHAPTER 19

Warren's friction with Richard could be felt, if not seen, in the form of a subtle undercurrent at AI*future*. I didn't know if the secret project Warren was working on wasn't such a secret or if there was whispered gossip about a potential merger.

Rona gave me a knowing look when I passed through the lobby. I wasn't surprised when she showed up in my doorway.

"They were at it again," she said, taking a seat across from my desk. "This time Richard closed the door right away, so Fannette took some folders over to the filing cabinet near his door so she could listen better. Richard said he had a potential buyer, and Warren exploded, yelling that Richard was taking the company in the wrong direction all because of that stupid flower shop. 'Pay back the money,' he said, 'so we can take our time finding the right acquisition partner.'"

"Did Fannette hear a company name mentioned?"

Rona had no more information. I assured her the cloak-and-dagger stuff would be over soon, although I knew nothing to back up my statement. *This can't go on*, I thought as I marched down to Warren's office. I wasn't sure what *this* was, but I needed to confront him.

Warren's door was open. He had to be somewhere in the office or down in the cafeteria because his lights were on, and a half-filled coffee mug sat on his desk. There was no one in the hall, so I stepped into the office and looked around. The credenza was covered with piles of manila file folders, the whiteboard listed milestones for NewAI with the dates erased, and the sole personal item, a silver-framed photo of Maya Malik, sat askew on a pile of facedown papers. I picked it up, intending to peel up the corners of the papers beneath, when I heard Warren behind me.

"Your wife is so lovely," I said, trying to sound nonchalant. "She must be due soon."

"Three more months." Warren's smile was as rare as a blue-footed booby. He perched on the corner of his desk. "I've been meaning to talk to you," he went on, "but I'd rather do it out of the office, perhaps over a drink."

I agreed, though I was mystified and more than a little nervous at the prospect.

■ ■ ■

Two evenings later, Warren and I faced each other across a high-top table at Burly's Bar and Grill. That Warren didn't want us to be seen was evident in his choice of this seedy spot far from the business crowd's usual watering holes. The waiter who approached us wore a stained white shirt and a tie that attempted, without success, to cover his beer belly. *Donald Trump*, I thought, *could give this guy a lesson on short-sheeting his tie to gain coverage*. Warren ordered a beer from the limited offering, and I ordered a Cabernet Sauvignon, though I anticipated it would disappoint.

"I've been watching you, Sylvie."

My fingers grew cold in my lap.

"You've been doing a very good job in your new role, better than I expected."

Tact was not Warren's long suit. "Thanks for the backhanded compliment."

Once the drinks arrived and the waiter departed, he took a large swallow and began. "First, this conversation is confidential."

I nodded, which seemed the logical response instead of walking out.

"I have a leak in my organization. Your ally, Sam, was nosing around Engineering, trying to find out why his precious NewAI is late, and someone disclosed information to him that was incomplete and misleading."

I wondered how Warren could know that when Sam had made it sound top secret. "Sam may be my friend, but he's our colleague in senior management, yours and mine. Why the hush-hush when you could just give the whole team more complete information?"

"Give me a little credit, Sylvie. I'm going to explain. The reason Sam can't know any of this is that he's unstable, and don't pretend that's news to you."

I knew Sam was capable of blowing his top like a pressure cooker, but I was convinced the delay in NewAI and the stress of an overseas assignment was making him worse. If I defended Sam to Warren, though, I was pretty sure I wouldn't get to hear the rest.

Warren leaned forward and crossed his arms on the small table. "NewAI is delayed in development," he said, "for a very good reason. I've pulled a couple of my people off it to work on exciting new technology. I've been collaborating with some associates on the outside, as well as those two AI*future* developers, on a side project I began on my own. I can't explain it fully right now. Let's just say some of what it does is to give greatly enhanced, natural language-writing capabilities to AI*future*'s existing applications, in fact to any AI application." Warren began to speak faster, warming to his subject. "Imagine the value to the military of undetectable disinformation, a powerful AI tool that could mimic and alter messages and orders going to foreign forces, leaders, drones, and even respond to human feelings."

"Aren't there a bunch of natural language competitors in that space already, and what about ChatGPT and now GPT-4?"

Warren went on, "Very good, Sylvie. There are, but trust me, mine is a unique capability."

I did trust him, although maybe I just wanted to trust him. I wasn't sure if I was more afraid of the potential uses of his software, the disinformation it could spread, or the manic expression on his face. My God, I was starting to think like Rip with his value judgments about AI. Who were these associates of Warren's and how were they getting paid? "Even if you think your software is groundbreaking, AI is changing so fast, companies are leapfrogging each other. Wouldn't it be a safer, smarter move to bide your time and put resources into NewAI?"

His mirthless laugh chilled me. "No competitor can touch me."

So arrogant. Did I know enough about his field to contradict him? "Could you use your tool to write a great novel? I would think a company like Amazon might want the capability to create, not just a few lines or essays, but an entire novel, a masterpiece. It would be as though Charles Dickens or James Joyce or any great writer were alive and creating again."

"AI can already write a novel. Some of Shakespeare too." He smirked. "Imagine the money saved if Amazon didn't need the content provided by writers at all."

Warren was amused, but the prospect of reading a novel created by software saddened me. I could acknowledge the financial benefit for publishers, but . . . "Feelings, Warren, great books are infused with feelings. The best ones come from the author's authentic emotions, from empathy for the characters. Software, robots, they have no emotions to express."

He was smug. "You have a very narrow view of what generative AI can do. Robots can be taught to convey emotions convincingly."

I knew that through machine learning, robots could become experts on even abstruse subjects, exceeding the knowledge of any PhD, but literature? If Warren thought robots could be taught to convey emotions, maybe people would start to prefer them to friends, even to spouses. Weren't there already sexbots on the market?

"Sylvie, you can't reveal any of this to Sam." Warren's face grew dark. "He's already spreading gossip about the company being sold. We need him to bring in revenue and stop distracting people. Once my software project is finished—soon—we'll be able to sell the company for a fortune."

Something was wrong. Why was I here? Before this, Warren had been so disparaging, so secretive. I excused myself to go to the ladies' room. I was hoping to sit and think for a moment, but the bathroom was unisex and poorly lit. The seat was up, and a few sheets of toilet paper clung to the damp floor. I leaned my back against the door.

If Warren were right about selling the company for big money, then Richard must be on board, but if that were the case, why were they having altercations in Richard's office? I was beginning to get it. A large company would probably be public, so the SEC would require the financials to be public, including Richard's disguised loan. If a smaller, private company acquired us, Richard might find a way for his loan to be forgiven.

When I returned to the table, I told Warren I only had a few minutes before I had to leave. "What do you want from me? Why did you share your secret?"

"I see Rona going into your office. Rona and Fannette are *partners*." The intolerant bastard smirked. "Richard wants to sell the company now, and I don't. Fannette knows all Richard's appointments and overhears some of his phone calls. She's sure not going to tell me, but you, Sylvie, you talk to Rona."

I wondered how Warren knew Rona came to my office. I hoped he was unaware that Fannette was already snooping for me. I'd made a commitment to Sam to find out if AI*future* were going to be acquired, because he wanted a heads up. Now Warren expected me to do the same thing for him, because unlike Sam, he wanted us to be acquired but not yet. *I was a fucking double agent.* My glass of cheap wine had done nothing to ease my stress. In fact, I was nauseated for any number of reasons. I picked up my purse. "I need to go."

"I'm glad we have an understanding," he said.

I was in sales. I knew this was his "presumptive close." I hadn't agreed we had an understanding. Despite that, I was flattered that he trusted me with the secret of his project.

That night I emailed Sam to tell him about the fragment of conversation Fannette had heard between Warren and Richard. I didn't know if Sam was aware that Richard had diverted company money to stake his wife in the flower business. When Harold first told me he had accounted for Richard's loan in AI*future*'s books, he'd asked me not to discuss it, but Rona and Fannette knew.

If Sam already knew, he'd say so in his return email. If not, he'd surely want to know what flower shop I was talking about. I was bone tired, and tired people have trouble keeping their lies and commitments straight. I hit send and closed my computer.

CHAPTER 20

The January thaw made me itch to run outside. A treadmill was an unsatisfying substitute. Rip and I set up a date to meet Saturday morning so we could try out a new park where the trails would not be as muddy as those at Cold Spring, and he could bring Dinger along for a run.

"Have you ever tried to clean mud out of the fur of a golden retriever?" he asked. "After my last run, he looked like one of those chocolate-dipped strawberries you find in an Edible Arrangement. Bathing him would release enough dirt to clog the sewers of a metropolis."

I bent down and scratched Dinger behind his ears. "I would do it, Dinger. Don't listen to that nasty man." I was rewarded with a wagging tail and a lick on my cheek. I had always loved dogs, but with my parents at the drugstore all day, there was no one around for walks. I knew there were people who went to work each day and expected their dogs to hold their urine all those hours, but that seemed like abuse to me, even before I knew the word for it.

Rip was right about the wider dry trails. A quarter of a mile down the path, we settled into a comfortable pace. "Enjoy this running weather, because there's snow forecasted for New England."

Weather was a safe subject, but I was desperate to talk with someone about what was happening at AI*future*. The night before, I'd dreamed a hawk was attacking the starlings outside our cafeteria windows. Despite my horror, I'd done nothing. I didn't need a soothsayer to interpret that dream for me. I needed a sounding board, and Rip was good at that when he wasn't lecturing me on the dangers of AI.

"Still training Kate?

"No, she's taking a break from the gym. I haven't seen her lately."

I felt safe confiding in him once I knew there wasn't any pillow talk with Kate. It helped, too, that Rip had met our management team at the Christmas party. He knew the players.

His eyebrows arched as I described Warren's request that I find out Richard's plans for our acquisition. When I told him I'd made the same commitment to Sam but for a different reason, he frowned.

I wasn't going to tell him what else I'd promised Sam, but the words rushed out like air from a balloon. Sam was hoping I'd expose Warren's side project or at least learn what it was, but I'd allowed myself to become a party to Warren's secret. I wondered at that moment if Warren had deliberately coopted me to keep me from revealing anything to the "hot head" with a "big mouth."

I watched my feet moving parallel to Rip's along the trail so I wouldn't have to look at his face. He was upset with me, but I needed to get everything out. I forced myself to recount my recruiting Rona and Fannette to spy. I used the word "recruiting" because it sounded less shameful than "using," but Rip's extended silence spoke to his disapproval. Dinger ran ahead of us, zigzagging with joy though the woods. At least someone was enjoying the run.

Rip put his hand on my arm to stop me, so we could stand face-to-face on the trail. "I hope you feel better after telling your whole story. A therapist would probably pat you on the back for honesty, but I won't."

Condemnation. I guess I expected that.

"People trust you, Sylvie."

I looked up at him, hopeful.

"Their trust pulls you toward them as though each one in turn was magnetic north. Their trust makes you want to reciprocate in some way."

"How can it be bad for people to trust me?"

"Maybe 'trust' is the wrong word. Too many people think you're with them, an ally. It's duplicitous."

I was less prepared for criticism than I thought. I held back tears and started running, increasing my pace to escape the woods. When the trail brought me back to the car, I knelt beside Dinger, my arms around his neck, my face in his fur. A few tears escaped into his silky coat before I regained control. Dinger would be discreet. A dog could be trusted, maybe more than I could.

■ ■ ■

By Sunday noon, I could hear the wind sighing in the trees, and my window framed a sky gray and mottled as old shingles. I was heating a bowl of chicken noodle soup in my microwave when delicate snowflakes began floating down. At first, they were so far apart I could count them as they descended. It didn't take long for a thick curtain of snow to obscure my view.

The snowfall would soon bury the running trails at the park, a thought that pleased me, as though snow could obliterate our words along with our footprints. No more running outdoors till spring. I'd see Rip only at the gym.

If he'd called me an idiot for getting myself into such a mess, it would have seemed my just due, but "duplicitous" was hurtful. It was a word connoting evil intent. That wasn't the way I saw myself, but then I wasn't sure of my motivation. If too many people who didn't trust each other thought I was their ally, I must be malleable and not in the good way.

My cell phone rang, and I was grateful to hear Eileen's voice, allowing me to set aside my disturbing thoughts. "I'm calling to tell you it's eighty-five degrees here, in case you were wondering. Has the blizzard begun yet?"

"Calling to gloat, are you? It happens to be beautiful outside."

"Yes, as long as you're inside."

"I'm wearing my favorite fleece pullover and enjoying a steaming bowl of chicken noodle soup. It's quite cozy here."

"I'm sipping a margarita, just saying."

"Okay, you win. I actually do miss you. Everything okay with Miguel?"

Eileen went into raptures describing their romance. "But that's not why I called. I was hoping you might be able to come down, even for a couple of days. Luis asked me to help Celia go through your mother's things. When I looked in her drawers, it felt wrong, like I was invading her privacy. I don't mean to stick you with the job, but some of her belongings might be of value to you—I mean sentimental value. Luis would be happy if you took them."

I didn't want Mother's clothes. Just wearing them to her funeral had made me uncomfortable. Anyway, I already had her jewelry and no place to wear it. Luis would never know if I shipped the clothes north and dumped them at Goodwill. I hated to admit it to myself but escaping AI*future* sounded oh so appealing. "Where's Carlos?"

"Don't worry. He's not around. He had some sort of argument with Luis and hasn't been here since."

I packed and caught the next flight.

CHAPTER 21

The smell of succulent bacon told me I wasn't at home even before I opened my eyes. Celia, how I wished I could take her home with me. I slipped into shorts and a T-shirt and hurried down for breakfast. When I arrived in the kitchen, Celia waved at me with a flowered oven mitt on her hand. "Coffee is on the counter."

I poured myself a mug and walked out to the patio, where Eileen and Miguel were sipping tall glasses of freshly squeezed orange juice.

"Hola," Eileen said, raising her glass and smiling broadly.

I parked my coffee on an end table and settled into a chaise. I'd left my sunglasses upstairs and didn't feel like going back up, so I shaded my eyes and took in the turquoise intensity of the ocean. The rhythm of the surf was calming, my shoulders were warmed by the sun, and I wondered how on earth I'd get myself to return to Boston. That was until I saw Carlos.

He'd slid open the glass doors and come out onto the patio. Carlos was striking in a yellow bathing suit with his broad shoulders, narrow hips, and tawny skin, but for me he'd lost the power to attract. His good looks were a weapon he used for preying on women.

"Sylvie, so nice of you to come back and visit us."

"I came down to help Eileen and Celia with Margaret's clothes. Of course, I especially wanted to see Luis."

"Yes, I bet you did," he said with a cryptic smile. "I hope you and I get a chance to catch up." He didn't wait for an answer but ran down the steps to the beach.

I glared at Eileen.

"Sorry," she said. "I don't know how he knew you were here. He hasn't been around at all." She looked at Miguel, who had a sheepish expression on his face.

"I might have let it slip. He's my brother. I'm not used to filtering what I say."

I lay back on the chaise and closed my eyes, hoping to retreat inside the only dark solitude available, but the sun came out from behind a cloud and turned the darkness under my lids red.

"Sylvie," Luis's guttural voice called out. I jumped up and a moment later was enveloped in his comforting arms. He laid his cheek on my hair. "I miss your mother so much, but seeing you helps. Thank you for coming."

His words were spoken from the heart, and though I was touched, his feelings discomfited me. I might look like my mother, but within I was my father's daughter. Maybe my father knew me better than I knew myself. "Pretzelita," he called me when I sat with my legs curled under me. "Sit straight on your chair," Mother commanded. Perhaps that contorted position was just the outward manifestation of my need to take on the shape desired by others. *Did he recognize that in me when I was a child?* I brushed aside the thought. It was only a nickname.

Luis put his hands on my shoulders. "I should have thought to give you your mother's clothes the last time you were here. It pains me to look at them, but if I can imagine you . . . you'll look beautiful." He meant to flatter me, but the idea of wearing Margaret's clothes creeped me out. I was a lousy stand-in.

The aroma of huevos rancheros wafted from the open doorway as Celia wheeled out a cart laden with a basket of warm buttered toast, muffins, a pitcher of orange juice, and a thermos of coffee. In the little space remaining on the white tablecloth were three strategically placed lilies, petals ruffled by the breeze. The arrangement looked too beautiful to disturb, let alone consume, but when we had finished, there was nothing left but two lonely blueberry muffins.

As soon as Luis excused himself, Miguel and Eileen pushed back their chairs. Eileen looked across at me and tilted her head toward the beach. "Going to let those boot-bound feet of yours loose in the sand?"

"I need to go upstairs and grab my bathing suit and sunglasses. Go ahead and start without me." When I came back down and returned to the patio, I slipped out of my sandals. Carlos, who'd been lying on one of the chaises, got up and turned in my direction. I started walking, but he must have come up behind me. I felt his hand on my arm. "No!" I jerked away, ready to run.

"Wait, Sylvie. I just wanted you to stop. I didn't mean to scare you."

"Carlos, you and I have nothing to talk about."

"Because of your mother, my father is very angry with me. She told him I raped you. I need you to tell him it's not true."

I pushed my wind-whipped hair out of my face. "Why would I tell him a lie?"

"Sylvie," he pleaded, "you know Luis has a bad heart, one that's been weakened by the trauma of your mother's death. He thinks of you as a daughter, and I can see you care about him. This is no time for an old man to be eating his guts out, angry at his son. I'm asking, not as a favor to me, but to him. Tell him your mother wasn't clear-headed because of her cancer. She misunderstood. Please let Luis die in peace. He doesn't believe what I tell him."

I was trapped, struggling with my desire to ease Luis's pain but mistrusting Carlos at the same time. He could charm the *Mona Lisa* into grinning. "I'm sorry, but I need time to think." I could see Eileen and Miguel, holding hands, ambling down the beach, but I wasn't ready to talk with Eileen or anyone yet. I ran down the steps and struck off in the opposite direction.

Carlos called after me, "Time is what Luis doesn't have."

Walking was difficult with each step sinking my feet into the hot sand. When I reached firmer footing in the dampness at the water's edge, I turned to assure myself Carlos was gone. My footsteps were leaving an imprint, a historical record that I'd walked there. Surely, some poet, perhaps many, had watched the surf erase footprints and written about the impermanence of life, but for me, there was a different message. I'd always let my footprints wash away at the behest of others. I was a transient.

My first inclination was to agree to Carlos's request, to bend the narrative of the rape for Luis's sake. Luis was no fool, though. He knew his son. The day after Carlos pinned me to the bed, Luis had invited me out to the garden and tried to explain why Carlos "expected the rose to have no thorns." Carlos was a prick. That's as close as Luis's euphemism came to the truth. Dying in peace had ceased being an option long before my arrival.

I had no difficulty avoiding Carlos for the rest of the day, since Eileen and I were still sorting Margaret's belongings when the sky outside the master bedroom window darkened. Luis had been generous with more than jewelry. Margaret must have reveled in patronizing the elegant shops at Bal Harbour with no limit on her spending.

When I was growing up in Reading, we frequented discount stores. We shopped sales and looked for designer labels at Marshalls and T.J.Maxx. I never felt deprived because I didn't see the inside of high-end shops, but my mother did. I could tell. She must have discarded the apparel she wore as a pharmacist's wife or perhaps ruined it after Dad died when she became a sloppy drunk. Maybe there's no other kind.

In Miami, her enormous walk-in closet was a visual feast of tropical hues punctuated with the sparkle of sequins and gold lamé, the airiness of lace and organdy and the sheen of satin. I was tempted to leave it all untouched, but as cancer had taken her body, my assignment was to take her possessions.

Eileen insisted I augment my wardrobe with garments that suited my personal and professional life. Though I doubted there would be many of those, I agreed, but only if she took any accessories appropriate for evenings in swanky settings. If she and Miguel remained a couple, she'd have use for beaded evening purses and gauzy wraps. Unfortunately, Eileen had much larger feet than Margaret, so the Jimmy Choo spike-heeled sandals were not an option.

When I tried on Margaret's clothes, I felt as though I were stepping back into my role as Ashton's wife. I'd had an expensive wardrobe during those years, and my smart-looking business outfits had been purchased on Ashton's nickel. Most of my mother's clothes were casual except for the evening gowns, a navy suit, and the black linen sheath I'd worn to her funeral.

I knew I wouldn't wear the halters Mother was so fond of, especially not the strapless ones, but some of the slacks and capris would work at home in the summer along with her blouses. Flashy prints were out, though. They just weren't me.

We packed shipping boxes as we sorted, and in the back of the closet, I noticed a few items pushed to the back of a high shelf. I fetched a stepstool and pulled them down. Among them was a man's plaid shirt.

"What's that doing in her closet?" Eileen asked.

I clutched the shirt to my heart. "It was my father's—his favorite." I held it to my nose, but his scent had dissipated with the intervening years. Just seeing it, though, made me picture him for a precious moment. Mother had claimed, "He was the love of my life." I'd thought it melodramatic at the time, but maybe that was why Eileen accused me of never cutting Margaret any slack.

When we finished with the closet, only the dresser was left. We made our weary way downstairs for dinner, and I was relieved to see Carlos wasn't joining us. The next day would be my last before flying back to Boston. He'd want my answer, and I dreaded giving it.

* * *

Luis came out to the patio the next morning and joined us at the table. Miguel asked Luis if he minded if he and Eileen excused themselves, and seeing his father's broad smile, took their coffee and muffins back to chaises on the far side of the patio. They had some arrangements they needed to discuss, according to Eileen, who gave me a coy smile before turning away. An engagement? Or perhaps just a move to Florida to live with Miguel? God, I hated that idea. I was thrilled for her but didn't relish the loss.

Carlos joined Luis and me as soon as Eileen and Miguel departed.

"I don't mean to be rude," I said, pushing back my chair, "but I have a document I have to review this morning, and I need to grab my laptop." Poor Luis, looking more grizzled and years older than when I'd visited in November, nodded, but his smile was gone.

When I came back down, I stationed myself on a stool at the outdoor bar with my back to the table. As I perused my emails, I could hear Carlos discussing his company, which he claimed was throwing off so much cash that he was considering becoming an angel investor in whatever viable technology start-up he could discover. "Sylvie, you work for an artificial intelligence company, right?" Carlos called over to me.

Luis cut him off. "Sylvie's leaving in the morning. She won't be able to help you with your research."

"Sorry to hear you're going so soon," Carlos replied. "Didn't you tell me you had something to discuss with Luis? I've got to head to my office anyway." A moment later, he disappeared through the sliding doors.

I left the bar and joined Luis at the table. "I wish I could stay longer, but . . ."

"I wish you could too, but we'll have to make do with short visits. What did you want to discuss with me?"

I had a pit in my stomach every time I thought about Luis's angst over Carlos, but I'd made up my mind not to lie about the rape. "Luis, I'm so sorry, but it seems as though my presence has been a source of distress in your once placid household. It may be a while before I'm back. When Carlos and I are here at the same time—well, I know you sense the tension."

"It's true, isn't it?" he asked. "The rape?"

"Yes, it's true."

His face seemed to droop. His eyes sunk deeper in their sockets.

I placed my hand over his. "The last thing I want to do is cause you more pain."

"You? My heartache from Carlos started long ago." He sighed. "Thank you for not bringing charges."

My anger at Carlos still burned, but its sparks had been smothered by a blanket of sorrow. "I couldn't bring myself to do that. Too many people would have been hurt." I picked up my laptop. "I'm going to finish this task upstairs. See you in a bit."

Why *hadn't* I brought charges? I'd given Luis only a partial answer. Anyone hearing the story of my rape would have found it open-and-shut, but I knew I'd slept with Carlos before—no persuasion required—and I knew I'd been every bit the seductress the night we'd gone clubbing in South Beach. A woman feeling guilty for her rape was a cliché, so why did I still feel rotten?

I hoped Carlos had been telling the truth when he said he was leaving for his office. It was so early in the day, avoiding him would have been difficult. He'd be back. I was sure of that. He'd ask what I'd said to his father. Had I followed his script?

A tightness took hold of my chest, a sense of urgency. I had to leave, today, not tomorrow. I pulled my sundress from the closet, my toiletries from the bathroom, and the few items I'd stowed in the drawers, and stuffed everything into my suitcase. The airline gave me a seat on a late afternoon flight, and I readily agreed to pay the penalty for changing my reservation.

I sat on the edge of the bed and took a few deep breaths. Feeling somewhat calmer, I went in search of Eileen and Miguel. I found them under the pergola that covered half the patio, shading it with lush jasmine vines. The two were nursing iced teas at a wrought iron cocktail table. They smiled as I approached. "I just wanted to let you know that something has come up at work, and, unfortunately, I need to head back to Boston this afternoon instead of tomorrow."

Miguel looked disappointed, but Eileen's eyes narrowed slightly. Before she could voice her suspicions, I told her I was dying to get in a swim and a walk on the beach before returning to the cold. I ran down the steps and onto the sand.

Fleeing was a pattern for me, but it was no solution. What was I going back to anyway but more problems: Warren's and Sam's expectations of me, Rip's disappointment? I had a sudden urge to disappear under the waves. I had too many commitments to too many people and had allowed them to tie me up in knots—Pretzelita.

Miguel had some business calls to make, so Eileen joined me on the beach. She offered me the frog scrunchie from her wrist, but I wanted to hang on to the feeling of the sea breeze in my hair. She used it instead to tie her own hair back in a ponytail.

“I’m so happy . . .” I began.

“I’m so concerned . . .” she said at the same time, uninterested in whatever platitudes were about to roll off my tongue. “You look like shit, Sylvie—not your looks, of course—but from worrying, and I don’t think it has to do with your mother’s closet. Spit it out.”

“If you make me tell you, I’ll want you to keep it from Miguel, and that’s just not fair to you.”

She stopped walking and looked at me, her face stern. “Our friendship doesn’t end because Miguel is in my life. Don’t make decisions for me. I want to know.”

In truth, I was relieved to tell her about Carlos and his demand.

She agreed that he would be furious to learn I’d told Luis the truth about the rape. “You did the right thing, though, so why are you running away?”

I was running away from Carlos, of course, and didn’t want to admit it, but I voiced my concern about the friction I’d brought to the household. Eileen raised an eyebrow but agreed reluctantly. I told her I’d called a ride service to take me to the airport, so I could leave without causing any more disruption, and asked her to ship everything we’d packed to my apartment.

We returned to the house so Eileen could see about the boxes and I could get changed to leave. Luis was in the living room reading his paper when I came down.

“Please take care of yourself,” I urged him. “I’m going to miss you.”

He stood and enveloped me in a bear hug, his stubble grazing my forehead. “I love you, Sylvie.”

I tightened my arms around his back. He didn’t seem to expect a reply but released me and started for the stairs. There were tears in his eyes, mine as well. I wiped them away with my sleeve and walked out the front door.

My ride was waiting, but so was Carlos. The driver opened the back door for me and took my bag to stow in the trunk. Carlos leaned against the inside of the open door. "Did you ease Luis's mind, as we discussed?"

"No, Carlos, I didn't lie for you. Your father knows you."

His eyes narrowed, his lips pressed together, his sensual features turned menacing. I tried to push past him to get in the car, but his body blocked me. As his face leaned into mine, I stepped back.

"This isn't over, Sylvie. You'll see." With that he turned away.

Breathless, I bolted into the back seat and slammed the door.

CHAPTER 22

I slept badly that night, shpilkes by Rip's description. Sam had just returned from Europe, and Warren was expecting to hear about Richard's secret suitor. Rip was disappointed in my choices at work, my fault, of course, for spilling my guts to him. What I hadn't expected was to be in mortal fear of Carlos. Sometime during the night, I'd had a nightmare. All I remembered was running from him, running for my life.

I'd promised to have lunch with Sam. The sky was slate gray, and I didn't need a forecast to tell me another storm was blowing in. A foot of snow covered the ground. Even in my fleece-lined boots, my feet felt the icy contrast to the warm Florida sand. Shivering, I looked over at Sam, whose chin was pulled into the neck of his jacket like a turtle's.

We drove to the mall and parked as close as we could to the Met Bar's entrance. The host seated us in an end booth, far from other diners. I wondered if he thought we were having a romantic tryst. It was way too cold for that. Neither of us wanted wine or beer, but I fortified myself with hot tea and lemon that warmed my throat and chest all the way down.

It was a good day for comfort food, so when the waiter suggested the soup of the day, butternut squash and lentil, I ordered a bowl. Sam asked for chili, extra spicy. His coat was off, but he'd kept his brown plaid scarf draped around his neck.

Although the restaurant wasn't cold, the tall glass windows allowed in the gloom, compelling me to sling my coat around my shoulders.

"So, fill me in," he said.

"You're the world traveler. You start."

Sam was in a talkative mood, so he went on at length about what was happening in Europe, where we didn't have our own offices but sold through distributors in each country. The distributors' salespeople had become productive quickly, probably because of Sam's investment of time and energy in bringing them up to speed on the capabilities of our software. Sam's revenue numbers looked good. He'd even managed to recruit a new distributor in Turkey.

"You've been away a long time. Susan must have been upset."

"No kidding. At first, I thought the problem was that she missed me." He looked down and shook his head. "Boy, did I have that wrong."

"You just got back. She hasn't had any help or moral support. Give her a little time, do something nice for her."

"Thanks for the suggestion, but we're past the wine-and-roses stage. She's seeing someone. I'm convinced of it." Sam went on to describe the anomalies in Susan's behavior and schedule. All I could do was listen and feel guilty, unable to tell him he was working overseas and I was in the United States because he was outspoken and I was Ms. Malleable.

I finally succeeded in changing the subject to how much he'd accomplished in Europe. "I bet Susan is proud of you for that. I'm not saying you should remind her you're a great meal ticket, but she'd have to admit it's nice to have all those commissions rolling in, especially since she's not working."

He shrugged. "You'd think."

Gentle snowflakes fell on the restaurant windows and slid down the glass. Sam turned his focus to what had happened during his absence. I couldn't tell him what I knew about

Warren's side project, and I hadn't spoken to Rona since my return from Miami. "What loan were you talking about in your email? I thought I'd wait till I was back to ask you."

I began to explain what I'd heard from Harold Astrove, but Sam interrupted me. "You mean Richard took company funds for a family investment? That makes him an embezzler." Sam's face was beginning to flush, with a spot on each cheek turning the color of his chili.

"Not really. It's a loan. Harold claimed it was accounted for as a company investment in Asia. Told me not to worry about it, like it was kosher. Even Rona knew, because Fannette overheard Richard arguing about the loan with Warren."

Sam pushed his bowl away, caught our waitress's eye, and made a scribble gesture on his palm. "Is that what the skinny pencil pusher told you? I don't believe for a minute that some flower shop is going to earn back that money, not in our lifetime! No wonder Richard wants to sell—probably looking for a private company that won't have to disclose the finances of an acquisition." My temper had a longer fuse than Sam's. I'd been indignant about Richard's loan when I went to Astrove for an explanation, but Sam proceeded directly to outrage.

By the time we left the mall, the north wind was blowing the snow in thick white curtains. My chest felt tight, but not from anxiety over the driving conditions. Tomorrow, Warren was sure to come looking for me, but I had nothing to tell him yet.

When we returned to the office, we found a large doormat spread just inside the glass doors. Rona sat behind the semicircular reception desk in a vivid red sweater with the merest hint of a camisole at the deep neckline. Her palm was face up like a traffic cop's. "Stop and stamp off the snow here, please."

Sam stared at her with fake horror. Rona got up and walked around her desk, revealing the rest of her ensemble. The sweater topped a clingy knit skirt with fake fur around the bottom. She looked like a cross between Mrs. Claus and Santa's mistress. My first reaction was *inappropriate*, but I remembered how Rip defended Kate's flamboyant attire at the Christmas party. If Kate was just being authentic, was the same true for Rona?

I wiped off my boots on the mat. Sam complied with exaggerated stomping. "When did we start hiring authoritarian women?" he asked.

Rona giggled.

"Good for you, Rona. Everything goes better when we're in charge."

Sam grumbled his way out of the lobby, but I lingered to talk with Rona. "I was only away for a few days, but it feels like forever." I lowered my voice. "Anything going on?"

"I'll come see you later," she whispered.

Rona appeared in my doorway at 3:30, just as my concentration was fading and I was contemplating a coffee break. When she left, I no longer needed caffeine. According to Fannette, Richard had gone for a couple of visits, long ones, to a company called Distributon. Afterward, he'd asked Fannette to collect archived financial records from Harold. Rona didn't know if that was important, but she wanted to pass it on.

I was aware of Distributon. They were a competitor of sorts but had no artificial intelligence capability, so I could see how we'd help them expand their market. They didn't have a good reputation for customer support, though, and the couple of small acquisitions they'd already made—well, Distributon was a bottom feeder, mostly interested in grabbing other companies' customer bases and firing their employees to reduce costs.

I sat at my desk, staring out the window at the snowfall that had begun at lunchtime. I could have enjoyed the magical kind with fat flakes drifting down, softening the windowsills of even our stark commercial building. Instead, I shivered watching the precipitation now on the cusp between sleet and freezing rain.

I had work I needed to focus on, but I also had commitments I'd made to both Warren and Sam and needed to tell them about Distributon. While I pondered how best to let them know and who should be first, I received a confidential email from Richard addressed to the executive team. Kate had resigned from her position at AI*future*.

Richard went on to ask that we inform our subordinates. With Kate gone, the sales force would once again be responsible for selling consulting services. Consultants would, for the time being, report to technical support. Richard requested that any further questions be directed to him in person rather than over email, text, or voicemail. *Further questions, indeed.*

I bolted for Richard's office. It didn't make sense that Kate would leave after such a short tenure at AI*future*. When I reached Richard's doorway, I saw Floyd seated at the conference table and Richard behind his desk. Warren was out of town and Sam in a conference call. Richard asked me to close the door and gestured toward a seat.

"Kate resigned?" I asked. "Just like that?"

Floyd responded, "We wanted to allow her to make a graceful exit. She was asked to leave."

"Because . . ."

"Sexual harassment."

"What?" My voice squeaked.

"Harold claimed she'd been asking him for confidential information about the company and wanting to barter sexual favors—made him uncomfortable."

What the fuck? I didn't think anyone but Harold's wife made him uncomfortable. When Harold quivered in Kate's presence, he made me uncomfortable. I didn't think CFOs got a hard-on for anything but net profit, but Harold was an exception.

Sure, I had become disenchanted with Kate after the Christmas party. When she showed up at the office hungover, my impression hadn't improved. Still, she and I had started off on good terms, and I respected her competence. Now I was the only woman on the executive team. We had precious little diversity at AI*future*, but if her departure afforded me job security, it was cold comfort, given that we might be acquired.

Richard got up from his desk and walked to the window, where he opened his vertical blinds and peered out. "It's piling up fast out there." He turned to me. "Sylvie, I assume you will let your people know that Kate has resigned. Tell them she's decided to become an independent consultant or whatever you think will play best."

Floyd pointed to his cell phone. "Just got a message that Route 128 is gridlocked. Accidents everywhere. I think we should consider early dismissal."

Richard hesitated, finally nodding his assent. I returned to my office to gather my things and saw that Richard had already sent a company-wide email about the storm.

■ ■ ■

Outside our building was a fairy tale landscape of snow-wrapped toy cars and cottony branches, topped with a sparkling layer of ice that sleet had deposited. Where there had been snowy mounds before with the stems of shrubs poking through, there were higher drifts obscuring all plant life. Employees looked like bundled gnomes battling to clear their windshields of the stubborn ice beneath the snow.

I turned on my ignition to get an assist from the heater and grabbed my scraper, but I was working against the storm, which seemed intent on foiling my best efforts. When at last I was ready to pull out of my space, my tires spun in protest. I rocked my car back and forth, but nothing worked. As I grew more desperate, I continued my frustrating efforts, though I knew I was probably flooding my engine.

Most cars were already gone, and snow again coated my back and side windows. I rested my forehead against the steering wheel and wondered if I would have to spend the night in my office. The minutes passed, marked only by the fruitless swipes of my windshield wipers.

Someone was calling me, rapping on the windshield with a scraper. Rip was out there, asking if I was okay. "You can't leave your engine running in this heavy a storm. It could be dangerous." He was yelling at me like I was a little kid.

"I'm stuck."

"Leave your car. Mine's already out. I'll take you home."

If I wanted to get back to Needham, Rip's car was the only way I was going to get there. I grabbed my purse and briefcase and stepped out into the storm, letting Rip lead the way. "How come you didn't get stuck?" I asked, aggravated by the injustice of it.

"Four-wheel drive and snow tires." He had an answer for everything. I pitched my belongings into the back seat and brushed as much snow off myself as I could before getting in. We drove toward the highway entrance, but as we approached, we could see the endless red taillights disappearing around the bend.

"Rip, this will take forever, and don't you have Dinger waiting for you at home?"

He was silent for a moment. "I live close by. Do you mind coming back to my apartment till I walk Dinger and the traffic eases?"

Since there was no practical alternative, I agreed. Rip lived half a mile from our building, yet the ride seemed interminable. When I turned my head to see how he was managing, the clenched jaw and riveted eyes answered my unspoken question. By the time we pulled into his driveway, I was ready to accept the hospitality of Attila the Hun.

Dinger was overjoyed to see us, but then that's the advantage of having a dog instead of a self-involved spouse. He was wagging his tail so hard it looked as though it were about to take off on its own like a kite. Rip put on Dinger's leash and went straight out, while I pulled off my boots and wet coat and collapsed into a well-worn brown corduroy club chair.

I don't know what I was expecting, but it wasn't a library in a living room. Garage sale bookcases, in every size and color, lined two walls. There were no matched collected works on display, only random titles shelved every which way.

Volumes on math, history, geography, religion, and science crowded novels and sports books. They were all fighting for breathing room, packed in like commuters in a subway car. If e-books and audio were replacing print volumes, you wouldn't know it from this apartment. I thought Rip was a know-it-all, but apparently he knew a lot.

There was little else in this small apartment besides a plain wooden table and chairs, a futon sofa, and vintage baseball posters of the Brooklyn Dodgers. A menorah sat on one windowsill with wax drips still attached. I had just repositioned myself, sinking further into the cozy reading chair, when Dinger came charging through the door ahead of his master. While Rip shed his soaked parka and gloves, Dinger shed his coat of snow by shaking it onto me.

I was fated to be cold and wet that day, a metaphor for something, I was sure. Although Rip chastised Dinger, he couldn't suppress his smile when he saw my clothes. "Sorry about that. I'm usually his target. I'm going to change into something dry. Do you want me to find—oh, I don't know—a three-piece suit for you? Actually, I still have a pair of sweatpants that shrunk in the dryer and a sweater that would at least be better than what you're wearing."

My slacks were still wet from the knees down, and Dinger had more than dampened my blouse, so I agreed. I was glad there was no full-length mirror in Rip's bedroom because I knew I looked ridiculous in his rolled-up sweatpants. His sweater had such a stretched neckline it kept slipping off one shoulder *Flashdance* style. Rip's laughter served as confirmation.

"That sweater is too small for me, so I guess I kind of stretched the neck getting in and out of it. At least you're dry." He offered me a beer. "Might make you feel better about how you look right now—well, maybe it'll just make you feel better."

"Don't you have anything hot?"

He was sheepish. "Just ramen noodles. Sorry. I was planning on getting to the supermarket today."

One glance out the window at the unrelenting snow made it clear I could be there for hours. Rip prepared the noodles in his microwave, and when he handed the bowl to me, I clutched it like a hand warmer. We sat down at his wobbly table, and I held my soup up in the air while he inserted a newspaper under the shorter leg.

"So, Rip, is this how you stay on top of the news?"

He groaned. "More corny jokes like that and I'm sending you back out into the snow."

I didn't argue the point, since more than anything, I wanted to dive into my ramen noodles. Rip nursed his beer while Dinger curled up at our feet.

Content, I let my thoughts wander, but they led me to an uncomfortable place. During our last run in the woods, Rip had chided me: "Too many people think you're with them, an ally. It's duplicitous." My kneejerk reaction had been resentment, although I knew there was some truth in his observation.

"I've been thinking about our last run, when you said I let people pull me as though they were magnets."

"Sylvie, we don't have to go back—"

"Is it wrong that I try to please, to accommodate if I can what other people want of me? I did that with my ex, Ashton, to a fault, but with Sam, Warren, and Richard at work—you think it's too much, even unethical?"

"Would you kill to please someone?"

"Of course not."

"So, the problem is what would make you draw the line? If each of your choices were a dot on the graph, an outlier would change you as a person when you faced new choices. It would change the moral trajectory of your life, the line of best fit." He drew an imaginary line on the table with his forefinger.

"Line of what?"

"Guess you don't remember your high school math. It's a straight line drawn on a graph as close to all the data points as possible. It crosses all, some, or none of them." Rip must have noticed my glassy-eyed stare. "Look, pretend you're putting dots on a graph for Ted Kennedy's choices. He made many good ones until the disaster at Chappaquiddick. What do you think that did to his moral line of best fit?"

"Point taken." I rinsed out my bowl at the sink, and Rip dropped his bottle into a box of recyclables in the corner of his kitchen. I turned my back to the sink. "I hate admitting it when you're right, but—"

"But you're too easily influenced?"

"No, I really should have four-wheel drive and snow tires."

Rip looked up at the ceiling, exasperated.

"No, seriously, I'll consider what you said about my 'line of best fit.' It hurts that you think less of me."

"Sylvie, you don't know what I'm thinking, at least not right now." He leaned in and kissed me. We stood facing each other for a moment, and I knew he wouldn't touch me again without a signal. I stepped forward and put my arms around him. For once, we were thinking the same thing.

CHAPTER 23

Eileen wasn't making sense. "I'm telling you it's true," she insisted. "Carlos went to see Ashton. I called you all last night but you didn't answer."

"My Ashton? Why would Ashton want to talk with my illicit lover, the one who gave him an excuse to dump me for infidelity?"

"As I recall your story, Ashton didn't know whose underwear was next to your bed, just that those black briefs weren't his."

"You appear to remember the sordid details of my story better than I do. Maybe you're right."

"All I know is that Miguel said Carlos was pursuing investment opportunities in artificial intelligence. Because he knows Ashton is a hotshot in your field, he's going to Boston. You'd think he'd find some other guru."

I tried to rationalize that this news meant nothing, that Eileen was just overwrought. I didn't think her heart could be beating as fast as mine, though. Carlos was unpredictable, and at that moment, despite Luis's gratitude, I wished I'd had put Carlos in jail for rape.

"I'm flying back to Boston as soon as I can get a flight—got a massage business to run. Your snowstorm screwed up the schedules."

"My snowstorm?"

"Guess I'm starting to think like a Floridian. See you soon."

Rip, who'd driven me home, was waiting for me to change my clothes. Our subsequent ride to the office took us through a transformed snowscape under a sun brilliant in the cerulean sky. It was the kind of day that beckoned to kids with sleds. In truth, it beckoned to anyone who'd ever been a kid. Though the parking lot at work had been plowed, my car sat in its hollowed-out tire tracks surrounded by an encircling snow drift that had kept the plow away.

The deep snow that so invited play worked against the swift arrival of a tow truck. It took an hour and a half till my car was rescued. At that point, buying a new set of tires didn't fit my schedule, let alone my budget.

When I finally reached my desk, I saw an email from Miguel that banished thoughts of tires from my mind. Luis's heart was failing. Nothing could be done short of a transplant, and he was unlikely to make it the top of the transplant list given his age.

Miguel's stated purpose was to give me a heads up, but he tacked on a sentence about Carlos's desire for my help in providing peace of mind to Luis. Carlos, who was in Boston, would get in touch with me. Perhaps I was reading my own suspicions into Miguel's email, but I was sure Carlos had pressured him to send it. I knew what "peace of mind" I was supposed to give Luis, the assurance that Carlos had never raped me. I was tired of Carlos's petitions, or maybe I was just tired. What was the point of holding out with Luis slipping away?

I felt a tightening in my chest. I was trapped between my affection for Luis and my visceral unwillingness to lie for Carlos. Did Miguel want me to accommodate Carlos in the name of family harmony? I couldn't tell for sure from his email, and Eileen had known nothing except that Carlos was in Boston to meet with Ashton.

Rip's admonitions about not bending to the wishes of

others seemed to appear like a pop-up ad on my laptop screen, but was Rip's advice practical or just the moralizing that's so easy when it's someone else's choices under scrutiny? Was Rip still a rebellious son of a rabbi, or was he trying to be my rabbi? Last night, we'd made love, insulated from the world by the blizzard outside Rip's snug apartment. Today, snowplows and tow trucks revealed reality, and it was anything but pretty.

Carlos didn't call. He just appeared at the office at five o' clock. Rona was on her way out, but he persuaded her to show him where my office was. He told her he was family and wanted to surprise me.

The fluorescent lights were unflattering to Carlos's complexion. His skin, bronze under the Florida sun, was yellow. Instead of a toned body in swim trunks, he seemed to have an ordinary physique, bundled as he was into a puffy black parka. "Are you surprised to see me, Sylvie?"

"I knew you were in town, because Miguel emailed me—the email you made him write for you about Luis's 'peace of mind.'"

"I didn't make Miguel do anything. He's my brother. We're close."

I doubted that was true. Luis had told me Carlos had always been resentful of his mother's favoring Miguel. At times Carlos and Miguel behaved like close brothers, as they had when we'd all gone clubbing in South Beach, but Carlos was capable of changing personas from charming to threatening in the space of a moment.

"I'm here," he continued, "because of my father. I told you in Miami that his heart condition was growing worse. Now he's slipping away from us, slipping away and doesn't seem to care." Carlos approached my desk and leaned across it. He was close enough for me to see the sweat on his forehead and the flare of his nostrils. "Luis has lost his will to fight because of you. You've burdened his heart with the lie that I'm a rapist. It's—time—to—make—it—right."

I heard the menace in his voice and wondered if I were alone in the building or if security were within earshot. I didn't think he would hurt me, at least not in my office, but if I didn't give him an answer, he wouldn't leave. If I gave him the answer he wanted, I'd have to follow through.

"I can't make things right because they already are. I told my mother what happened and she told Luis the truth. You raped me."

Carlos scowled and his fingers began to curl. I held my breath, certain he could hear the pounding in my chest. I thought he was going to hit me, but he didn't. I thought he was going to yell, but he didn't. His jaw tightened as his eyes drilled into mine. I forced myself to return his gaze and will him out the door.

"You'll regret your decision, Sylvie. I'm not done with you."

After he left, I realized I was trembling. I collected my belongings and went down to BodySculpt. Rip was with a client, but I asked Rob if he'd mind my waiting in the locker room. I knew Rip might be tied up for an hour. All I cared about, though, was not leaving the building unescorted.

■ ■ ■

Eileen called me as soon as she returned to Boston. She hadn't wanted to leave Miguel, but her regular clients had been calling to find out when they could schedule appointments. She was heavily booked already but asked if I could come by her studio during her dinner break and bring a couple of sandwiches.

Eileen's studio was a tiny anteroom offering a view of her massage table through the back door. There were two tan wicker chairs with a small table between them, a couple of potted palms, and an indistinct pastel print of a reclining woman. The colors were all variants of beige, New Age piano music tinkled softly in the background, and the scent of lavender hung in the air. The idea was to get clients to relax in anticipation of becoming relaxed. At work, I would have disparaged this as preparing to prepare, but Eileen knew her business, which differed from mine.

I arrived at six and saw her five o'clock client leaving, a woman with the same indentations on her face that I had after a half hour with my face squashed into Eileen's massage table headrest. We hugged and sat down on either side of the table. When I handed her the turkey sandwich she'd requested, I saw it.

"Oh my God, look at that diamond." I grabbed her hand. No need to mention how much it resembled the ring Ashton had given me and that I'd thrown in his face.

"I couldn't wait to tell you. At first, Miguel just wanted us to move in together, and I really wanted to, but my clients . . . I wasn't ready to lose my massage practice. When he drove me to the airport, he said he understood we hadn't known each other very long and he was asking for a big commitment, so he wanted me to know he was serious. Out came the ring box. I was stunned. If it hadn't been for the honking cars behind us, I would have stayed in my bucket seat."

"Wow, hope you had your sunglasses on."

She pulled her hand away. "You don't think it's ostentatious, do you?"

"Just teasing, silly." What cause had I to make Eileen anxious just because the worse things went for me in that tropical mansion, the better they went for her? "Glad I talked you into leaving behind your poinsettia and coming with me for Thanksgiving."

Eileen looked at her watch. "I don't have much time before my seven o'clock. Have one other thing to talk to you about, to warn you." She held up her forefinger and took a giant bite of her sandwich, which propelled mayonnaise down her chin. I handed her a napkin but returned my sandwich to my lap.

"Miguel told me Carlos is angry. Is this still about your refusing to lie to Luis about the rape? Why is that so important, especially now? The poor man is dying." She shook her head, puzzled. "It just doesn't compute."

I wished I had an answer. I brought her up to date on Carlos's visit to my office, but I didn't want her to know how scared I'd been.

"Sylvie, are you nuts? He could have hurt you. I know artificial intelligence is a hot new field, but Miguel told me Carlos was never interested in technology before. It's just an excuse to harass you."

"Well, now that he's harassed me, he'll probably go home."

Eileen looked as though she were about to protest, but a sixtyish woman in a red down parka appeared in the doorway. She apologized for being early and interrupting us as I rewrapped my sandwich and grabbed the empty wrapper from Eileen's. I told her I was just leaving and was rewarded for my haste with a dollop of mayonnaise on my empty ring finger.

CHAPTER 24

Two days later, Sam and I met at Starbucks for breakfast. The tables were closer together than in Rebecca's Café, but our cafeteria could be crowded in the morning. We were short on time, given Sam's flight to Munich that afternoon, and I didn't want friendly interruptions from colleagues interfering with our conversation. I needed to tell Sam about Richard's meetings at Distributon.

"Those losers have enough cash to acquire us?" The familiar flush rose from Sam's collar.

"Apparently so. They're a private company, so their financials aren't public, but I did a little research. They're looking to expand their markets but need AI solutions to do that."

As I watched the barista behind the counter make change for a customer, I realized there might be something I could do that would help Sam as well as Warren. "What if I stick some orders 'in my drawer' and delay booking them? Right now, the US is bringing in more revenue than Europe, and you're dealing with different distributors in each country. For some of my sales reps who are doing well, the delay wouldn't hurt them. I can tell them it's just insurance in case they have a slow month when they don't make quota."

"That's going to hurt the way your numbers look relative to your forecast and make trouble for you with Richard."

"That's the point. If it looks like the company's bookings are slowing, it might delay Richard from making a deal with a potential acquirer." I didn't tell Sam that a delay might enable Warren to complete his secret project and get us a more lucrative deal with a big public company. Sam grumbled about a delay not doing much for us, but at least a corporate suitor better than Distributon might come along.

"I'm not happy about your taking on this risk, Sylvie."

I assured him it would work out, although as I walked back to my car, I wondered if the source of my plan was bravery or too much caffeine.

Later that evening, Warren called me at home on my cell. He said he didn't want to be seen together except when required at work. It seemed melodramatic, but I had no desire to revisit the seedy bar he had taken me to when he'd wanted to share his secret project. Where would we need to hide next? I had a sudden vision of us being spotted by someone from work as we conferred behind the refrigerators at Home Depot. Would we have to claim we were moving in together?

"Have you learned anything further about Richard's plan? He knows I'm angry about his so-called loan, so he's clammed up."

I told Warren about Richard's lengthy visits to Distributon, and he agreed they'd make sense as a potential acquirer, albeit an unappealing one. I remembered my conversation with Richard when he'd promoted me and asked me to make AI*future* look larger than life. I guessed he was doing a first-class job of that himself with Distributon.

"We need to stop him," Warren said. I could imagine his dark eyebrows drawing together into a V-shaped unibrow.

"I think I can delay him." I told Warren about my plan to hold back on booking some orders from my more successful sales reps, so company revenue would miss its target. If it were noticed, I'd just claim to have miscalculated slightly while trying to smooth our US revenue across several months.

I didn't tell him I'd already shared this suggestion with Sam. Warren and Sam had asked the same favor of me, to gather intelligence, so I wasn't really a double agent. No need for each to know about the other. Although the thought of Rip's line of best fit nagged at me, I was hardly the first sales executive to temporarily stick an order in the drawer. What was the downside?

* * *

January was unusually strong for the first month of the fiscal year. Sales organizations usually ran like hell in December to bring in as much business as possible and beat their quotas. Winter had been good to AI*future* even though NewAI was still stuck in engineering, Sam's complaints notwithstanding.

I'd had no problem holding back on bookings, although one large order that was supposed to go in was unexpectedly canceled by the customer. That left my February numbers in a hole and caused Richard to call me into his office. Though it had been only a few months since he'd said he was promoting me, I felt good about what I had accomplished with the US. Surely one hiccup wouldn't matter.

Richard sat behind his broad mahogany desk. He looked taller, even regal, which made me wonder if he'd cranked up the height of his chair. He usually came over to his conference table to talk with me instead of remaining behind the polished authority of his desk. He didn't ask me to sit down, but I dropped into one of the visitor chairs opposite him anyway. I didn't want to be yelled at standing up.

"Do you remember what I warned you about when we met to discuss your promotion?"

I sorted through my memories, but it seemed there was more than one admonition to remember.

"I warned you that our investors from your ex-husband's venture capital firm were short on patience."

"They're upset with AI*future*'s revenue?" I was puzzled, given the steady growth in US sales since I was promoted on the fly. Kind of a miracle, really. Without Manny, my North Star, to mentor me, I'd made my quota.

"Your ex called me on a personal matter. Well, business but also personal. A new investor has been to see him, one with very substantial resources that Ashton would like to have added to one of Tory Partners's new venture funds. The investor said he'd provide the money if Ashton would help him with a personal matter.

"Apparently, you have a family connection with this investor, and as Ashton tells it, you have falsely accused the man of rape. Ashton claims you accused him without filing a police report. Perhaps this isn't fair, Sylvie, but Ashton claims this accusation is of a pattern with past behavior. I want you to put an end to it. I don't need this pressure right now."

Carlos! I realized my hands were clutching the arms of my chair. I wondered if smoke were coming out of my ears, which would have made sense given the heat in my chest. I'd never heard of a venture capitalist getting involved with a potential investor's private life. I wasn't sure whom I wanted to kill more, Ashton or Carlos. *Did I really have to tell my CEO that I was held down and penetrated against my will?* "Not fair doesn't begin to cover it. My integrity has to be sold for some venture fund?"

Richard looked pained. I gave him points for that.

"I'm sorry, but, yes, I'm asking you to drop the matter."

Matter? This was just a matter to these men. I might have led Carlos on during our romantic night at South Beach, but whatever guilty feelings I still harbored slipped away and were replaced by rage. I could barely speak. "I didn't lie!" I got up and started for the door. "I have a meeting. I'll need to get back to you tomorrow."

■ ■ ■

That evening, as Rip and I lay intertwined on my couch, I drew comfort from the strength of his arms around me. I had never told Rip about Carlos. We'd provided glimpses into our respective pasts as they'd been relevant to our conversations, but in a gym, subjects may last only as long as fifteen repetitions of a bicep curl or until you can no longer talk while holding your body straight in a plank.

My personal and professional lives had been in a head-on collision, and I wasn't sure even the jaws of life could save me. I needed to talk to someone, but I was afraid to tell Rip about my first hookup with Carlos and how it had finished off my marriage. What would Rip think of me, he of the perpetual warnings about altering my line of best fit? I couldn't explain the rape, though, and Carlos's expectations, without starting at the beginning.

I extricated myself and turned to look squarely at Rip's face while I told him my story. I braced myself for his disapproval. "I got chewed out today by my CEO. I was not exactly deferential, because he was asking me to do something unconscionable."

Rip's eyebrows drew together.

By the time I finished, it was 11:00 p.m. He interrupted me only once, after I told him about the night Carlos and I had hooked up consensually and how it had precipitated my divorce.

"Did you love Ashton?"

"I don't think I knew what love was. I wanted the trappings of being in love and married, never recognizing the hollow core of our relationship. I certainly didn't love Carlos."

"It sounds like you're the one who's trapped now by both Ashton and Carlos. What are you going to do?" With a sardonic curl to his mouth, he asked, "Could artificial intelligence advise you, maybe figure out the optimal decision?"

"That was a cheap shot. What the hell does AI have to do with it?"

"Decide one way, and you keep your job at the price of your integrity. Decide the other, and you have the opposite outcome. Wouldn't you have to teach your artificial brain how to value your job versus integrity, in which case you would already have to know what your decision should be? Or maybe your machine would eventually learn what the decision should be because it teaches itself from tons of data, right?"

I jumped up from the couch, angrier with myself than with him. Why did I care about being straight with him or reading the disapproval in his eyes when all he was thinking about was preaching his anti-AI message? "You know, Rip, your father was right. You really should have been a rabbi. Everything's a teaching moment for you—how to do exercises right to become fit, how to keep your line of best fit right or straight or whatever. I thought you were going to help me. Go home, Rabbi, and preach to Dinger. I'm sure he'll be fascinated."

Rip sat for a moment, his face contorted by fury or injury. I couldn't tell and didn't care. He said nothing, just grabbed his parka. I thought I'd hear the door slam, but he closed it quietly behind him, somehow a more final gesture.

CHAPTER 25

I couldn't complain that Eileen's call woke me up. Although it was 1:00 a.m., I was lying in bed staring at the ceiling, replaying my falling-out with Rip.

"Sylvie, Luis had a massive heart attack. Celia went upstairs to check on him and discovered he was gone."

"Poor Luis. At least the end came fast." I blinked back tears.

"Miguel's upset because he wasn't there. Out of town on business, same as Carlos. I'm sorry to wake you, but I'm flying to Miami in the morning, and I was hoping . . . you'll come, won't you?"

I knew where Carlos had been—in Boston harassing me. Still, I couldn't leave Richard hanging, assuming he was hanging and hadn't already decided to fire me. No matter how I felt, whether it was like crawling into a hole or scratching his eyes out with one of those cufflinks he was always buffing, I'd have to leave right after talking to him and drive to the airport, where Carlos might be on the same flight. I'd sooner travel in the baggage compartment than see him. I promised Eileen I'd fly out as early as I could.

How is it that the death of those we care about shocks us even when we can see it coming at a distance? Sleep eluded me. I was possessed by morbid thoughts, worried about who might next slip away, although I couldn't say why. I'd already lost both parents and a sweet man who loved me like a daughter.

Friends—losing a friend could be worse, leaving an empty space, like a tree that you don't realize is anchoring a landscape till it's felled by lightning. People who love animals mourn them as though they were family, better than family. Hadn't I seen the love and loyalty between Dinger and Rip? Dinger, burying his face in Rip's chest, tail wagging, and Rip, massaging Dinger's neck and kissing the top of his furry head. Rip—I didn't want to think about him.

Richard was expecting me in his office at 8:30 a.m. It should have been easy to be on time, but as so often happens after wakeful nights, sleep drew its curtain at 4:00 or maybe 5:00. I slept through my alarm and had to race for the office, or what passes for racing during commuting hours. I hated the feeling of having dressed in such haste that I might not have noticed wearing two different shoes or having lipstick on my teeth.

"Sylvie." Richard acknowledged my arrival with a nod. He didn't invite me to sit down nor did I wait for a seat to be offered.

I took a deep breath and began. "I have no reason to amend what I said yesterday. I was raped by Ashton's prospective investor and never lied about it. I didn't report the rape to the police because of family ramifications."

Richard gestured toward the chair in front of his desk, and I perched on the edge of the seat. "I'm not going to question you about your 'family ramifications.' In fact, I might have put off Ashton's request, because you managed to hit the ground running as US sales executive, but now, well, I was disappointed in your performance this past month, well below forecast. If our revenue doesn't continue to rise, I may have to act on Ashton's concerns."

This was a reprieve of sorts, although temporary. Carlos might not keep after me, now that Luis was dead, but my strategy of sticking orders in the drawer wasn't going to work, not if Richard was going to scrutinize my bookings. "We had an unwelcome surprise last month, just a blip. I don't see us missing quota again this quarter or next." I noted the sour look on Richard's face and he looked down at his laptop as if he had lost interest in me. A minute went by before he looked up.

"That's all, Sylvie. I expect you to take the gloves off. No more missing your numbers, and clean up your personal mess, please."

"I need to travel to Miami for my stepfather's funeral, but I'll stay in touch with my sales reps while I'm away. I can address the personal issues you mentioned at the same time."

He responded with a curt nod that in no way signaled approval.

■ ■ ■

With great relief, I noted that Carlos wasn't at the gate for my flight. What were the odds anyway? He'd probably left as soon as he heard about his father. When I arrived at the estate, which had become quite literally part of Luis's estate, Eileen greeted me. "Don't worry. Carlos is staying at his own place."

We went upstairs, where I collapsed on the guestroom bed. Eileen plunked herself down on a wicker rocker. As bone weary from emotional stress as sleeplessness, I wondered if I were losing touch with reality, expecting Carlos to jump out from behind every palm tree like a tropical bogeyman. I propped myself up on one elbow. "I hope he's finished harassing me. After all, Luis is dead."

Eileen raised an eyebrow. "Are you trying to convince me or yourself? Why don't you take a nap, and I'll come get you for dinner."

I closed my eyes and wished I were anywhere but Miami, but no alternative came to mind. I wasn't in the least tempted by anticipation of the sun's heat, the bracing ocean waves, and the warm sand giving way beneath my feet. They couldn't be restorative with my mind in such turmoil. Avoiding Rip in Boston, avoiding Carlos in Miami—how did I manage to be in full retreat?

Dinner was quiet and simple, served to the two of us by a hollow-eyed Celia. When I hugged her, I felt the wetness of her tears through my blouse. "Such a difficult time," I said.

"I've worked here for more than thirty years. He was a wonderful man and a good father, better than that Carlos deserved." I thought of Celia as discreet, but grief can give voice to angry thoughts.

Miguel had given Eileen the schedule. The wake would be early tomorrow with mass later. The burial was for family only, but Miguel hoped to put together a memorial service for his father in a week or two. There was no time for Luis's far-flung friends and family to arrive in time for the wake. At a memorial service, people would have a chance to honor Luis and tell the stories that no doubt went back to Cuba.

Eileen turned to Sylvie. "There's a will that the family attorney wants to read while you're here. You know you're in it, right?"

"I know my mother wanted it that way, but that's all I know. It doesn't seem right to be talking about assets so soon after Luis's death."

Eileen sighed. "I get it, but Miguel said the lawyer insists on your presence. I won't be there, of course. I'm not family yet, but Miguel and I have set a date, June 1, and you'd better be there as maid of honor."

"Don't know if I'm still considered a maid after a divorce, probably a matron, but it would definitely be an honor to be at your side. What a shame, though, that Luis didn't live to see you and Miguel at the altar."

"At least I had a little bit of a chance to get to know him and see how much like him Miguel is."

"You're lucky, Eileen. Both sons inherited his charm and good looks, but Miguel got all the sweetness genes. Carlos just got the gift wrap. Once you get past that, you find that what's inside is broken."

Eileen had sad eyes. "Don't worry, Syl. Everything will be all right. Soon you'll be on your way back to Boston and your normal life."

There was no normal in my life, whether in Miami or Boston. I had a talent for tainting geography. Pretty soon, I'd have to head for Pago Pago.

* * *

The wake was more difficult for me than I expected. Luis's coffin was open. He looked alive and close enough to hug. The mortician's artistry impressed me. Luis wore a handsome blue suit, undoubtedly pinned in the back to fit his wasted body. Though his face looked less troubled in repose than it had the last time I'd seen him, I wondered if he had really suffered more from his son's disappointing behavior than his loss of Margaret. Carlos was fully capable of making up the whole thing about Luis's state of mind.

Luis was well respected in Miami and throughout the Cuban community. Despite the absence of distant friends and relatives, the wake was crowded. When I spotted Carlos staring at me, I went out to the vestibule to sign the guest book.

An expensively dressed woman in her seventies saw my signature and touched my arm. "Are you Margaret's daughter?"

I nodded.

"I don't know if you were aware of your mother's contribution to the Cuban Relief Center. She gave a lot of time—a real administrative whiz, that woman. Allowed our volunteers to do more hands-on work in Miami. Luis doted on her too. So sad that they're both gone now." She shook her head.

I didn't think of my mother as the do-gooder type, but to be fair, she wouldn't have had any spare time when she and Dad owned the pharmacy. To be fair—when was I last fair to her? It was a little late to cut her some slack.

I sat through the mass, inattentive and uncomfortable. My parents were nonobservant Protestants, so I had rarely attended church. At Christmastime, I'd seen bits of Catholic services on TV, including the ritual and magnificent setting of whatever great cathedral was being featured. Why was so much of the service in Latin? Did people understand what they were saying, and if they didn't, why didn't it bother them?

Maybe the same could be said about Jewish services filled with Hebrew prayers. That was a question for Rip. Then I remembered Rip and I were over. I wasn't sure what I believed, but I knew I was a lot closer to being an atheist than a theist.

A pall hung over the house and seemed to obscure its beauty. Celia went about her chores robotically, and I asked Eileen if Celia would be staying on. Eileen didn't know what was going to happen to the house, its contents, and the staff.

"Wait till tomorrow," she replied. "You'll know the answer when the will is read."

■ ■ ■

The lawyer, Alberto Aceba, was a short bald man in his sixties, attired in a white suit. The suit reminded me of John Travolta, but the body was twice as wide. He ushered us into an over air-conditioned conference room and gestured toward the chairs surrounding a circular table. Since there were only three of us and Aceba attending, two of the chairs were unoccupied. I sat next to Aceba and put my bag on the chair next to me to ensure Carlos would not sit beside me. He sat on the other side of Aceba and gave me a look that made the room feel even colder.

The lawyer placed a folder on the table in front of him and folded his hands. "You may not be aware of this fact, but lawyers no longer need or are required to read wills aloud to beneficiaries, not in any state. Copies of the will are usually mailed. There are, however, circumstances when it is desirable to pull the family together for a reading, usually when there is a chance the terms of the will could cause confusion."

As Aceba opened the folder, I felt the tension in the room ratchet up as though he were stripping the insulation off a live wire. What "confusion" was he referring to? He withdrew a document and began to read aloud the last will and testament of Luis Rodriguez. The boilerplate sections sounded familiar, lulling me along. When I heard the words "Luis's stepdaughter, Sylvie," I was jolted back to full attention.

Luis had left 20 percent of his financial assets to me, which I considered a gift of stunning proportions. Miguel would inherit 40 percent plus the Miami oceanfront estate and its contents to do with as he wished. Eileen would be happy about that. She loved the house. To Carlos, who sat rigid as stone in his chair, Luis left 40 percent of his financial assets, but the money was to be divided between two trust funds for the benefit of Carlos, one managed by Miguel and one by me. If Miguel or I were deceased, the other trustee would manage both trusts.

Carlos, with lips pursed and eyes narrowed, said not a word. He clearly understood that no money was coming directly to him unless it was disbursed from one of the trusts. There were additional paragraphs describing various contingencies and what would happen if Carlos had children or died. He would also have to continue supporting the child he had fathered with his previous rape victim until that child turned twenty-one. Luis had called it a seduction—a euphemism, no doubt.

Despite the legalese I didn't entirely understand, one thing was clear: Luis had intended to punish and humiliate Carlos by making him come to me for his annual disbursement from the half of his trust I managed. He would hate that. He would hate me. Luis must have told Carlos about his changed will. I couldn't blame Luis for wanting to see his son's reaction, to ensure Carlos understood the consequences of his actions.

I saw with clarity why Carlos needed me to withdraw my rape accusation. He needed me to comply so Luis would destroy his new will. What bullshit Carlos had made up—that I should put poor Luis's mind at rest—not to mention the fact that Carlos was willing to wreck my career at AI*future* to bring me to heel.

At least Carlos would have his brother managing half his inheritance. Miguel would be a softer touch for his entreaties, while I would be perceived as an unceasing obstacle to be pushed against. I'd endure his antagonism for a lifetime. *Oh, Luis, you didn't think this through.*

It occurred to me that I might be in danger only when Miguel and I returned to the house. Aceba had said that if either Miguel or I predeceased Carlos, our share of the trust would be added to the share managed by the other trustee. Mine would revert to Miguel, and wouldn't that be a far more comfortable arrangement for Carlos?

That evening, Eileen perched at the end of my bed while I sat cross-legged, clutching a pillow to my chest. The lamplight reflected off the facets of her diamond, and I noticed her capable fingers, now adorned by manicured and polished nails. Funky was giving way to something else in Eileen, but I hoped she wouldn't change in any fundamental way for Miguel's sake. I doubted he would ask it. Anyway, pleasing others was my specialty, not hers.

"Do you think I'm getting carried away?" I asked. "Am I being paranoid?"

"I can understand your concern. Carlos is an Aries, and everyone knows they have anger issues. I have to admit Miguel said Carlos is enraged, but Carlos knew about the changes to the will before Luis died. I think he'll settle down and become his charming, devious self again. After all, it's over. Luis is dead, and the will is settled. You need a break from worrying. I'm going back downstairs for Cabernet and a couple of glasses."

When Eileen returned with three goblets, Miguel was beside her. They set up the bar on my dresser. With full glasses in our hands, we looked at one another waiting for someone to make an appropriate toast.

"To my father, Luis," Miguel said. "May he finally rest in peace." We sipped the full-bodied wine, but despite Eileen's good intentions, it did nothing to lighten the solemn moment. "Don't worry, Sylvie," he said. "My brother isn't that crazy. He'd never hurt you."

CHAPTER 26

I was grateful to be home from Florida. All I wanted to do was hide out in my bedroom, turn off my cell, and bury my laptop under a snowdrift. There were no elderly people left in my life who were in danger of imminent death, so I expected no urgent phone calls requiring a trip out of town. Even though there was money coming my way from Miami, under the circumstances, I didn't want to think about it.

Rip would be pleased, if we were on speaking terms, that I could now afford to buy a four-wheel-drive car and snow tires. Our last evening together had ended with such acrimonious words, I couldn't imagine going to the gym and seeing him, let alone training with him. To hell with my fitness level, moral and otherwise.

I sat on my quilt and ran my fingers over the wedding-ring stitching. It belonged anywhere but on *my* bed. I picked at one of the loose stitches. Having bad taste in men was such a cliché, I hated to think it applied to me, yet every man I hooked up with wanted to change me in some way. Is that what I wanted? How could anyone love me for myself if I wasn't sure who I was?

Eileen was right about Ashton. He was like Dr. Aylmer in Hawthorne's story, "The Birth-Mark," unsatisfied with less than physical perfection in his wife. Georgiana's desire to please him cost her dearly. She drank his potion, which lightened her birthmark. When it disappeared completely, she died. At least I escaped from my divorce with my life. Rip, on the other hand, wanted to hold me to his standard of morality, nothing less than perfection on the inside, or at least perpetual awareness of my line of best fit.

Before I left for the office, I checked my email. I figured if I knocked out a few messages before going, it would ease my reentry. A note from Kate was as unexpected as its content. "Can we meet for a drink after work?"

I didn't want to see her, but I gave in to my curiosity. After all, I did believe she'd been fired for bogus reasons. The sexual harassment accusation had made no sense until I learned that Harold Astrove's wife had a brother on our board. Still, AI*future* was lucky Kate hadn't brought a wrongful termination suit. Maybe that wasn't her style. Maybe she preferred subterfuge.

We met at 6:00 p.m. three days later at the Embassy Suites cocktail lounge. Kate looked better than the last time I'd seen her, or maybe she just looked sober. She wore a white pantsuit, which made her red curls stand out even more, and she attracted plenty of attention at the bar when she got up from her table to give me a quick hug.

"You look great," I said. "You've obviously landed on your feet."

"No thanks to AI*future*," she replied with a wry smile, "Distributon offered me essentially the same job for more money." She sat back in her chair looking satisfied with herself. "What are you drinking, Sylvie? I'm buying."

I wondered if the reason for our meeting was for Kate to crow over her good luck after AI*future* screwed her, but by the time I was halfway through my glass of wine, she surprised me with her real intent. "You may not know this, but our CEO is talking to Richard about our acquiring AI*future*."

No point in letting Kate know I'd already heard.

She continued. "Richard treated me like shit when he fired me from AI*future*. Harold Astrove is a liar whose wife makes him grovel. There's no way I'd work with those assholes again." She shook her fist at the imaginary assholes at our table.

"Kate, don't you think you're being a little melodramatic? You don't know which of those 'assholes' would get to keep their executive positions in a combined company."

"Yes, I do. We just lost our CFO, so Harold Astrove would get the job. I don't want that devious lecher anywhere near me."

I remembered when Kate had been smug about hooking up with that "devious lecher" and getting information out of him. How much had changed since our lunch at Legal Seafood. The truth was I didn't want AI*future* to merge with Distributon any more than Kate did, but my effort to slow things down by holding back sales orders had backfired. "I get it, but I have no role in Richard's negotiations. What do you expect of me?"

Kate drained her wineglass. "I was hoping you'd tell our CEO about Richard's so-called loan for his wife's flower shop. That would either prevent the deal or change the leverage in a negotiation."

"Are you serious, Kate? That would be a career-ending move for me. Why don't you deliver the poison pill yourself? You work for Distributon." I reached for my bag.

"Wait." She put her hand on my arm. "It's more complicated than that. When Richard was letting me go, I threatened to bring a wrongful termination suit against AI*future*. He knew he was letting me go for bogus reasons and wanted to avoid a suit, so he offered me a lot of money if I'd sign a nondisclosure agreement. Without knowing how long I'd be out of work, I had to take the deal. If I violate my NDA, AI*future* could sue me."

I felt that familiar urge to go along, to be on her side, and, after all, I could think of a good reason. She'd been screwed just because Harold Astrove's wife was both vindictive and well-connected. Whatever I thought of Kate, she deserved better, and wouldn't I be helping my company?

With Kate's plan, perhaps I could squash the Distributon deal so Warren could finish the software that would make us attractive to a large public company. Richard might oppose that, but he couldn't prevent a hostile takeover. I looked down and realized I had worked my cocktail napkin into a twist. Somehow, I could always come up with a reason to go along.

"I hate to say no, Kate, but I just can't do it. It's too big an ask. It would be wrong. I wish you good luck—really I do." I stood up, and she began to protest.

"This would be good for you. Please reconsider."

I didn't trust myself, so I made a swift exit, mumbling, "Sorry, sorry," as I left the bar.

* * *

That evening I opened my email to find a message from Rob Linde: "Sylvie, we haven't seen you at BodySculpt recently. Should I release your standing appointment with Rip? I hate to lose you as a client, but I have a waiting list. Please call me."

I didn't call right away because I found myself choked up. I was not going to cry over Rip. At least that's what I told myself as I wiped off the tears that had dripped onto my keyboard. I punched in Rob's number on my cell, but I had barely begun to speak before my eyes became wet again.

"Sylvie, are you still there?"

Trying hard to keep the huskiness out of my voice, I said, "Sorry, but I've been tied up with family issues since the recent loss of my stepfather. Best to give my slot away for now. If I'm able to come back at some future point, I'll be fine working with whatever trainer is available."

It was Rob's turn to leave the conversation on pause. He must have known Rip and I were seeing each other, because he asked me if I were sure. At that point, there was little in my life I felt sure about besides the pain I'd feel encountering Rip.

■ ■ ■

I didn't hear from Kate again, nor did I have reason to contact her. I did wonder, though, if she had approached anyone besides me to tell her CEO about AI*future*'s cash position. I decided to email Warren to see if we could get together, but I heard nothing until 6:00 p.m., when he entered my office, closed the door, and dropped into the seat opposite me. He looked tired and claimed he was beat from trying to finish his secret software application before Richard made commitments to an outside company. "Any news?" he asked.

I told him about my drink with Kate and updated him on her new position at Distributon. "She's got a sweet deal over there and is adamant about keeping AI*future* from screwing it up for her. She wanted me to tell her CEO about Richard's so-called loan, hoping that the truth about our financial situation would prevent the deal. Of course, she's pissed off at us in general because of the way she was treated." I explained the NDA terms she'd agreed to before leaving AI*future*.

Warren leaned back in his chair and put his hands behind his head. The wheels in his brain never stopped spinning. "If she does find a way around the NDA she signed and tips off her CEO, that might at least slow down an acquisition till I can finish my software and find a major acquirer." He sat up and faced me. "You're not going to help on this, right?"

I shook my head. His gaze made me feel he was one step ahead of me, ahead of everyone. I worried he might not be telling me the truth about when his groundbreaking software would be finished. In the meantime, I was managing a group of sales reps waiting breathlessly for the NewAI product Warren had slow walked.

* * *

My heart seemed to be beating double time. I wondered if it were possible for someone my age to have a heart problem. I packed up and left the office early. A long walk around my neighborhood would calm me down and maybe make up for my canceled appointments at the gym.

Despite the snow, the sidewalks were mostly clear, and I restricted myself to streets illuminated well enough to light my way through the winter darkness. I hated to admit it, but I really missed exercise. I'd become addicted to it, or maybe just addicted to Rip. I was almost home when I realized a car was following me. I quickened my pace and soon was power walking. If I ran, it would be obvious I was frightened, which, of course, I was.

I hadn't noticed before how few houses along my road had lighted windows. No one would hear me scream. I suspected the retirees living in those homes were snowbirds who flew to Florida for the winter. As the car drew abreast of me, I recognized Carlos's voice calling out my name. Florida had come to me.

For a moment, I was almost relieved to see someone I knew at the wheel, but the grim set of his mouth made my chest tighten. "Sylvie, when I arrived at your apartment and you didn't answer my knock, I gave up and drove away. I spotted a woman walking but couldn't believe you would be out on such a frigid night. I turned around and followed you back."

"I imagine it would seem frigid to someone from Miami. Why are you here?"

"I need to talk to you. Can I come in?"

"That's a bad idea. You should have called instead of stalking me."

He got out of his car and slammed the door, his face dark with anger under the purplish halide streetlamp. Another twenty yards to safety, and if I sprinted, I could beat him.

I took off, listening for his footsteps as I ran. I tried to pivot and change direction, but the plowed sidewalk had become icy. My boots failed me. I landed on my back in a snowdrift, feeling the shock of snow pushing down my collar and into my sleeves. My fingers were becoming numb from struggling to get up without the gloves I'd somehow lost. A heavy weight landed on me and held me down.

"Don't fight me, Sylvie. Lie still."

I struggled against him but only dug myself deeper. I tried to scream, but he clapped his gloved hand over my mouth, jamming snow into my throat.

"I'm not going to hurt you . . . yet," he said. "Give back my money, and I'll leave you alone, dear stepsister." He pressed his groin into me, harder and harder, his hand reaching under my coat, then under my sweater. "You're a gold-digging interloper, just like your mother."

I was sinking, choking.

"What's happening here?" asked an indignant voice.

The weight slipped backward off me. "Thank God," Carlos said. "Can you help us? She fell, and I tried to pull her up. I must have lost my footing in the same place she did and fell on top of her. I think I broke my ankle."

The Black woman looming over us was tall and bulky in a white down parka and hood. She extended a hand to Carlos, who struggled to his feet, wincing and holding his right foot off the ground. "You okay, hon?" she asked while reaching down with her long arms to lift me to a sitting position.

"He molested me." I forced the words out, although I could hardly breathe. Her eyes narrowed.

Carlos raised his palms. "Look at her." He nodded in my direction. "She's in shock. Do you think any man would be physically capable of molesting a woman in a snowbank on a night like this?" He limped toward his car. "Last time I'll be a good Samaritan."

She let him go and reached down to help me gain my footing. "I'm Mary Jo Carter. I live in that blue Cape over there." She pointed to a sweet, snow-covered house set back from the road. "I was going to get a snack from the kitchen when I saw what I thought was a man face down in a drift."

"Mary Jo, I'm so grateful. When I saw you in that white coat and hood, I thought you were my guardian angel."

She smiled. "Believe me, I'm no angel. You look a little shaky, though. Let me take you home."

"I'm fine, and I'm almost there."

She took my arm and walked me the rest of the way.

■ ■ ■

I didn't go to work the next morning, though I wasn't ill. I had a sick feeling in my stomach each time I relived my helplessness under Carlos. Thinking I was in danger from him had seemed paranoid before, but the terror of choking on snow while icy gloves pushed under my sweater toward my breasts . . .

I wanted no part of Carlos's trust fund, but refusing it, or whatever I'd have to do legally to give up my trusteeship, would be to surrender to a person who wanted me to know he could always overpower me. I had to get back in control. If only I could talk to Eileen, I could figure out what to do. She was my sanity check. I couldn't bring myself to call her, though. She'd be in the position of having to tell Miguel, who was still coping with his father's death. If she didn't tell him, she'd be keeping a secret from him about his own brother.

I googled "restraining order" and discovered I'd need evidence like a police report to take one out against Carlos. A temporary one would be easier to get than a permanent one, but how could I prove what had happened without a witness? Eileen wasn't an eyewitness to my rape, but I'd told her the basics of the story on the plane ride home. Maybe Mary Jo Carter could help.

I closed my laptop and went to see if my jacket had dried. The insides of the arms were still damp, and I shuddered remembering the icy wetness seeping into the cuffs as Carlos pressed himself against me. I pulled a fleece windbreaker off its hanger, not warm enough for this weather, but Mary Jo's house was close. Shouldn't I take a thank-you gift? I had nothing in the house but wine, so I grabbed a bottle of Malbec. *Hope she's not one of those people who never touches the stuff.*

Mary Jo answered the door in her white parka. I apologized for catching her on her way out, but she had just arrived home and invited me in. She was a nurse and had just finished a shift. When she took off her parka, she was in blue scrubs. "I'm sorry. You were probably about to change your clothes."

"Oh, hon, you didn't have to bring me anything, and don't apologize. It's fine. Before I married Leon, I had a similar experience, not in a snowbank, in a hospital supply room. I know just how you feel."

She gestured toward her sleek black sofa. Mary Jo's house was bigger on the inside than it appeared from the outside. Walls had been removed, so the living room, dining area, and kitchen were open. Tasteful low-voltage ceiling lights illuminated modern furnishings including a white area rug.

I sat down on the leather sofa, unsure of how to begin as Mary Jo began to brew coffee. "Join me?" she asked.

I agreed. While she set up mugs and spoons on a tray, I looked out the window, easily spotting the hollowed-out snowbank where Carlos had overpowered me. I kept coming back to the word "overpowered." More than the grinding and groping, it was my helplessness that traumatized me.

When Mary Jo's large mugs of steaming coffee were on the glass-topped coffee table in front of us, I remembered my dinner in the late fall with Eileen. We had topped it off with venti cups of steaming coffee from Starbucks and talked about my hot stepbrothers in Miami. It seemed like a lifetime had passed since then. Mary Jo was looking at me.

"Sylvie, you're still upset about that incident last night, aren't you?"

If only it had been an incident and nothing more, I wouldn't be sitting on Mary Jo's couch. I sipped my coffee and began to explain who Carlos was and my reasons for fearing him.

"So, he was just pretending to be a passerby?"

"He was stalking me. Our encounter was no accident. I want to take out a restraining order against him, but I have scant evidence to give the police. I have a friend—she's out of town now—who knows the whole unsavory story. I can ask her to be a witness of sorts, but I thought I'd ask you first. You saw what happened. Would you be willing to come with me to the police? You hardly know me and I'm asking a lot, but I'm just so desperate."

"Sylvie, I can only tell what I saw, not what was happening between your two bodies. Is that going to help?"

"I don't really know. I've never been down this road before."

Mary Jo picked up her mug, took a few sips, and looked out her window. Perhaps she was summoning the memory of what she'd seen. "You're in danger, so how can I say no?"

* * *

I was glad I decided to research how to proceed, because I discovered I would need to go to the district court in Dedham to get the necessary forms and file an affidavit, and I wouldn't need Mary Jo for that. I wouldn't qualify for a restraining order, because I had no evidence of being raped. I hadn't filed a police report.

What I qualified for was a harassment order. The judge could provide a temporary one ex parte, that is, without notifying Carlos. Once the police located and served him, the judge would set a date for the ten-day hearing, where Carlos could defend himself and contest the order.

The important thing was that Carlos would not be able to threaten or assault me in the interim. He'd have to remain a set distance away from me, and he couldn't call, email, contact me on social media, or go to my home or office.

■ ■ ■

After returning home from the courthouse, I locked the front door and wandered aimlessly around my apartment. I lay down on my bed thinking a nap would calm me. No such luck. I couldn't sleep and, worse yet, found my thoughts wandering to Rip, whom, I hated to admit, I missed. I sat on the edge of the bed, head in hands. How did I get myself so tangled up?

Rip was mad at me. So was Kate, not that she was any great loss. Sam didn't know what was going on because he was still away, but when he found out I'd kept from him my agreement to help Warren, he would not be pleased. Only Warren, whom I never liked, was on my side. Eileen was loyal, of course, but I was about to put her in an awkward position by taking out a harassment order against her soon-to-be brother-in-law.

I went into my kitchen and poured myself a large glass of Pinot Noir. After a few generous swallows to bolster my courage, I sat down at the table and called Eileen. "Are you in town yet or still in Miami?"

"Still with Miguel, Syl."

"Oh, okay. It's just . . . I was hoping we could get together."

"I'm sorry. What's going on?"

I described my encounter with Carlos. "He called me a 'gold-digging interloper' and wants me to give the money in the trust back to him." When I got to the part about Carlos pinning me down in the snowbank and lying to my neighbor, she was horrified.

"My God! I have to tell Miguel."

"I hate dragging you two into the middle of this, but I can't help myself. I wouldn't even be calling if I didn't need to ask an important favor."

"Anything, Syl."

I told her about the harassment order and Mary Jo Carter's offer of assistance. "I'll need more evidence against Carlos for the hearing, and only you can provide that. I'm waiting for a call from the judge."

"You shouldn't have to go through this alone. Of course I'll help you. I'll check the flights when we get off the phone."

"You're a saint, Eileen. Thanks."

■ ■ ■

At 8:00 the next morning, the judge's administrative assistant called and put him on the line. He asked me about each of my antagonistic encounters with Carlos and agreed to provide me with a temporary harassment order. He warned I'd need to produce more evidence at the hearing. I gave the judge Carlos's email, home address, and cell number so the police could serve him, but my voice shook a little at the end of the call. I was worried about the process I was setting in motion, but I was even more worried about what Carlos might do next.

CHAPTER 27

What I really needed was to hide, but that would have been impractical given my AI*future* responsibilities. Instead, I decided to shop for a new car. I drove to the Subaru dealership closest to Needham and selected a royal blue SUV. At first, I berated myself for following Rip's advice, given that we were no longer together, but I rationalized that I was simply learning from my mistakes.

I asked for snow tires, and despite the dealer's assuring me I wouldn't need them, I insisted. Never again did I want to hear my wheels spinning a rut clear down to the earth's core. I shuddered—too much like sinking into the snow under Carlos's weight.

When the car was ready the following day, I picked it up and continued to the airport to get Eileen. It was my least favorite kind of winter day: rain mixed with snow, slush underfoot, snowbanks capped with soot. Worse yet, my beautiful new car was getting dirty. I wanted to be upbeat for Eileen's sake but the only cheering prospect I could come up with was picturing her in a white gown, walking down the aisle to a smiling Miguel.

I spotted her coming through the automatic doors at the baggage level, tan and striking compared to those around her in their dull winter coats and boots. She hadn't abandoned her unique style, but she had clearly gone upscale. Her asymmetrical skirt and top were contrasting shades of teal, and her gold and turquoise earrings swung with her long dark hair. God bless Miguel. Eileen deserved to be indulged.

The only incongruity was her old winter jacket, thrown on, I imagined, at the carousel after she claimed her suitcase. As I watched her approach, I realized that jacket would soon be replaced by a stylish wrap, all she would need for fending off tropical evening breezes.

I stepped out of the car and waved. She flung her bag into the back seat and jumped in next to me, leaning over to give me a quick squeeze.

"Thanks for picking me up. I'm sorry about the mess Carlos has created for you."

"I'm the one who should be sorry. The mess is all because of me. Maybe Carlos is right. I am an interloper."

"Stop apologizing. I would never have met Miguel if it weren't for you. Remember? Luis meant well, but now things kind of suck. How can I help?"

I told Eileen about the date of the hearing and the information I hoped she could provide. She hadn't heard anything about Carlos besides what I'd told her, and he hadn't been in touch with Miguel either. As much as I feared seeing Carlos, not knowing where he was or what he was up to was just as scary.

* * *

When the day for the hearing came, we picked up Mary Jo on our way.

"I've heard about you," Eileen said, shaking Mary Jo's hand with both of hers. "You're the guardian angel."

Mary Jo shook her head. "From what I understand, that's you, hon."

I told them they could share the title if they got into the car, otherwise we'd miss the hearing.

We arrived at the courtroom after Carlos and his lawyer. I hadn't hired a lawyer because I was sure Eileen's testimony would be compelling. The judge hadn't had a problem providing me with a temporary harassment order, so my hope was he would extend it for at least a year.

I thought perhaps Carlos had brought a lawyer to intimidate me, as if the formality of the courtroom itself wasn't enough to raise my blood pressure. It was designed to inspire respect for justice, the judge, and the trial process. The raised bench flanked by flags, high ceilings, ornate paneling, and polished tables reinforced the image.

Eileen didn't disappoint. She spoke with confidence about the rape that took place the night before Thanksgiving and Carlos's anger at his father's arrangements for the trust. She made it clear that as Miguel's fiancée, she was in a position to understand the family dynamics.

Mary Jo recounted the story I'd already told the judge about Carlos's attack when I was returning home from my walk. I supplied what transpired between Carlos and me in that snowbank, since that was the part Mary Jo hadn't seen.

After I took my place in the witness chair, Carlos's lawyer approached me. "Ms. Manhardt, after this alleged rape, did you file a police report?"

I was ready for the question but had trouble keeping my voice steady explaining the circumstances. "When Carlos pinned me to my bed, we were in a room next to my mother and stepfather's bedroom. I couldn't yell for help. My stepfather had a bad heart . . ." I looked up at the judge, suddenly at a loss for words.

My hesitation was all the lawyer needed. He leaned in close to me, sneering. "Are you sure you weren't giving in to your own passions? That's a tough position to force a woman into, especially without a weapon."

"No! It happens to millions of women," I protested.

"No? But you'd had consensual sex with my client on another occasion. You were quite smitten with him. Cost you your marriage."

I looked over at Eileen, who had a look of horror on her face. Wasn't this what men always said? There was no rape. *You wanted it.*

If I'd been smart enough to bring a lawyer, she would have objected at that point. Carlos's lawyer wasn't asking a question. He was making a speech, one intended to make me lose my composure. It worked. I was rattled.

Before I could respond without sputtering, he claimed I'd managed to worm my way into my stepfather's affections in order to damage his client's interests. How was Carlos supposed to request a fair disbursement from the trust without talking to me? That's all he wanted to do, talk. He wasn't a stalker. Far from it.

I tried to control the rage that was making my voice shake. "When Carlos was smothering me in a snowdrift and humping me beneath him, he wasn't trying to have a conversation. When his hands were under my shirt, he wasn't trying . . ."

The judge's face showed no sign of sympathy. He refused to extend the temporary harassment order for lack of evidence. Carlos shook hands with his lawyer while I sat in my chair, incredulous. Eileen took my arm and pulled me out of the courtroom, sparing me the humiliation of shedding hot, angry tears in front of Carlos.

"What a bunch of shitheads!" Eileen vented as we emerged from the courthouse.

Mary Jo just shook her head. A chilly wind whipping around the corner made us bend our heads on the way to my car.

"Let's go back to your place and consider our options," Eileen suggested.

Mary Jo apologized for not being able to do more for me, but I assured her she'd been a true friend. When we dropped her off at home, I got out of the car and hugged her. "I'm so very grateful."

■ ■ ■

I was about to make coffee when Eileen intervened. "Has to be hot chocolate, after a disappointment, not coffee. It's good for the soul."

"I thought that was chicken soup."

"Not after losses in court." While I microwaved water for instant hot chocolate, Eileen slumped over my kitchen table. "I'm going to call Miguel and let him know everything that's happened. Maybe he can arrange some kind of an intervention with Carlos."

"Seriously? I mean, I know you're trying to help, but Carlos would be impervious to an intervention."

Eileen blew on the surface of the hot chocolate I placed in front of her. "You have a point," she said, "but let me try." She was silent for a moment. "Look, this is probably the worst time to tell you, but I'm closing down my massage therapy practice and moving to Miami to live with Miguel."

"Of course. I've been expecting that." The tears I tried to hold back contradicted my matter-of-fact statement. I hated myself for laying a guilt trip on Eileen. "I'm sorry for crying. I didn't mean to steal your joy."

"Oh, Sylvie, it may be a happy time, but it's sad too, and we both know it. I'll miss you terribly." She came around the table and hugged me. I wiped my eyes with a napkin and took a swallow of my hot chocolate.

"Restorative," I lied. "You were right." I wondered if there were such a thing as running out of tears, like running out of printer ink. I must be close to my limit.

"Seems to me, since Miguel holds the purse strings on the other half of Carlos's trust, he can pressure his brother and make him behave."

"If Carlos were being rational, maybe, but this has turned into some kind of vendetta. I'm no shrink, but I think he's losing it."

CHAPTER 28

The next few days were quiet by my new definition of the word: no sign of Carlos. I eased up on my reflexive glances behind me to see if a car were following. The snowdrifts, which had never seemed threatening until Carlos pinned me down, were melting, as the bitterest cold of the winter abated. My only regret was the absence of a blizzard in which to test my new SUV's traction.

The sales reps who worked for me were still booking business, but the chorus clamoring for NewAI was growing louder, as it was among Sam's distributors in Europe. Without it, we were losing sales to competitors. I needed to take on Warren, no matter how groundbreaking he thought his secret software was, and get him to devote more resources to NewAI. I wasn't sure if Sam had gone so far as to deliver an ultimatum to Richard: *NewAI or I'm out of here*. Because of my worries over Carlos, my head hadn't really been in the game.

The relative quiet I was enjoying ended abruptly, but because of Richard, not Carlos. His early morning text, "Get into the office immediately!" was more potent than a double espresso and had me racing up Route 128 like it was the Autobahn.

When I reached Richard's office, he barked at me to come in and close the door. Without saying another word, he swung his monitor around and hit play. I stared at the screen and watched in disbelief as a person, who appeared for all the world to be me, urged the CEO of Distributon to expand his due diligence into the finances of AI*future*, in particular into an investment in Asia that might be a misrepresentation. The clone of me said she knew that what she was doing was highly irregular, but she felt compelled to come forward.

Richard turned his monitor back around and regarded me with narrowed eyes. "Just who do you think you are? You've wrecked a delicate negotiation with Distributon by spouting lies about AI*future*."

"Richard, that . . . that's not me! It's some sort of clever fake. I would never—" My hands trembled.

"Yeah, right." He glared at me and stood up. "That's all, but you can be sure this isn't over."

I fled to my office, closed the door, and leaned my back against it. I needed to talk to Sam, but I was so rattled I couldn't remember how to make an international call to his cell phone. I fired off a high-priority email telling him it was urgent that he call me. I held on to my cell expecting it to ring at any moment. No such luck.

Who could hate me enough to cause so much harm? No one came to mind but Kate. She was the one who wanted to wreck the acquisition, wanted me to wreck it. Before I could call her, my phone rang. "Sam, thank God it's you."

"What's going on?"

"I'm in serious trouble." I told him about my meeting with Kate, who had joined Distributon and wanted me to stop the acquisition.

"Stopping it would be great."

"No, Sam, not the way she wanted me to do it, by exposing Richard's loan. She'd signed an NDA with AI*future*, so she couldn't reveal it herself."

"So that's why you're in trouble. You did it."

"No, I turned her down, but here's the crazy part." I described the video Richard had received. "Sam, it was me, not someone pretending to be me. How the fuck did Kate do that? I've never been recorded in a video, at least not since I was a toddler."

"With AI software. There are several products available on the internet, although I'm probably out of date. You should research it. At any rate, I don't think Kate could come up to speed and do it that fast. She doesn't have the expertise."

Sam didn't think Richard would fire me even with Distributon out of the picture. "Don't forget that you know about his loan. Firing you puts him at greater risk. Also, he's still looking for someone to acquire us, and he can't afford a hitch in his revenue stream. That's only true in the short term, but we're both safe for now. He even promised me he'd push Warren to get NewAI out the door. Of course, knowing Richard, he might just have been blowing smoke up my skirt."

I collapsed into my desk chair, released my cell phone from my sweaty grip, and leaned my head back. I wanted to leave the building, even for half an hour at Starbucks, where I could collect my thoughts over a comforting drink like a hot chocolate. I was afraid to go, though, possessed by an irrational fear that Richard would lock the front door behind me.

I contacted each of the sales reps who reported to me, as much to keep myself focused on work as to check on the status of their deals. By the end of the day, I was relieved that I hadn't yet heard from Richard. If he were going to fire me, he'd have to call me at home, an unlikely prospect. Home was a sanctuary, if a lonely one. At least, it would provide the solitude I needed to think through what was happening to me. I was haunted by the video of a veritable doppelganger speaking the words I'd refused to say.

I wished I could talk to Rip. I missed him, but with some distance from our breakup, I was hard-pressed to say who was more at fault. Rip never missed an opportunity to disparage my professional commitment to AI, but he hadn't attacked me personally, just said I had a decision to make. I made the right one too, refusing to recant my claim that Carlos had raped me, despite the pressure from Richard. Rip didn't know that, though, because I was too busy accusing him of sermonizing. He'd walked away for good.

I sat on my couch trying to summon up the feeling of being encircled by his arms, his warm breath in my hair. I wanted him back, wanted him enough to apologize, wanted him enough to act on impulse and call his cell. Rip didn't answer, though. Kate did.

"Hi, Sylvie."

Damn caller ID. "Sorry, Kate, I must have butt-dialed Rip's number." I couldn't end the call fast enough. I was the butthead, not realizing Rip would move on. It hadn't taken long, but then Kate had probably resumed training with him, if you could call it that.

I'd seen her workout clothes: low-cut leopard-print leotard, a thong between her legs, the display of skin reminiscent of her provocative Christmas party dress. I imagined Rip still thought her "authentic." I was alone, so there was no reason to hold back my tears, except there weren't any. My throat felt tight, my head heavy, and I didn't know how to comfort myself. I grabbed a bottle of wine from my living room and a glass from the kitchen. Hot chocolate would not be up to the task.

* * *

Sam had given me the right advice. Google led me to a wealth of information about deepfakes and how far the software to create them had progressed. Generative AI was exploding and with it the capability to create any desired images, even violent ones. Artificially intelligent "beings" had capabilities that exceeded what their developers initially thought possible.

Without a lot of data, almost anyone could create the content of a person's writing or speech.

All that was needed to synthesize my voice was a sample. Although deepfake videos were crude at first, now the creator could start with any picture, even a Facebook photo, and soon the target would be starring in her own porn video.

Who but Warren had the sophistication to mimic me so convincingly? Why would he do it when he'd made me his confidante? If I were right, I needed to confront him. If wrong, he could help me figure this out. I texted him asking to meet first thing tomorrow. "Sorry," he replied. "Out of town for a day or two. Not sure yet. Will let you know." Perhaps he was avoiding me, or maybe I was suffering from well-deserved paranoia.

I remembered Rip telling me about the history and legends of the golem and how, over time, the golem had become more of a threatening, evil creature. People believed in the golem, the way people would increasingly believe in AI. At first, many of us wouldn't want a computer deciding the strategy for our surgery or picking us up for a driverless taxi ride. Eventually, though, it would become as commonplace as the software on our cell phones. We'd accept it.

We've already accepted it. Every time we did a Google search or talked to Siri or Alexa, an AI algorithm decided what to tell us. We couldn't even ask for information about can openers without being inundated for weeks with ads for can openers. We can't even look for incontinence underpants for our hypothetical Aunt Sadie without being contacted by every company in the world that sells them.

Humans already have some of their organs controlled by implanted sensors and devices like pacemakers and defibrillators connected wirelessly to computers. If the combination of robotics and AI can produce individuals who are superior to humans in every way, won't we become superfluous? Will we all need to have a wireless smart chip implanted in our brains to keep up? Right now, brain implant research is directed at helping the disabled, but when it's available to all of us, won't we want our brains to be able to access all the information on the internet so we can be as smart as our robots?

I couldn't read any more. It was as terrifying as it was riveting. I didn't want to think about what hackers could do with this technology if it were implanted in our brains. Maybe the crazies wearing aluminum foil hats to deter surveillance weren't so crazy. AI was here and would keep coming whether we wanted it or not, just like cloning. Dolly the sheep had been the first one cloned, and hadn't Barbra Streisand cloned her dog twice, at fifty thousand dollars a pop?

If something *can* be done through science or technology, it *will* be done, by someone somewhere, rules be damned. I felt sick to my stomach. I was a perfect example of an individual injured by AI used maliciously. I snapped shut my laptop to close off any more disturbing information.

CHAPTER 29

Morning—another day gone and still no word from Richard. Was this his idea of sensory deprivation torture? I entered the lobby expecting to be accosted by security. Instead, it seemed Sam was right. Richard had decided to keep us employed until he could find another corporate suitor for AI*future*. He was putting his proverbial house on the market, and Sam and I were furniture being kept around as part of the staging. I needed advice, but from whom? On arriving at my office, I dropped into my desk chair and leaned back, unready to check email or texts for fear of what I might find.

I thought back to the day Sam, worried and frustrated, first talked to me about Richard's putting the company on the auction block. Sam had been freaked out because he'd discovered Warren had a hush-hush project draining development resources from NewAI. He wouldn't tell me how he'd found out, but I had a feeling Manfred Schmidt, the enigmatic software engineer with a cottontail man-bun, was a possibility. Manfred was an avid poker player who'd reached out to Sam to fill in when he and his friends were short a player.

I texted Manfred, asking if he had a few minutes to provide me with some technical advice, given that Warren was out of the office. He agreed and an hour later we met at a corner table in the cafeteria. I'd once thought Manfred was just one of Warren's unassertive engineers with glasses sliding down his nose and a scurrying walk, but if anyone was going to be deferential today, it was me.

"Have you seen this video?" I asked, pushing my tablet across the table.

His pale eyebrows rose as he watched. "Um, did you get in trouble for that?'

"A shitload of trouble, only that isn't me! Please don't ask me about the content, which isn't exactly accurate. Someone is trying to destroy me professionally, and I don't know why. I thought you might have an idea who around here has the technical skill and the AI software to produce that."

Manfred leaned back in his chair and pushed his glasses onto the bridge of his nose. He looked out the window, and I followed his gaze, although there was nothing out there but black branches reaching for the gunmetal-gray sky. I couldn't tell if he had no answers or was trying to decide how much to reveal.

He finally met my gaze. "I know Warren is a colleague of yours in senior management, but maybe you don't know him as well as you think you do." Manfred pulled his chair closer even though there was nobody within earshot. "This has to be confidential."

I nodded.

"I don't know everything, but what I do know is that Warren has considerable technical expertise and is very well connected in the industry. I don't just mean that he has a big network. He has friends involved with cutting-edge AI technology. If he can't accomplish something quickly himself, he knows people who can."

I wanted Manfred to be more specific than vague allusions to AI experts, but he refused. Warren might be behind the video, whether he made it personally or not. I thought back to our conversation at Burly's Bar and Grill, when he'd confided in me what his secret project was. It seemed he had at least some of the capabilities needed to create that video. "So, Manfred, you're not telling me Warren did it, just that he's the only person in the company who could get it done fast. Strange . . . I thought I had a close relationship with him."

Manfred looked at me with pity in his eyes. "No such thing. He'll throw anyone under the bus, and he's good at it." He looked at his watch. "I have a team meeting in fifteen minutes. If you don't have any more questions for me, I'd like to leave now—separately from you."

■ ■ ■

The next morning, I saw Warren's car in the parking lot. *This is it*, I thought, but before I had a chance to get to my office and text him, Rona came out from behind the reception desk and whispered, "Can I walk with you to your office?" She looked nervous, repeatedly pushing the same stray curl behind her ear until we arrived. She asked if she could close my door.

"Fannette's scared. She thinks she's going to get fired because Richard caught her lingering by his door. She told him she was just about to ask if she could run out for a prescription, but she's sure he knew she was listening."

"Please tell Fannette not to worry. Unless she went after Richard with a meat cleaver, he's not going to fire her. I think he's trying to avoid making changes right now. He'd have to do a lot of interviewing to find an executive administrator as good as Fannette."

Rona's hands were clenched in her lap, her bangle bracelets standing up on her wrists. "I hope you're right, because Fannette heard some private stuff. Warren was telling Richard to pay back the money he borrowed, but Richard lost his temper. Yelled at Warren that he couldn't because his wife's flower shop was going under. Warren stormed out and practically squashed Fannette behind the door. That's how Richard spotted her."

"Rona, if it really goes that far, I'll go to HR. Floyd might be able to talk him out of it." I didn't think Floyd could talk Richard out anything, but I wanted to reassure Rona.

Fannette's news startled me. Retail businesses sometimes fail, but failing so fast meant an incompetently written business plan, undercapitalization, poor management, or an act of God. Since the last major earthquake in Boston was in the 1700s, I figured an act of God could be ruled out. The Newbury Street flower shop would never allow Richard to pay back the money he'd taken from AI*future*.

Our auditors had come in early January. When they finished their audit, who knows what anomalies they'd report or when they'd expect AI*future* to fix them. Richard was running out of time. He must be desperately hoping the auditors fell for Harold's sleight of hand in hiding his loan. I wasn't sure what would happen if the audit went to our board. Maybe nothing. They were all handpicked cronies of Richard's. Since Warren understood Richard's predicament, wouldn't that increase the pressure on him to complete his secret project? Maybe Warren had a plan B.

Back at the reception desk, Rona rang my extension to let me know I had a visitor in the lobby. The thought that it might be Carlos chilled me. Instead, I found Rip, shifting from one foot to the other, dressed in jeans and boots instead of a tracksuit. The purple bags under his eyes made him look as though he hadn't slept in a week.

"I'm sorry for interrupting you at work, but I was hoping you could spare a few minutes." He lowered his voice. "I called your cell several times, but you didn't pick up."

"Let's go downstairs and grab a coffee." I was glad there were other people on the elevator so we didn't have to talk. He was right. After Kate had answered the phone in his apartment, I had ignored his calls. I was in enough pain from the incriminating video Richard had received and had neither the time nor the desire to pick at the scab over my wounded feelings for Rip.

I'd left my wallet in the office. Rip offered to pay though he wanted nothing for himself. More awkwardness. We found a table in the back, and he sat across from me, allowing full daylight to illuminate his drawn face and dejected expression. I resisted the urge to tell him how awful he looked and waited for him to speak.

"I'm not working at BodySculpt anymore. Rob fired me."

"How. . . why? I thought you'd been close friends since—well, forever."

"I'm afraid I crossed a line. I'd been training Kate, and then somehow she persuaded me to give her private exercise sessions outside the gym."

"Somehow?"

"I said no at first, but she offered to come to my apartment so I wouldn't have to travel to hers. She was going to pay me more than I'd get at BodySculpt, and since I wouldn't be using Rob's facility, I wouldn't have to share my fee with him."

"Sounds like a sweet deal." I tried unsuccessfully to keep the acid out of my voice.

"Rob didn't think so, although I'm not sure how he figured out what I was doing. I started feeling paranoid, like someone was following me. At any rate, he said I was poaching a customer, which is against the terms of my contract, and he was pissed."

"Knowing Kate as I do, I'm guessing the deal was even sweeter than what you've described." It would have been satisfying to point out to Rip that his poor choice would drag down his line of best fit, but I'd already taken a cheap shot, and I could see he was miserable. He had the same hangdog look on his face as Dinger did after he'd chewed something forbidden.

He looked up at me. "Sylvie, I'm sorry about everything. Can we start over?"

I couldn't risk getting hurt again. "We can start over, but from the beginning, not from where we left off."

He nodded.

"If you're out of a job, though, how are you supporting yourself?"

"I have some savings, and I've started advertising private training sessions. Several people have responded. It seems there's an underserved market in obese men and women too self-conscious to train at a gym."

We made no plans, just leaving it at an agreement to get together. I sat for a moment after he left, not ready to resume worrying about my AI*future* problems. I was glad I'd see Rip again but felt sorry for him. Losing Rob's friendship probably hurt him more than losing his job. No wonder he looked weary.

A message awaited me when I sat down at my desk, an email from Richard asking me to come down to his office as soon as I returned. *This is it*, I thought, kind of an anticlimax after so many days of expecting to be fired. Fannette was at her desk but was looking down at a folder. Maybe she didn't greet me because she knew I was headed to the gallows.

As I entered Richard's office, he came around his desk, gesturing toward his conference table. I didn't wait to be asked and closed his door before sitting, hands clasped in my lap. I didn't want them on the table where Richard would be able to see how stressed I was.

"Sylvie, I have a proposition for you." As he leaned in, I struggled with myself to keep from leaning back. "I suspect Warren," he said, "of diverting resources from NewAI to some kind of private project. If you'd like to save your job, find out what it is."

I wanted to shout at him: *How could you not already know?*

He continued, "I can't do it myself, because the company may be entering delicate negotiations, and I don't want to spook him."

Interesting choice of words. If anything, I was already a spy. I couldn't tell Richard that I knew about Warren's secret project, because if I betrayed Warren, he might put out another deepfake video of me, a worse one. If I told Sam that Richard was suspicious of Warren, it would confirm Sam's belief that Warren was slow-walking NewAI. If Sam were to blow up, it would be bad for everyone, destroying whatever balance still existed in the relationships among company executives.

I was trapped and understood full well that if I were fired or even quit without another job, I'd be screwed in the industry. The money I'd inherited from Luis would protect me financially, but what about my reputation? Worse, I'd be giving credence to Ashton's claim that I was unstable. The only people in my life I could trust were Eileen, who was in Miami, and Rip, whose recent activities were weak in the trust department.

I returned to my office and stood looking out at the parking lot, the carscape in neat rows. Such a variety of sedans, station wagons, SUVs, and sports cars, and yet all had one thing in common: they were standing at attention, facing the building, and confined to their parking lanes. We could choose our own brands, models, and colors, but we had to toe the line.

Richard hadn't said how soon I needed to get back to him, but I devoted the rest of the day to my real job as opposed to my spying assignments. Being a double agent was bad enough. I'd never heard of a triple agent—sounded like the final season of some tired TV drama.

It was tough to focus on my sales reps, who'd been bugging me about NewAI. At first, they asked only in meetings, then in more frequent emails, and now, with new urgency, in imploring text messages. They named specific customers and deals that would be won by our competitors who had functionality in their software we couldn't match without NewAI. How long could I tell my reps to hang in there when I was barely doing it myself?

I met Rip for dinner after work at a burger place in the Burlington Mall, neutral territory safe from the siren song of our apartments. He promised the restaurant had plenty of choices besides burgers, but when we entered, the savory smell of grilled beef drove any thoughts of salad from my mind. We were seated in a booth by a wall of windows overlooking the parking lot.

I wanted to tell him about my dilemma, no, trilemma, but I was chicken. When I chugged half of my beer, Rip's eyebrows rose. I decided to start with the good news, so I told him the story of Kate's asking me to blow the whistle on Richard and warn the CEO of Distributon.

The fact that my story made Kate look bad didn't bother me in the least. The important thing was that I'd said no. She'd played on my sympathies, but I walked away.

"Good for you," he said. "I'm afraid, though, I'm no longer in a position to judge other people's choices."

The server delivered my cheeseburger, a guilty pleasure. When I took a large bite, juice ran down my chin, eliciting Rip's first smile of the evening.

"You'd better slow down. I don't want to have to perform a Heimlich maneuver in the restaurant aisle."

I was embarrassed by my gluttonous appetite but also by the image that flashed into my head of Rip standing behind me, wrapping his arms around me. I put down my burger and dabbed my chin with a napkin. "Stress eating," I said. "I'm having a lot of problems at work. There's no way to get out of the trap I'm in except to leave the company, which is pretty much the same thing as leaving the industry."

"Doesn't sound so bad to me. You could become a dog walker or a gardener, something outdoorsy."

"Dog walking in a blizzard? No, thanks. Gardening? Too seasonal. Wait, maybe I could be a trainer."

I got no response to that one, just another raised eyebrow.

"Tell me about your trap."

"No judging?"

Rip crossed his heart. I wasn't sure he could resist, but I told him my story, starting with Warren and Burly's Bar and Grill.

"Oh, yeah, I know that place," he said and turned his thumb down.

Rip ate, and I talked. By the time I finished, my burger was cold, my appetite gone. Rip shook his head slowly, but his eyes were sympathetic. He took my hand in his. I meant to pull it away, but his tenderness filled a hole I'd tried to ignore. I lowered my head to hide the tears that had begun to leak out, pointless since they were landing on the table.

"I don't want you to think this is a ploy to get you back to my apartment, but I really do need to walk Dinger." He pleaded with me. "Let's talk this through; come back with me."

I looked out the window to escape his appealing face and decide what to do, a futile effort since I already knew I'd go with him. A car sat parked, motor running, in the circle outside the restaurant's street entrance. Before I turned back to Rip, fear coursed through me. The driver was Carlos. I had to be sure.

"Yes, I'll go back with you. Do you mind paying? I have to run to the cash machine. Can I meet you at the American Girl store entrance?" I didn't wait for his answer but grabbed my coat and ran. I reached the other mall entrance before Rip. I pulled my cell phone from my bag and texted Eileen to ask if she knew where Carlos was. *Silly to be panicky*, I thought. Eileen doesn't keep tabs on Carlos. She called.

"Sylvie, I miss you. Any chance you can fly down for a long weekend?"

"I only wish. I can't get away right now, but listen, do you happen to know where Carlos is?"

"We haven't seen him in weeks. Miguel gave him his annual payment from the trust, and since then he's gone silent.

He knows Miguel is pissed at him for harassing you, so it's not surprising he hasn't come around. Why are you asking?"

I saw Rip striding down the hall. When he saw me with my phone against my ear, he slowed down. "Gotta go, talk soon." I clicked off my phone as he reached me, pressed the automatic door opener, and stepped outside.

"Are you okay? You've gone kind of pale."

"Just the lighting in the mall." I was afraid to tell him about Carlos since our last conversation about him hadn't gone well. I couldn't help looking back over my shoulder, though, so much so Rip noticed.

"Are there treasury agents trailing you for back taxes?"

"Of course not. Let's just get back to the car." I picked up my pace. "I'll explain later."

■ ■ ■

As soon as we entered Rip's apartment, Dinger jumped up and mopped my face with wet doggie kisses. I told him to sit, and as I leaned down to embrace him, his honey-colored tail swept the floor. "I missed you too, Dinger. What a sweet boy you are." With each stroke of my hand down his furry back, fine hairs floated up from his coat.

"I hope you're planning to vacuum before you go," Rip said, grabbing Dinger's leash off a table by the door.

"Sure. That's what I'll be doing while you're walking him."

Rip made a face at me before disappearing outside. I took off my coat and sat down in the living room. I was uneasy about telling him I thought I'd seen Carlos outside the restaurant. Vacuuming wasn't a half-bad idea for dispelling my nervous energy.

How was I supposed to explain what had happened since the episode when Ashton first got involved with Carlos as a potential investor, and I refused to recant my rape accusation? No matter Rip's reaction, I had to try not to be defensive. If I lashed out again and told him he should have become a rabbi, I'd strain my relationship with him, just like his father had, this time permanently.

When Rip returned and paused in the doorway to remove his parka, ski hat, and boots, Dinger trotted over to me, tail wagging, and pushed his muzzle under my hand in a bid for resumed petting. No misunderstanding there—clear communication. I rested my cheek on Dinger's damp head, impressed by how dependable his love was. Perhaps, to enjoy a relationship that was uncomplicated, I needed a dog of my own.

For a moment I felt I belonged there, in Rip's apartment, the three of us together at the end of the day, maybe every day. I pushed the image away. Fantasizing would only lead to hurt. "I'm sorry I freaked out at the mall, but I think Carlos is stalking me again."

"Stalking? Oh, c'mon." He sat down on the futon sofa across from me. I reminded him of my hot-and-cold relationship with Carlos and described how complicated it had become after Luis found out about the rape and put his assets into a trust. At my description of Miguel's and my roles as trustees, Rip's mouth hung open.

"You control half the inheritance of someone who hates you? What does he expect you to do, give it back?"

"Turn it over to Miguel, who Carlos thinks will be a more generous trustee. Trouble is, Miguel doesn't want it. He's angry at his brother, and it probably doesn't help that Miguel is marrying my best friend."

When I told Rip about my unsuccessful effort to take out a harassment order against Carlos, he shook his head. "That guy is dangerous. No wonder you imagine you're seeing him everywhere. Too bad you can't get the police to surveil him."

"Rip, you do know that surveillance is an AI application, don't you? Sorry, I couldn't resist."

"Humph."

I couldn't help laughing. "No one says 'humph' anymore."

I managed to get a weak smile out of him.

"I'm talking too much. What do you have to drink?"

He retrieved two cold beers from his refrigerator and pulled open his dishwasher to retrieve a glass. "Don't bother for me. Just bring over the bottles."

I perused Rip's wall of books slowly enough to take note of some of the titles on the spines. "I wish I could spend a week or a month holed up here, just reading."

He handed me my beer. "That's probably not practical, but . . ." He looked at his watch. "It's pretty late, and we're still not finished catching up. Would you consider staying over? I could sleep on the couch."

We hadn't finished discussing my trilemma, and I felt guilty for monopolizing the conversation when I knew he must be in pain from his rift with Rob. "I'll stay, but it's your turn to talk."

Rip nodded. "Thanks."

As soon as he touched my arm, I knew no one would sleep on the couch that night.

CHAPTER 30

The next morning, Rip brought two steaming cups of coffee to his tiny kitchen table. "You said I had to do the talking today, so tell me what you want to know."

"Maybe you can begin by explaining something. Why does my trying to please people make you so angry? Even if it's true that I have a failing, you've been more than disapproving. I feel as though I struck a nerve."

He sighed. "You're really going to make me go back there?"

"You're kidding. This goes back to childhood?"

"I was fifteen and had just saved up enough money for an expensive pair of baseball cleats and a Dodgers jersey. Even though the Dodgers had been in LA for decades, my father thought they were traitors. I guess I kind of wanted to piss him off. Wearing those cleats, I felt like Dorothy in *The Wizard of Oz*. I could click them three times and hit a home run."

"Okay, now you're making this up."

"I'm not." He crossed his heart. "My father came into my bedroom one night and sat down on my bed. He was still in a suit, so I knew he'd been tied up with meetings or seeing congregants till late. He looked tired. 'I know you'll be taking the college boards soon, so we need to be thinking about schools.' That was the conversation I'd dreaded. I was descended from a line of rabbis and knew I was expected to enter rabbinical training at the Hebrew Union College. It was bullshit to act like I had a choice."

"I wanted to play college baseball and do something like coaching after that. He'd laughed off those ideas when I was a little kid, but not that day. When I said, 'I'm not going to be a rabbi,' he grew red in the face, got up from my bed, and took a step toward me. His temper had always frightened me, although his congregants never saw that side of him. He picked up my cleats from the floor and my jersey from the bed, walked out the door of our apartment, and went down to the building entrance, where he heaved the shoes into the street. He had a good arm. Rain was coming down in sheets, and a passing car ran over them. By the time I pushed past him, he'd tossed my new jersey into the branches of a tree where it snagged high off the ground and drooped like a wet flag.

"When I retrieved the cleats, they were crushed. I looked up into the branches where my jersey was hanging, but it might as well have been on top of the Empire State Building. I was glad it was raining, so no one could see I was crying." Rip gazed into his coffee mug as though it were a crystal ball revealing the past instead of the future. I covered his hand with mine.

"Sorry," he said. "It probably doesn't sound like such a big deal to you, but we scarcely talked to each other after that, even though I went to Hebrew Union College for two miserable years, miserable for both of us. Then he died, and it was too late to make things right, years wasted. You asked why I was on your case about being Ms. Malleable. Pleasing my father made neither of us happy."

■ ■ ■

Unfortunately, the glow from being back with Rip did not extend to my office. I still had to figure out how to keep my job. Richard had made it clear: report back to him on Warren's suspected side project or else.

Rona caught me as I returned to the office after lunch. "Did you hear?" she asked, fidgeting with excitement. "Warren's wife, Maya, is having her baby now. He went rushing out to the hospital, looking pretty worried. Things must be happening fast because they took her by ambulance."

I could think of several reasons why an ambulance would be needed, none of them good. I thanked Rona and asked her to please keep me posted. After depositing my briefcase and purse in my office, I walked down to software engineering to find Manfred. I spotted him leaning forward in his chair, riveted to his screen.

"Manfred?"

He looked up, startled.

"Heard anything yet about Maya Malik?"

He shook his head.

I continued down the hall to Warren's office, lingering for a moment in his doorway, as I looked around. No one seemed aware of me, so I walked in. Although I was sure I was unobserved, I tried to look as though I were retrieving some folder I needed, something Warren would have passed on to me if he hadn't left in such a hurry. I checked out his bookcase, glanced at the papers on his desk, and pulled at the file drawer beneath. It was unlocked. Only an emergency could have led Warren to such an oversight. All the typed folder labels were related to engineering projects, except one, handwritten with the letters "S.M."

My heart stopped beating for a moment. A file labeled with my initials couldn't be a coincidence. It seemed to be empty, but I removed it anyway and found a flash drive nestled in the bottom. After tucking it away in my pocket, I replaced the folder and slipped out into the hall. Once back in my office, I inserted the drive into the port on my laptop. There I was on video, betraying Richard, telling Distributon what they needed to know about irregularities in our finances. What was most interesting was the date on the file, two days before Distributon had received it. Warren hadn't downloaded this video. He'd created it.

Rona looked in from my doorway. "Sylvie, Warren's baby is okay—a girl—but there was some kind of complication, serious hemorrhaging. Warren told Richard that Maya's condition isn't good."

Since Warren wouldn't return to the office until tomorrow best case, I decided to report to Richard on what I knew about Warren's side project. Richard's office door was open. He faced his window, arms hanging and shoulders slumped.

"Richard?"

He straightened and turned to face me.

"I heard about Warren and Maya. Touch and go, I guess."

"At least for now. I'm concerned for them, of course, but I'm also concerned about the implications for the company."

I imagined he was worried about how he could pay back the money he'd taken from AI*future*, given what I'd heard about his wife's florist business. Richard was still answerable to our board of directors, even if they were his buddies. Fiduciary responsibility and all that. He could be fired.

I almost felt sorry for him, but not quite. "You wanted to know if Warren had a side project that was getting in the way of his department's producing NewAI. He does. I don't know that much about it, but I think it's some sort of natural language solution, maybe an enhancement to ChatGPT or GPT-4. He claims it's far more sophisticated than anything currently available." I was feeling dangerously exposed. Richard had given me an ultimatum—get the information or get fired, but I didn't want him to think Warren had taken me into his confidence at an earlier time.

"And you uncovered this how?"

"You know, just ear to the ground." I knew how he loved clichés.

I watched Richard return to his desk chair and put his head in his hands. I had the sense he was so lost in thought he'd forgotten I was there. Time to make a discreet exit. Fannette watched me walk out, so I nodded as I left.

When I finally collapsed into my chair and glanced at my monitor, I saw an endless array of emails, but my cell phone's text alert was competing for my attention. I was amazed to see it was a message from Warren, who was supposed to be at the hospital with his wife.

"Meet me tonight at Burly's, 6:00 p.m." He didn't even ask if I were free, as though I would drop everything to show up for his command performance. Whatever his urgent need was to talk to me, my need to confront him was more urgent still. I called Rip to cancel our plans for the evening.

■ ■ ■

Burly's hadn't improved since my last visit. If anything, it looked seedier than before, an impression reinforced by the approach of the same waiter with a different shirt and tie, as stained as the ones he'd worn last time. Warren hadn't arrived yet, so I commandeered one of the high-top tables and ordered a beer. No point in trying their Cabernet again, since I remembered what a weak sister it was to a quality wine.

When Warren blew in, disheveled as though a gust of wind had had its way with him, I couldn't help but feel pity. "Maya?" I asked.

He shook his head. "Very weak."

"Warren, should you even be here?"

He shrugged.

The waiter took Warren's drink order, which to my surprise, was a double scotch. I was halfway through my beer when his drink arrived. He took a swallow, and before I could say a word, started with his own accusation. "So, searching my office, you found the flash drive with your video. I assume you saw the date on the file too. Didn't think you were the type to take advantage of someone who was racing off to the hospital."

"You want me to feel guilty when you're the one who created a deepfake video of me sabotaging Richard's merger with Distributon? Not only did you set me up to be fired and ruin Richard's deal, you tainted me. I'm finished in this industry."

When Warren started laughing, I thought he might be demented from stress. "Oh, Sylvie, you're even more naive than I thought. I knew Richard wouldn't fire you when he was actively looking for an acquisition partner. Unfortunately, since you were so virtuous in turning down Kate's request, I needed another way to inform the Distributon CEO about Richard's loan."

"You could have told him yourself. Why did I have to be the fall guy—just for your enjoyment?"

"I couldn't take the risk myself because of important things I have in the works. You were expendable and wouldn't suffer any meaningful consequences."

Expendable? I remembered what Manfred had said about Warren's not hesitating to throw people under the bus. "There must be something seriously wrong with you!"

"This isn't personal, Sylvie. It's just business. Anyone would have done the same. I'm leaving AI*future*, and it would have happened today if Maya hadn't had her emergency."

"The text generator? That's what you told me when we met here. You also asked me to use Rona and Fannette as my spies to find out Richard's acquisition plans." I could feel bile rising in my throat.

"Sorry, I had to fib a little to keep a watch on Richard. I did it for the greater good. My associates and I are starting a company capable of creating extraordinary deepfake videos, text, robotics, and so much more. We already have a customer—the US military—and the necessary capital to create the business.

Every country's military and every politician will need this technology. They're probably working on it themselves. I'm taking with me two of my engineers who've been helping."

I fell back in my chair, too appalled to know where to start. "You're a real shit, Warren. I suppose NewAI will never be finished either."

He shook his head.

"And using AI to kill people doesn't bother you?"

"Of course not. The drones we already have are saving the lives of US combat troops, even as they kill enemy soldiers. Everyone's using this technology. If it makes you feel better, I'm sure we can find a place for you in my new company, not as an executive, since you have no experience working with the military, but perhaps in sales."

So many thoughts were running through my head, I thought my brain would explode. Warren threw some cash down on the table. "I have to run. Maya's expecting me." He was out the door, but I remained riveted to my chair.

I needed to leave, needed to go for a run, but outside the plate glass window, it was dark and cold. Perhaps another drink would help calm me down. I looked around Burly's, where the paint was peeling off the walls, the commercial carpeting was discolored, and a cobalt-blue beer sign behind the bar was missing a couple of bulbs. The sign said simply BE__, as though expecting more than mere existence was unrealistic, let alone expecting a beer. I paid the check and walked out.

I was too weary to see another human, even Rip. I got into my car and drove home, but instead of my usual hurried lead-foot mode, I drove ever more slowly until the car behind me flashed its lights. My mind was racing, but my foot was coming off the accelerator. I turned over responsibility for maintaining my speed to cruise control so my mind would be free to imagine scenes of torture in which Warren was the victim, not of a rack or waterboarding, but of workplace nightmares.

I imagined Warren giving a public presentation on AI in a vast auditorium and forgetting what he wanted to say, while his PowerPoint slides vanished from his computer. Soon a hostile audience barked at him for his inadequate knowledge of the subject. I imagined Richard humiliating and firing him for piss-poor performance in front of our board of directors. I saw him emerging from the men's room with a strip of toilet paper hanging down from the back of his pants and flapping in the breeze as he strode through the office to meet customers in the lobby. Everyone he passed was doubled over with laughter. Worse yet, he smelled like shit.

Once I was in my own kitchen, I made myself coffee, although I never drink it this late in the day. Even the aroma as it brewed was bracing. I didn't expect to sleep that night anyway. The right person to talk to was Sam, but not until I figured out what time zone he was in. By tomorrow, after Warren talked to Richard, the company would be in collective shock. Every one of my sales reps would have their resumes on the street if they didn't already.

I was tempted to let voicemail take the message from my ringing phone, until I saw that it was Eileen. I tried not to sound tense, but my voice was shaking when I answered.

"Sylvie, are you okay?"

"Not really, but it's just work stuff, and I'm wired from too much coffee." I could picture Eileen curled up on a cushiony floral sofa, her diaphanous turquoise robe blending in with the upholstery.

"I wanted to warn you."

"Why are you whispering?"

"Wait a second . . . okay, Miguel just left."

"Is something wrong between you?"

"No, no, nothing like that. It's about Carlos. His behavior has become erratic. He was at the Bal Harbour Shops and began stalking a young woman. When she stopped to look in a store window, he came up behind her and pressed his body against hers. Her scream brought the security guards running."

"Was he arrested?"

"You know Carlos. He charmed his way out of it, offering heartfelt apologies to the woman, whom he said he mistook for a girlfriend. It was supposed to be a joke. The guards let him go, but an acquaintance of ours who was shopping there called to tell Miguel the story. What Carlos did was bad enough without the humiliation for Miguel of having a friend witness it."

"Did Miguel talk to Carlos about it?"

"He tried a bunch of times, but Carlos didn't answer his cell. There have been other incidents: bar fights and groping accusations. Sylvie, I'm afraid for you."

I told her not to worry, that I was back with Rip, who could be my protector. I tried to laugh although I didn't believe what I was saying, and I knew she wouldn't either. "One question, Eileen, why didn't you want Miguel to know you were calling me?"

"It's hard to explain. He's angry at Carlos, but he also understands why Carlos is furious with their father. I don't think Miguel ever got over feeling guilty about how much more their mother loved him than Carlos. It wasn't Miguel's fault. It wasn't your fault either that Luis made you a trustee over Carlos's inheritance. Why does family stuff get so complicated?"

I was the last person to have an answer to that question. I promised Eileen I'd be careful, but when we ended our call, I felt even more weighed down than I had after leaving Burly's bar. What if I could no longer count on Miguel's support? Worse yet, I was creating dueling loyalties for Eileen.

I looked at my watch. It was the middle of the night in Europe. I could leave Sam a voicemail, but when he woke up, it would be the middle of the night here. He'd probably hear about Warren's departure from multiple sources, but an email would have to do until I could speak with him directly.

It seemed like a million years ago that my biggest worry was proving to Ashton I could be successful without a prominent husband managing my life. Did success in business even matter if there were people like Warren who had no problem exploiting a trusted colleague? Maybe Warren's greatest talent wasn't technological. He could compartmentalize with ease his business and personal lives.

CHAPTER 31

Although I thought I had spent most of the night watching the green digital numbers change on my bedside clock, I must have slept. I checked my phone for the anticipated message from Sam, which, as I had expected, said he was flying home ASAP.

As I sped up Route 128, my sunroof framed a cloudless blue sky. If only I were on my way to meet Rip and Dinger for a run. I wondered if Manfred Schmidt was one of the engineers Warren was taking with him to his new company. It seemed unlikely. Manfred didn't like Warren. If he were staying, and a bigger if—if I were staying—Manfred might be able to finish NewAI.

By 8:00 a.m., there were more agitated voices out in the hall than usual. A text from Richard asked the executive team to meet in his office at 9:00—attendance required! Clearly, neither Warren nor Sam would be there. That left Harold Astrove, Floyd Buckley, and me.

When I arrived, I was surprised to see Floyd looking the most distressed of the four of us as we gathered around the table in Richard's office. "Word has leaked out from software engineering, Richard," Floyd began. "People have started lining up outside HR wanting to know what Warren's departure means for the company's product development and how it will affect them personally, especially if they have stock options. Morale is—"

"I don't care about morale right now," Richard snapped. "Just make something up. You're not getting paid to be a social worker."

Harold Astrove looked down at his spreadsheets. I noticed his usual frameless glasses had been replaced by larger tortoiseshell frames. I wondered if his wife broke his first pair on purpose. Perhaps he felt better hidden behind these, although he looked like an undernourished owl.

Richard continued, "Since Floyd has let the cat out of the bag, we might as well acknowledge that Warren has been leading a double professional life, one as head of software engineering here and one using AI*future*'s time and resources to help develop his new technology."

"Didn't he sign a standard employment agreement that prevents him from taking any AI*future* work product out of the company?" Harold looked at Richard expectantly.

I'd never seen Richard so tight-lipped, not even after he saw my deepfake video. The answer he gave Harold obviously pained him. "Warren claimed he'd gotten into a pissing fight with a previous employer over what software was his and what was theirs. Said he wouldn't sign an agreement with that clause in it, and we'd just have to trust that he'd bring enormous benefit to the company."

"Ha!" I hadn't meant to say that out loud.

Richard scowled at me. "We're going to be fine," he said, "and this conversation doesn't leave the room. I'll update Sam when he flies in. Since the Distribution deal has gone south"—he paused to give me a dirty look—"I have found another suitor, or I should say, they have found us. It's UndauntedAI."

Harold looked up. "How are they going to finance the deal?"

"We haven't worked all that out yet, but probably it would be some sort of cash for stock arrangement or maybe a stock swap. I'll let you know."

"I assume you'll include me in the negotiation." The owl's assertiveness surprised me, but of course he was right.

"When the time comes, Harold."

* * *

Sam wanted to meet me for dinner, even though he sounded exhausted from his flight. I suggested a bistro halfway between our homes, but he insisted on coming to Needham. If I'd had time to shop, I would have offered to cook. Instead, we settled on a quiet place in town. The restaurant was fairly empty, given how early it was on a weeknight, but it had amber sconces that created a pleasant glow and cozy booths. I wished I were in a mood more in sync with the atmosphere.

"You look wiped out. Why did you want to meet here?"

"You mean, didn't I want to go home? Fuck that. It's not my home anymore. Susan has filed for divorce, and she has her boyfriend staying at the house. She says he's not her boyfriend, just a mason working on the renovation of our bathroom, but after he lays the tile, he lays Susan."

Despite the attempt at gallows humor, his face was grim. What was there to say about Sam's second divorce besides 'I'm sorry'? We ordered drinks, wine for me and a double scotch for him. I figured the scotch would take the edge off, but it didn't. When the conversation turned to work, his restless finger-drumming was accompanied by a familiar flush in his face.

"I knew it! I knew Warren would pull some kind of shit," he said. Now he's leaving with two of our engineers, NewAI will never be finished, you and I won't be able to close any new business, and Richard is so desperate he'll sell the company to Ugly Stepsisters Incorporated to wipe out his debt." He threw back the rest of his scotch and glared at me. "How did this happen, Sylvie? I thought you had your ear to the ground."

"I thought he was developing an AI text generator of some sort. He misled me."

Sam exploded. "You knew what he was up to and you didn't tell me? Didn't you promise to find out what his secret project was and let me know?"

"I'm sorry. It got complicated. I thought I could keep tabs on what he was doing by keeping his trust. He wanted me to dig into what Richard was planning for an acquisition."

"Keeping his trust? How did that work out for you? He lied to you about his project, got you in trouble with a deepfake video, and now he's bailing on AI*future*."

"You're right, okay? I said I was sorry. Look, I'm hungry. If you're finished fuming, let's eat and get out of here." My shoulders ached from tightening them. I looked around for the waiter and ordered another glass of wine and a burger. Sam just wanted chicken soup. Said his stomach was still in an uproar from airline food.

He sat across from me, scowling, until his face suddenly brightened. "For starters, I'm going to make a deepfake video of Warren."

"Who'll care? He's gone on to another company, his own. They're preparing to ink a contract with the defense department for their first product."

"Great. I'm sure Warren offered to sell his AI software to foreign militaries too, ethics be damned."

No surprise Sam was stressed out between a pending divorce and Warren's bailing on AI*future*, but he looked unhinged. I wondered what Manfred's reaction would be to Sam's idea for a deepfake video. While I agreed that Warren wouldn't hesitate to sell his product to US adversaries, there was nothing to be done about it. We couldn't prove it.

As hungry as I'd been, it took only a few bites of my savory burger before it tasted mealy in my mouth. While my stomach churned, Sam seemed to have no problem slurping up his soup and mopping the bottom of the bowl with a slice of bread. He paused, spoon in the air, and vowed to contact Manfred that night about sourcing a video. "Are you in, Sylvie?"

"No, I just can't. I know Warren's a shit, but . . . no."

Sam's face fell, but he didn't protest. Maybe his scotch was finally kicking in. Outside under the streetlight, he looked even more haggard than before.

"Go to sleep, Sam. You need some rest." I probably didn't look much better than Sam and should have gone straight home to bed, but instead I called Rip's number from my car.

When he opened the front door, I practically fell into his arms. His hug felt like life-saving medicine. Dinger's greeting was more exuberant but no less welcome. It's self-serving, I know, but I like to think dogs are excellent judges of character. A friend once told me dogs will love anyone who feeds them, but I think Dinger is more discerning than that.

I handed Rip my coat and headed for the one comfortable reading chair in his living room. Dinger put his paws on my lap, but I cut Rip off before he could correct him. "Dinger, I love you too. I wish everyone had such sincere brown eyes. I'm sure you'd never lie to me."

Rip pulled up a chair. "I never thought I'd be jealous of my dog's eyes. How could a neutered golden retriever be such a ladies' man?"

"I can think of some males I'd like to see neutered. I just came from dinner with Sam. I think he's losing it."

"I thought he was one of the good guys."

"He is, but I'm worried about his plan for getting back at Warren. I understand the reasons for his state of mind, but I think maybe he needs a shrink."

Rip sighed. "Doesn't everyone? Lately it's seemed even my training clients are coming to me with their problems. Do I look like a shrink to you?"

Not that I didn't have Rip's face memorized, but I reached out and ran my hand over his stubbled cheeks and chin. "Maybe not a shrink, but grow a beard and lose the shabby sweatshirt, and I could see you as a rabbi. Of course, I've told you that before. Do you think if your father hadn't been so insistent about it, you might have had an interest? God knows, you sound like one often enough." My shoulders tightened as I anticipated his anger, but he held it back.

He stood abruptly. "Want a beer?"

"After my two glasses of wine with Sam? I'll pass, thanks. I couldn't even finish my dinner, the conversation was so disturbing."

I joined him in the kitchen while he searched his refrigerator. "There's nothing in there. How tough could it be to find a can of beer?"

He pulled out the large package that had been blocking his view. "Excuse me, Miss Snarky. I was planning to roast this chicken for you. I even called my mother for her recipe."

I wondered what he'd told his mother. Did she think I was the one who should be roasting a chicken for Rip? My thoughts flew in several directions at once. Crazy—I was so tired.

"Rip, I'm sorry. I'm probably terrible company right now." I put my arms around him.

He put down his beer and stroked my hair. "You must be pretty upset to try coming between me and my beer." He led me back to the couch. "What's going on?"

"Warren's leaving has screwed up everything, including my dinner tonight with Sam. He was furious and not a little jetlagged. His plan for getting back at Warren is to create a deepfake video that would screw up Warren's deal with the military."

"You're not going to help him, are you? Remember, there are plenty of other people I could roast this chicken for."

"No, I'm not. I've seen firsthand the damage deepfake

videos can do. I guess researchers and software developers should think about how their applications could be misused."

Rip shrugged. "How do you weigh one against the other? It kind of depends on your personal ethics, doesn't it? That's what worries me. I don't care how much data we feed robots, initially their morality will be based on our own assumptions, our own confused morality that isn't even universal. Is it an eye for an eye or turn the other cheek? Would you buy a car, Sylvie, that was programmed to sacrifice you and your passenger to save five pedestrians in the middle of the road? I doubt it, even though the car would be acting for the greater good."

Why did Rip always have to make so much sense? How many people who are engaged in product development or sales think about the potential misuse of what they're developing or selling? We focus on the benefits, the patients saved in the operating room, the elderly helped by robotic caregivers, the rescue teams guided by GPS, or the urgent communications carried by smartphone. I never gave this much thought. My noble motivation in working for AI*future* was proving to my ex-husband I could be successful without him.

Rip was watching me, waiting for me to respond.

"Okay," I agreed, "you're partially right. We're on a risky path, but it's not as if humans don't make mistakes too. The AI software in the 737 Max caused two plane crashes, but AI on the whole has made air travel safer. Human error causes automobile crashes, but AI has given us accident-avoidance features in our cars. AI ethics is a hot topic. Institutions, companies, even countries are trying to set down rules.

"Sam will be angry with me, but I won't help him. I agree with him that Warren deserves to be punished, but good intentions don't compensate for bad actions. There's enough fake stuff on the internet without Sam's adding another deepfake video. The amount of disinformation out there is terrifying."

Rip tapped my head with his forefinger. "Remember the golem. In Jewish folklore he was invented from clay to help people, yet he sometimes turned on them."

I grabbed Rip's hand and held on to it. He took my other hand and pulled me out of my chair to kiss me. As his lips moved slowly down my neck, he whispered in my ear, "I think it's possible I'm in love with you."

I wrapped my arms tightly around him and whispered back, "I hope so."

CHAPTER 32

I was late to work the next day because I took my time driving home to shower and change. Not only was I still under the spell of the night before, but I had no desire to return to the maelstrom of my office. My sales reps were still filling my email with questions I couldn't answer about Warren's departure and the status of NewAI. When Rona showed up in my doorway to let me know Richard was having new private conversations about mergers, my day seemed complete, and it was only 11:00 a.m.

Rona's voice, no louder than a whisper, uttered one word: "UndauntedAI." She wanted to know if I had heard of them. "Are they a good company, or should Fannette and I get out? If one of us goes, the other goes too. Sylvie, I wouldn't dare ask that of anyone but you."

I noticed that Rona had linked her fate and Fannette's, not bothering to hide their relationship. "Heard of them? Yes, but that's about it. I think they sell sales management software. I don't even know how big they are." Rona left my office looking as worried as when she came in. I'd never seen her with less than perfect makeup, but while she was with me, she'd been biting her lower lip, which left it outlined in lip liner but strangely devoid of color.

I felt sorry for her. Without research, though, I couldn't advise them. At this point, I couldn't even advise myself. I walked to my window and viewed the orderly commercial landscape, cars parked just so between the lines, grass and shrubs carefully tended, sidewalks swept, all giving the impression that winter or summer, the corporate inhabitants of these buildings had everything under control. Inside the offices of AI*future*, we were in the woods, where trees were strangled by bittersweet vines and poison ivy lurked. I was trying to succeed, and I was, but some part of me knew there was no thriving here. I couldn't keep reacting to events. Somehow, I had to get ahead.

Harold Astrove was in his office and did not look happy to see me. "If you're here to pump me for information, forget it. I don't know anything."

I sat down uninvited. "Harold, that's bullshit, and you know it." If possible, he looked thinner than usual. His watery eyes were large behind his new glasses that looked too wide for his face. "If we're getting acquired by UndauntedAI, you must know something."

He threw down his pen and swiveled his chair. "Richard's back is up against the wall, especially with his wife's florist business failing and the auditor's report showing . . . shall we call them 'anomalies'? That should be no surprise to you, especially since you were instrumental in causing the Distributon deal to fall through, so what do you expect me to say?"

"That wasn't my fault. The video was a deepfake. Richard said the new deal is with UndauntedAI."

Harold pushed his glasses up on the bridge of his nose and looked away from me.

"What's likely to happen? Isn't Richard worried their due diligence will turn up the phony Asian investment?"

Harold stood up. "Richard's going to pull the executives together over the next few days. These things take time. You'll just have to wait."

Wait to get screwed, I thought, but took his cue and walked back to my office.

■ ■ ■

Rip called my cell at the end of the day. "I've been thinking about . . . well, I know this will sound strange. I haven't been to religious services in several years. I kind of have an urge to go. There's a Reform Jewish temple in a town out by Route 495, and I was thinking you might want to go with me Friday night."

The urge he was describing seemed to come out of left field, but I checked myself before the baseball metaphor slipped out. I agreed to go. I hadn't been to a temple or synagogue—I wasn't sure which to call it—since I was a kid attending a couple of friends' bat mitzvahs. I couldn't remember much because we were only thirteen and trying to keep the rabbi from noticing we were giggling behind our prayerbooks.

■ ■ ■

When Rip picked me up, he was wearing a blue dress shirt, gray slacks, and a navy blazer. Even his stubble was gone.

"You look handsome," I said as I climbed into his car. Being dressed up was no big deal to me as it was often a professional requirement, but I hadn't seen Rip spiffed up since the AI*future* Christmas party. He thanked me but looked discomfited by the compliment, as though I were drawing attention to his seriousness of purpose.

As we were about to enter the sanctuary, he took my hand. We sat on an aisle near the back, sparing me the embarrassment of sitting where everyone could see I knew none of the prayers. Why I felt embarrassed by that, I don't know. It just seemed like wearing a sign, NOT JEWISH.

Sitting up front would have been more exposure than Rip was ready for too, although, as the service progressed, I couldn't see why. He read Hebrew fluently and knew many of the prayers by heart. He seemed enthralled, and why not? He was comfortable here, a prodigal son, no matter how many years had gone by.

I'm not sure what I expected, perhaps a long gray beard, but instead the rabbi was a middle-aged man with a ready smile, who seemed to have a good rapport with the congregation. I was raised as a nonobservant Protestant. Several times, I'd attended church with a Catholic boyfriend and found praying in Latin to be bizarre. In this house of worship, the Hebrew also seemed pointless to me.

I understood the significance of Hebrew to Jews, but why not have every word of the service in English or French or whatever your native language was? There wasn't enough time to read all the translations at the bottom of the page, and I wanted to understand what I was saying, especially since I had doubts about most of it.

I hadn't discussed religion much with Rip and didn't want to admit that whenever I attended a service, my mind wandered. It seemed like a failure of character, especially amid so much talk about the soul. Did I have a Christian soul and Rip, a Jewish one? The idea of a soul was so appealing, an ineffable something that was part of us all, wholly separate from intelligence.

My brain kept nibbling at the edges of that concept, and I couldn't get it to stop. I'd learned so much about neural networks and artificial intelligence that I suspected someday robots would have souls. At least, we'd have no way of knowing if they didn't.

What if a robot professed to having a soul and displayed spiritual feelings identical to ours? Could a robot be moved by a sunset? Could it have yearnings? What if our souls were just a bunch of electrical impulses, a helpful adaptation for human survival? Maybe animals have souls too, or perhaps none of us do.

Why do we think we need a soul? Aren't a head and a heart together enough? A silicon heart would have a superior duty cycle to a human one. A robot would have the advantage of never becoming brokenhearted unless we programmed it to display those feelings. Why do I keep asking why when it's simpler to avoid these issues?

"What do you think?" Rip whispered.

"Beautiful," I lied.

Rip was quiet in the car, alone with his thoughts, so I reclined my seat and closed my eyes. If he knew the ideas plaguing me during the service, he'd surely have me burned at the stake for heresy. Or maybe not. Hadn't he told me that Judaism was a religion that encouraged questioning: "the truth can withstand scrutiny." Unfortunately, some fakes can too.

* * *

Richard worked at warp speed to complete our merger with UndauntedAI. Even though he called it a merger, word traveled fast that they were acquiring us. The terms of the deal were secret for now. Sam was suspicious, though I couldn't decide if his suspicions were reasonable or if he was paranoid. Several employees in accounting and marketing had appointments with Floyd for exit interviews, information that came to me from Rona even before I found out from Richard at staff meetings.

After hearing news from the highly efficient but often incorrect rumor mill, I received word from Richard about a compulsory meeting Friday morning. The executives from UndauntedAI were coming in for a series of presentations by the respective heads of each of our functional areas.

"Sam and Sylvie, we need to strike while the iron is hot."

I suppressed a groan. "Each of you has an important role to play. I want you to put the best possible spin on our pipelines. 'B' sales opportunities should be shown as 'A's' that will close this quarter. Anything with a 50 percent chance of closing this month should be described as a sure thing."

I pointed out that all our forecasted business was slipping out or even away because we didn't have NewAI.

Sam turned to me. "Don't you get it? He wants us to lie."

Richard jumped to his feet. "Spin, not lie. Think positive. Manfred, NewAI is close to release. Right?"

Manfred, who had been appointed acting head of software engineering in Warren's place, regarded Richard with a blank stare. I thought I saw his pink nose twitch, but I could have imagined it during the interminable pause, made more so by Sam's eyes drilling into Manfred's.

"The Greeks the Romans will beat," he replied. "That was the Delphic Oracle's reply when asked who would win the battle between the Greeks and the Romans. My answer to you is that it depends. NewAI could be finished in a heartbeat if we applied fresh resources, but engineering doesn't have any. On the other hand, even though the Romans won, the people walking around Greece today are Greeks, not Romans. Ergo, it depends how you look at it."

Sam turned to Richard. "This guy," he gestured toward Manfred, "has gone round the bend. You're never going to pull this off, Richard."

Richard looked stunned, but it occurred to me that Manfred had been clever playing up his reputation for eccentricity to avoid making a commitment. When Richard abruptly ended the meeting, he asked Harold Astrove to remain. Manfred fled. Sam, Floyd, and I filed out slowly, heads down. It felt like a funeral procession. I wasn't the only one struggling to "think positive."

Back in my office, I sent an email to my sales reps asking for updated forecasts. I could imagine the grumbling that would greet my message, but Richard had left me no alternative. I wasn't going to be pleasantly surprised. I was sure of that.

On my way out of the building that evening, I looked into

BodySculpt and saw a familiar scene but with unfamiliar faces. So much had changed since I'd acted on impulse and walked in that door. Rob and Rip had been a comedy act together. I'd so enjoyed their repartee, I'd committed to training sessions on the spot. Now I was an executive. Instead of scraping along, I had an inheritance, and though I didn't have a sleek car, I had a practical one. Most important, I had Rip, or at least I hoped I did.

Heavy traffic on Route 128 gave me too much time to think about work, so when my cell phone rang, Eileen's voice was a welcome diversion.

"I miss you," she said. "Why can't you come down here?"

I could almost hear the waves and inhale the fragrance of Luis's rose garden. "Please don't tempt me, because I'd love nothing more than to hop on a plane. AI*future* is in the middle of merger negotiations. You can't imagine how crazy it's making everyone."

"Well, you're right there. The only experience I have with mergers is the one I'm contemplating with Miguel. Don't forget, June 1."

"I'm not sure that gives me enough time to lose ten pounds, find someone to do my hair and nails, and get new eyebrows tattooed on."

"You're my matron of honor. You just need to buy a dress, a mauve one."

"How will I find one of those? I can't even pronounce it. My mother always made it rhyme with 'clove.' You pronounce it like 'maudlin.'"

"Fine, think about 'maudlin' when you're shopping for a dress, and see where that gets you!"

I was trying to come up with a snappy retort when I heard Miguel's voice in the background.

Eileen covered her microphone when she answered him. "Sorry, Syl, we're about to leave for dinner. I just wanted to let you know that we've located Carlos. He's been in Boston for a while, doing what I don't know. Just be careful."

Of course Carlos was in town. Adding him to my problems made it a regular pile-on. As soon as I got home, I poured myself a glass of Cabernet in preparation for my pity party. Halfway through, which doesn't take long when you're chugging, I heard a knock. Mary Jo Carter stood on my doorstep.

"I'm collecting in our neighborhood," she said, "donations for heart research. Can you help, Sylvie?"

I swung my door wide open and looked past Mary Jo toward a car parked on our street. Mary Jo turned too.

"Hey, isn't that the guy you wanted the harassment order for? Is he stalking you?"

I couldn't see much of the driver's head, but I saw enough to know it was Carlos. "I think so. It's hard to tell for sure in this light."

"That's the guy. I remember him. Don't you think you should call the police?"

"I can handle it. Don't worry." I handed Mary Jo a twenty-dollar bill as a contribution. "Would you like to come in? I was just having a glass of wine."

"No thanks, hon. I've got more houses to hit tonight. Nice to see you, though. Raincheck?"

I agreed enthusiastically, and as Mary Jo turned to go, she said, "Thanks again for the donation, and please be careful."

First Eileen and now Mary Jo telling me to be careful. No one had given me so many warnings since I was a kid, but what was in it for Carlos, or any stalker, to just park out there? It seemed crazy, and crazy behavior was unpredictable. I shivered and checked that my front door was locked.

CHAPTER 33

Eileen texted me she was coming to Boston. I was surprised, since early spring in Boston is muddy and cold. Made perfect sense from her perspective to insist I come to Florida, but she must have been really worried about me, because she texted a couple of hours later with her flight information.

The next evening, her plane was delayed an hour, and the thought of hanging out in the cell phone lot was unpalatable. I sprang for the fee in the garage and went into the terminal. With no ticket, I couldn't go through security, so I parked myself at a table in the food court just off the airline check-in counters. Just as I was settling in with a hot cup of coffee and an obscenely large chocolate chip cookie, I spotted venture capital royalty in the form of my ex-husband.

Ashton was smartly turned out, as usual, with designer jeans, a suede jacket, and Gucci loafers. He placed his handsome leather attaché case on the floor beside him while he hoisted his suitcase onto the scale. While the attendant printed out his baggage receipt, Ashton looked around the terminal and spotted me. There was no place to hide except under the table, so I nodded to acknowledge him. Ashton chose to interpret that as an invitation.

He purchased coffee, although there were better choices on the other side of security. "Share your table for old time's sake?" He didn't wait for a response but sat down opposite me.

I decided to take the offensive. "Whatever happened with your potential big shot investor, Carlos Rodriguez? You know, the one who said I falsely accused him of rape."

With coffee cup in midair, Ashton frowned. Catching him off balance rarely happened. It was a small thing, but I was pleased to see his momentary discomfort.

"I haven't gotten him to invest yet, but I'm certain it will happen soon," he said. "I guess that caused a bit of a problem for you at work, but . . . ancient history, right? You remember what I used to tell you: politics is the job; you gotta play them."

"Yes, well I've managed to stay employed without your advice. Been promoted, too: US sales executive."

His smile was patronizing as he got up to leave. There was a sign asking customers to discard their trash, but, of course, Ashton didn't. I waited for his parting shot. He pulled his briefcase out from under the table. "I'm glad you took to heart everything I taught you about business."

I laughed. "I learned a lot from you, Ashton, but not about business."

He stared at me, then without a word walked away.

Eileen texted that her flight was at the gate, so we arranged to meet in the baggage area. Seeing her more than made up for my unpleasant encounter with Ashton.

"You have no idea how happy I am to see you." My eyes welled up.

Eileen backed away and held me by the shoulders. "What a liar you are, Syl. You are very definitely not all right."

On the way back to Needham, I quizzed her on her wedding plans to keep the conversation away from my state of mind. I figured the wedding was a subject Eileen could turn into a doctoral thesis. She didn't disappoint. She'd brought a photograph of her dress, which I couldn't look at while I was driving. I was expecting something funky, Eileen being Eileen, but the dress she described had a fitted lace bodice, a deeply scooped sweetheart neckline, and sheer full sleeves ending in tight lace cuffs. She'd be wearing her hair up to show off the earrings, pearls trimmed with diamonds, that had belonged to Miguel's mother. He'd insisted.

Eileen was still going strong when we arrived at my apartment. The ceremony would be at the church, the reception at a boutique hotel, and Eileen wanted to shop with me for my mauve dress during her visit. I was laughing when we got out of the car until I spotted Carlos partway up the street. Unfortunately, Eileen followed my gaze as the car moved away.

"Shit, that's Carlos," she said. "I knew you needed me here."

"Unless you brought a loaded revolver with you, I'm not sure how you can protect me. I think he's decided if he harasses me or scares me enough, I'll give up my trusteeship. I'm just about ready to do that, too, but then I remind myself he's a rapist I should have had arrested."

"So, you're punishing yourself?"

"I'm doing what Luis wanted. I am a little worried, though, that he'll see Rip and me together and decide to go after Rip to hurt me.

"Speaking of Rip"—Eileen settled herself into my sofa and grabbed a throw pillow for her head—"I want to hear how he went from trainer to lover. Leave nothing out."

"Don't get too comfortable. That would take half the night, and I'm beat. I thought maybe I'd arrange for you to meet him instead." Eileen smiled and gave me a thumbs-up.

■ ■ ■

The next morning, I called Rip. I gave him two choices: he could go shopping with Eileen and me for my matron of honor gown or meet us for dinner.

"I actually have another idea. Would Eileen be interested in going for a run? The weather's improving, and I know a place in Weston where we haven't been before. The trails are wide enough for three."

"I don't know how you could turn down the chance to shop with us, but let me check with her. Hold on."

Eileen was in the kitchen making herself tea, so I didn't have to go far.

"Rip, you're on. Are you bringing Dinger?"

"Of course."

"That will make it all worthwhile." We arranged to meet Sunday morning, which pleased Eileen since it left all of Saturday for shopping. An entire day with Eileen would be fun. A day of shopping, not so much. It might take hours to find a mauve dress. Why couldn't she have picked something easy like blue? I was about to suggest looking online first, but if mauve turned out to be as scarce as a UFO, it might be good for Eileen to find that out and perhaps fall in love with a different color.

We started at Saks in Boston. I listened to Eileen's rapturous description of the peonies, calla lilies, and roses planned for the bouquets, and as she extolled the virtues of mauve organdy dresses, it was hard not to be caught up in her enthusiasm. As much as I was dreading trekking from one store to another, it felt like a great relief to be worrying about nothing but flowers, silk, and satin.

As we approached the gown department, I readied myself for the glory of sequined and beaded prom dresses. Eileen dove into the rack and the next thing I heard was a triumphant, "You see! I told you." She pulled out a mauve dress as though she were unfurling a flag. The lace shoulder straps and bodice and the deep scoop neck gave the gown a Victorian feel that entranced Eileen.

I'd never bought a dress with so many zeroes in the price and couldn't imagine ever wearing it again, but if it pleased Eileen, I didn't care. A representative from the alterations department joined us in the fitting room five minutes later.

We were done, and my fears of being dragged from store to store were dispelled. Nothing left to do but treat ourselves to a celebratory lunch.

Eileen sprang for Champagne.

"Salud!" We clinked glasses.

Champagne goes down like ginger ale, so it didn't take long for Eileen to urge a second glass on me. "I hate to spoil your fun, but we have to run with Rip tomorrow."

"I'm sure he'll take it easy if I'm there."

"Not a chance. He's a tyrant, and I'm out of shape. I can't remember the last time I went for a run."

"If Carlos were stalking me, I wouldn't go for a run either."

"He's just trying to scare me. I'm not worried." Another lie.

■ ■ ■

The next morning, I looked out the window and saw a perfect early spring day, buds on the shrubs and tree branches and grass that was surely greener than even a day ago. Eileen was still in pajamas, sleepy-eyed and sipping tea from a mug at my kitchen table.

"Boy, are you lucky," I said. "We could have had a hurricane today, and Rip would have shown no mercy."

She raised an eyebrow. "I brought an umbrella and galoshes, so there, mean girl."

"Save the galoshes for your wedding day." I ducked as Eileen threw her wet teabag at me.

It took us half an hour to get to Cat Rock Park. I was looking forward to exploring its eighty acres. I was also praying its trails were flat. The entrance was at the end of a residential cul-de-sac that included a small traffic circle and generous parking area. Rip was late, so we got out and tried to stretch our tight muscles.

"Ugh," Eileen complained. "This is a bad omen. We should leave immediately."

"Uh-oh, too late."

Rip pulled into the adjacent parking spot and waved. "Sorry to keep you waiting. Happy to meet the famous Eileen." He got out and released Dinger, who ran to me, tail wagging, and jumped up to give me a sloppy kiss.

"Rip, I just noticed there's a sign that says only Weston residents can use the parking area and trails on weekends. Is there somewhere else we can go?" Eileen laughed and knelt down to embrace Dinger. "What a sweetheart."

Rip grinned at her but didn't get a chance to answer me before a black sedan came rocketing down the street and headed straight for us. Dinger got between the car and me, bumping me aside. Rip grabbed Eileen, who had fallen hard after the car grazed her.

"Bastard!" Eileen screamed, recognizing Carlos, who careened around the circle and sped up the street.

The sound of screeching tires and screams brought residents spilling from their houses. In a daze, I sat frozen on the ground and watched Rip trying to help Eileen, who groaned in pain. It took a moment before I realized Dinger had been hit. He lay on the ground bloody and still. For a second, my eyes locked on Rip's before he ran to Dinger.

In a moment he was on his knees, bending tenderly over his pet, cradling Dinger's bloody head. Though Rip didn't make a sound, his shoulders began to shake. Eileen was crying, too, but I was too stunned for tears.

The people gathering around us kept their distance from Rip and Dinger. Eileen was clutching her leg, injured too badly to get up. I stayed with her as the sirens drew closer, while onlookers took photos of the scene with their phones.

When the EMTs arrived, they lifted Eileen gently onto a gurney and wheeled her to the ambulance. I asked the driver his destination: Newton-Wellesley Hospital. "I'll only be two minutes behind you," I assured Eileen and squeezed her hand.

Rip looked so shaken, I wondered if he were in shock. The police officer at his side offered to remove Dinger, but Rip waved him away. One of the homeowners offered him a towel. The blood on his face was streaked with tears. I crouched next to him. "What can I do to help?"

"There's nothing to be done. I don't want the police to take him. I need to be with him right now. Go to Eileen; she needs you."

I was reluctant to leave him, but a policeman interrupted. He'd already talked to witnesses and understood that we knew the driver. I eagerly gave him all the information about Carlos I had with me on my phone.

"So, you think this was deliberate?" he asked.

"I'm sure of it."

He took my phone number and address, thanked me for my help, and said they'd be in touch. Alone in my car, I let the tears come. Wiping them away with the sleeve of my running jacket, I tried to stay focused on the road. Eileen needed me, but so did Rip. I ached for the two people I most cared about in my life. I was the cause of this disaster. If only I'd chosen a different path, Carlos wouldn't have been driven to this murderous assault.

Eileen was in the emergency room in a curtained cubicle. The ER doc had sent her to X-ray right away. Her face brightened when she saw me. "Want to be first to sign my cast?"

"So, it is broken. I'm really sorry. Carlos is furious with me but ended up hurting you and Rip. Maybe he figured out that was the best way to make me miserable."

"That's ridiculous. You're not responsible for what a madman does."

"Yesterday seems like a dream—Champagne, silk dresses. Now your visit is ruined. Miguel will hate me."

"Not you, but Carlos, who most definitely will not be Miguel's best man. He'll probably be in prison by the wedding anyway."

I marveled at her resilience. A nurse came in to let Eileen know she'd be taken shortly to have her cast put on. As I sank down on her bed, deflated, she pointed out that my running pants were ripped. Just abrasions underneath, I assured her, which seemed minor under the circumstances. She instructed me to at least get myself a cup of coffee in the cafeteria—no point sitting around the ER, since she wouldn't be walking out anytime soon.

The cafeteria was quiet. The clock on the wall said 11:30, not quite lunchtime. I'd beaten the crowd. I took a minute to sit at a table and collect my thoughts. I felt so guilty about Dinger and sorry for Rip. How he loved that dog. This mess, my mess, shouldn't have involved him at all. I called his cell but ended up in voicemail. What was I going to say anyway? I knew he'd be inconsolable.

When I returned to the ER, Eileen was gone. I went out to the waiting room figuring they'd let me know when she returned. Checking my texts, I discovered someone from the police department wanted to ask me more questions about Carlos.

A nurse came out to notify me Eileen was back in the ER and ready for discharge, so I saved the message for later. I found her sitting on the edge of her bed, crutches close by. "I guess I won't be running up any hills for a while," she said. "Poor Rip, I feel sorrier for him than for myself."

"I haven't been able to reach him. He looked devastated."

"I'm sorry, Syl. Carlos is a sick asshole."

"He's more than an asshole. He's a criminal."

I helped Eileen into my car and threw her crutches into the back seat.

My cell phone rang as soon as we arrived at the apartment. A police sergeant wanted to let me know they'd caught Carlos Rodriguez, but Carlos claimed the accident was a misunderstanding. "He didn't deny the speeding and alleged he was only trying to scare you. I understand the two of you have some history. He acknowledged that his plan had gone badly and said he felt terrible about the dog he didn't even know he'd hit."

"Did he mention that his soon-to-be sister-in-law has a broken leg because of him? Sergeant, he knew exactly what he was doing. He headed straight for us and came close to killing three people as well as the dog."

Eileen was looking at me wide-eyed as my voice rose.

"You have to put this guy away!"

The sergeant paused. "We'll be contacting the other two people he allegedly targeted so we can meet with them, probably tomorrow at the station house." He assured me Carlos had broken the law and would be held over for arraignment until the DA specified charges. Malicious animal cruelty was punishable by jail time and a fine, and, in this case, there were many witnesses who had offered to testify.

When I got off the phone, I asked Eileen if she'd spoken to Miguel. "On his way up here," she replied. "I called him from the hospital. I didn't want to upset him, but you can imagine how well that went. It was all I could do to keep him from hiring a private jet."

My refrigerator and freezer were pretty bare, which wasn't normally a problem. I promised my trip to the market would be quick and took Eileen's prescription for pain medicine with me. Despite my hurrying, I returned to find Eileen looking weary, dejected, and pale. I was impressed that she'd been able to run on adrenaline as long as she had.

"That police officer called me while you were out. Carlos told him you had a history of making false accusations against him. He has a lawyer now too. He got him through your ex. Carlos told Ashton the same story he did last time, you know, the one about the made-up rape."

"He's going to get away with it, isn't he? The same way as before when I couldn't get the harassment order, only this time it's going to be Rip who doesn't get justice for Dinger."

"Have you reached him?"

"Still just voicemail. Not like him at all. I'm worried."

When I insisted she lie down on her bed in the guestroom, she gave me no argument. I put an extra pillow under her leg and asked her what she'd like for dinner, but she had already drifted off.

Miguel's flight arrived in the evening. He checked into an airport hotel for the night so he wouldn't disturb Eileen. I told him what had happened, at least from my point of view, which turned out to be the same as Eileen's.

I heard the despair in his voice. "Sylvie, I'm so sorry. Carlos has needed help for many years, but he just won't listen to anyone. I'm still the younger brother who stole his mother's love, and he wants me to feel guilty about it. He's good at that. Even though he's older, I feel responsible for him. If he had killed Eileen . . ."

Poor Miguel. Luis must have felt the same way—responsible for a son who made him furious. I could think of no words of comfort for Miguel, who would always have to look out for Carlos. He wasn't the kind of person to abandon his brother. "Don't worry about Eileen. She's resilient, and there's no way she's going to walk down the aisle with crutches."

We agreed to touch base in the morning.

* * *

As I predicted, Eileen felt much better after a night's sleep, fortified as she was by breakfast and pain meds. She was standing, supported by crutches, when Miguel arrived. He rushed over to her, then stopped, uncertain how to embrace her. Eileen planted her crutches, leaned forward, and gave him a noisy kiss.

Leaving them alone seemed like a good idea, especially since I was becoming frantic over Rip's silence. I drove to his apartment and let myself in with the key he'd given me. I wasn't sure what I was expecting. He wasn't the kind of serious drinker to be passed out on the bed. The kitchen was neater than usual, although Dinger's bowls were still on the floor. Rip's bed was made too. I sat down and pulled out my cell to send him a text. "I'm sitting in your empty apartment. Really worried about you! Please call."

I'd already called my office to say I wouldn't be in today, but I couldn't think of what to do except drive to my building and talk to Rob at BodySculpt. I didn't think he and Rip had been in touch since Rob had fired him. They were lifelong friends, though, so maybe they had patched things up.

Rob was surprised to see me. Months had passed since I'd been at the gym. He'd seen the story about the accident on the local news and asked how I was doing.

"I'm fine. It's Rip I'm worried about. I can't find him. He and I are usually in close touch." I felt myself blushing.

"Yes, I know." He smiled. "It's taken a while, but Rip and I have restored our friendship. He felt pretty bad about what he had done, which was so out of character."

"Kate has that effect on people. I'm glad that's behind us."

"All I know, Sylvie, is that he thought he might be going out of town and asked if I'd be able to take Dinger for a couple of days. Said you were up to your neck in problems at work. Yesterday changed everything, of course. He was crushed when Dinger died. Called to say he was leaving immediately."

"Leaving for where?"

"Brooklyn, where his mother lives. He said he had some business to take care of in New York." He shrugged. "That's all I know."

"But—"

Two clients came up to the counter to check in for their appointments, so I had to move out of the way. What point was there in harassing Rob when he was as much in the dark as I was? If Rip wanted me to know what he was doing, he would have told me.

Before my mother died, she'd made it sound as though she and my father were soulmates, not at all the way I remembered their marriage. Actually, she said he was the love of her life. I guess the two weren't the same. Rip had said it was "possible" he was in love with me. I can see now that love doesn't necessarily include the soulmate part. Maybe a robot could be a reasonable facsimile of a loving partner. Given my experience being married to Ashton, a robot could have done the job better.

CHAPTER 34

Richard wanted my head on a pike for disappearing at such a critical time for AI*future*. The UndauntedAI executives were coming back in. I didn't know much about the actual process of due diligence, but it seemed to me UndauntedAI was in as big a hurry as a smitten suitor. I wondered if they had secrets of their own. As for Richard, he was keeping his cards close to the vest, to use one of his favorite expressions, so I imagined there was an agreement to wipe out his loan.

Having heard the details about our technology from Manfred and analyzed the financial information provided by Harold, they needed some final reassurance. According to Richard, they were concerned our strong past performance might not continue into the future, a fear I knew was valid.

I was supposed to assure them that our deals were all going to close in the timeframes and for the dollars we had forecasted. Fiction, pure fiction. I know what Ashton's advice would have been: *Hold your nose and do it. That's the way the game is played.* I know what Rip's advice would have been: *Your choices influence who you become and how you decide your next choices. They change you*—Rip's infamous line of best fit.

"Headache?" Sam asked. I'd been holding my head in my hands when he appeared in my office doorway. He didn't wait for an answer. "Richard told you what we need to do next to close the deal on this merger, right?"

I wondered if I looked as haggard as Sam. Haggard was an especially bad look on a woman. Guys can get away with it. "I can't present fake numbers. I just can't. What are you doing?"

Sam sat down on the corner of my desk and leaned in. "You have to, Sylvie. Do you know how many people you'll be screwing if you don't? It's not your problem if UndauntedAI has blinders on. This is no time for the moral high ground. Just do it and live to fight another day."

"Not you too. I thought it was only Richard who resorted to clichés." I was too tense to stay in my chair and retreated to my window. Outside was the familiar, predictable scene, neatly landscaped commercial buildings and rows of cars. Inside this building, inside AI*future's* offices, the landscape had become ugly and unpredictable, like a portrait in the attic. I turned to Sam. "You're going to lie?"

"I don't know what will happen to our stock if AI*future* goes under. With Warren's abandoning NewAI and Harold's hiding the loan Richard can no longer afford to pay back, we could go bankrupt. Between the alimony and child support I'm going to be paying, I really need this deal to go through. You've always been a team player, Sylvie. I'm begging you. Please go along."

Sam's cell phone rang, and he walked toward the hall to take the call. He turned at the door and mouthed "please."

Fuck. A friend was pleading with me to help, not Richard but Sam. He was right. I'd always gone along. Wouldn't going along serve the greater good? Was that the moral path in life or just in commerce, where the greater good to be served is the interest of the stockholders?

How wonderful it must be to believe right and wrong are easy choices, I thought. *All you have to do is look in whatever holy book you happen to think came from the heavens via some earthly sage.*

But what did believers do with the gray between right and wrong? Pretend it didn't exist and feed it into the paper shredder? It amazed me how hard people would work to avoid using their brains. Didn't they believe God gave them judgment for a reason?

I tasted blood. I was angry, biting my lip. I hated facing this dilemma, so I was blaming everyone else, all those faceless people who didn't struggle with hard choices. Who exactly would that be? No one.

Driving home that evening, I kept seeing Sam's face, pleading, almost in tears. He was right. If I didn't go along, I risked screwing up everyone's stock options. That could happen anyway, given whatever deal was negotiated. Damn Rip and his line of best fit. When choices affected other people, choosing was no longer an intellectual exercise. You ended up eating your guts out.

■ ■ ■

Eileen and Miguel had been to the police station while I was at work and had discussed the case with two officers. It appeared Carlos's lawyer wanted him released on bail, claiming Carlos's version of events was more reasonable than that of the eyewitnesses. According to the lawyer, everyone in law enforcement knows eyewitnesses are notoriously inaccurate. The bystanders were dog lovers who were letting their emotions color the truth.

The police wanted to locate Rip to get his statement. I collapsed on my couch, suddenly exhausted, and let my briefcase slip to the floor. I told Eileen and Miguel what Rob at BodySculpt had said. Eileen dropped down beside me.

"How disappointing," she said. "I hate to leave you like this."

"You're leaving?"

"We have a morning flight. Miguel has to get back to work, and I need to get home to rest my leg properly."

Miguel sat on my other side and put his arm around me. "Carlos is in custody. You're safe, and we'll be in close touch."

"Of course." I tried to keep from crying and making them feel guilty, although in truth, I felt as though everyone were abandoning me. "Makes perfect sense. Nothing to be gained by staying."

Eileen frowned, but I patted her hand.

"Go pack up while I get dinner going. Nothing like meatballs and spaghetti to make us forget our troubles."

■ ■ ■

I went into the office early the next morning and pored over the forecasts each of my sales reps had turned in. I was sure word had leaked out about our negotiations with UndauntedAI, but I no longer cared. I was not surprised to see a temp at the reception desk. Both Rona and Fannette had already turned in their resignations.

I closed the door of my office and examined my reps' forecasts, compiling them into the most optimistic view of our potential revenue I could conjure up. I emailed it to Richard and sat back to wait. It took him only five minutes to appear in my doorway, clutching a creased printout of my forecast. "This is it, Sylvie? The best you can do?"

My fear of insubordination was replaced by indignation. "Yes, Richard, I've never been as good at writing fairy tales as Warren is. My sales reps are losing deals because NewAI has less substance than a hologram. The forecast you're holding is wildly optimistic, which, I believe, is what you asked for. If you want to edit it, be my guest, but don't ask me to defend it."

"What does that mean?"

"When UndauntedAI comes in on Friday, I'm going to have an acute case of the flu with a fever so high I won't be able to get out of bed. Don't call me. Don't ask me to videoconference. You're welcome to stand behind those numbers, but if questioned, I will not. I won't contradict them either. I'll be too ill to talk." I held my hands up. "See, I took the gloves off just like you told me to."

Richard said not a word to me the rest of the week, which was fine by me. I told Sam my decision, and he too fell silent, which was not fine. My mood was so gloomy I couldn't imagine anything depressing me further. Then Rip returned.

CHAPTER 35

I stood in the middle of Rip's living room, the room where I had found such comfort and warmth from his wall of books and cozy reading chair, and listened to his brief, lame apology, outrage and resentment rising inside me like a newly stoked fire.

"Rip, 'sorry' doesn't cut it. You picked a traumatic time for all of us, not just you, and vanished. Did it occur to you I might be worried?"

He avoided my gaze, which made my need to provoke a response grow stronger.

"Even the police were looking for you, trying to track you down. What kind of a person does that?" I didn't mean to make my anger balloon into something huge, a Goodyear blimp hovering over our entire relationship, but I couldn't stop myself. "You're a hypocrite who has no business lecturing anyone on ethics."

Rip hung his head. Having said what I came to say, I turned to leave.

"Sylvie, please don't go. I didn't want to tell you yet, but you're forcing my hand. I've decided to become a rabbi."

I took my hand off the doorknob. "Are you serious?"

"I went to New York to stay with my mother while I talked with the admissions people at Hebrew Union College.

I already have two years of credits. You were right about me. The only reason I turned away from the rabbinate was because I resented my father's trying to control my life."

"But why now, at this particular moment? Why did you disappear?"

Rip started to pace across the living room and back. "I was falling apart. First, I hooked up with Kate, then Rob fired me, then Dinger was killed. I felt like a kid who'd built a castle out of blocks, and someone started pulling out the bottom ones. The someone was me. I didn't recognize myself."

"Kate's a manipulator."

"Yes, but it was my error in judgment that made me moonlight as her trainer. When that creep, Carlos, showed up, he created yet another problem between you and me. I argued with you about your choices like I wasn't making bad choices myself."

"Carlos was my problem. I never meant for him to become yours."

Rip stopped pacing and reached for my hand. "It doesn't matter. You were right about me. I was always moralizing like some street corner preacher with a sign that says, 'Jesus loves you.' I want to help people, but they need a reason to trust me. I may not be perfect, but at least if I go into the rabbinate, they'll be able to trust my knowledge and training. Maybe I'll even be able to trust myself."

He looked so miserable, I couldn't bring myself to walk out the door. I returned to the living room and perched on the edge of his reading chair. "Why couldn't you talk to me before you disappeared? Is it . . . you don't have feelings for me anymore? If that's why you're leaving, just say it."

He knelt in front of me and took my hands. "Sylvie, you're so wrong. I'm in love with you. That's what made the decision to leave so hard. A rabbi can't have a wife who's not Jewish, and even if I knew you wanted to be my wife, it would be unfair to pressure you into converting. Judaism doesn't proselytize like some other faiths. I'm the guy who kept telling you not to try to please everyone. How could I ask you to please me?"

My brain was numb. Rip wanted to be a rabbi, and he also wanted to marry me, at least at some point. He couldn't do both because I was a Protestant. He was right. My parents may not have been observant, but we went to church on the holidays. I may have questioned my religious beliefs, but I never questioned my religious identity. The Sabbath service Rip and I had attended together—interesting, yes—but Jewish stars where there should have been crosses. Could a temple ever feel like home to me? Didn't it have to if I were married to a rabbi? On the other hand, could I honestly say the church felt like home to me?

Rip dropped my hands and stood. "I'm sorry. I didn't mean to dump all that on you. Of course you're confused. I kept struggling with how to tell you. I'm a coward."

"How soon are you leaving?"

"My lease is up next month, so I need to start packing. My mother is willing to have me live at home till I finish the degree."

I wondered if his mother had room for all his books. I didn't ask, though. I needed to begin the process of separating from him. Like an addict who gives up her addiction, I would have to take it day by day. Time to start day one without Rip. I told him I was going home to think things over, but really, there was nothing to think about. I'd been dumped before, but I'd never lost a guy to God.

■ ■ ■

Because Rip had been unavailable to provide evidence to the police, Carlos's lawyer succeeded in getting him released on bail. Carlos was instructed not to leave the state. His passport was also confiscated.

Eileen called and warned me to be careful. I assured her Carlos was not stupid enough to risk his bail, nor was he likely to come after me when that would mean going straight to jail. I was not as confident as I tried to sound, because Carlos could no longer be relied upon to behave rationally. I didn't think I persuaded Eileen.

The prosecutor called to let me know Carlos's lawyer wanted to talk about a plea deal. I begged him to delay the meeting.

"Rip—I mean Fielding Harris—has come back to town. I'll have him contact you."

He agreed to wait.

"One last question, who put up bail?"

"I believe it was an Ashton Manhardt. Do you know him?"

"Thank you for the information."

That fucking asshole. I'll kill him! Ashton was the one who found Carlos a lawyer, so I should have known he would bail him out too. Ashton never tired of screwing me. I felt as though an electric current was coursing through my chest.

I took some deep breaths to calm myself. I had to reach Rip, although I suspected he might duck my call. No answer. I left a detailed message on his voicemail begging him to follow through with the police.

■ ■ ■

I was sure I would hear from Sam before the week was out, but instead I received a call from Warren.

"Sylvie, I've been wondering how you're doing and thought perhaps you'd meet me for a drink to catch up. I have a proposition for you."

My stomach lurched. Refusing would be the best response, but I was curious about his proposition. I'd heard little about his new venture or their major opportunity with the defense department. He was persona non grata at AI*future*, since he'd quit the company with NewAI not even close to finished. Gossip about him had dried up.

Warren no longer seemed worried about secrecy because he met me at a gastropub near the office. The wraparound bar was huge. The lighting was bright enough to attract the see-and-be-seen crowd, mostly single or at least without wedding rings. I almost didn't recognize Warren with his beard and mustache. He wore a black T-shirt and black jeans, the Steve-Jobs-with-facial-hair look. He appeared more keyed up than usual, his fingers tapping the table.

I ordered a glass of Malbec, hoping it would take the edge off. It didn't. "How are Maya and the baby doing?" I asked, expecting a more descriptive answer than "coming along." Warren had no interest in pleasantries.

The hawk swooped in. "I've heard you're not on board with the acquisition, and I thought perhaps I had misunderstood. You know, I still own a lot of AI*future* stock. I have a stake in this deal, and you do too."

If he felt so strongly about his stake in the company, why did he leave? "Perhaps I should remind you your departure left us without a NewAI product to speak of. Weren't you the one who wanted to hold out for a bigger acquisition partner?"

"Let's not rehash the past. You'll help both of us if you push this deal through by forecasting substantial revenue."

"Which would be a lie."

"Grow up, Sylvie. You're not responsible if their due diligence is inadequate. Plus, there's more in this for you than cashing in your stock. Persuade UndauntedAI, and I'll have a high-paying sales job waiting for you at my new company."

He looked satisfied with himself, and why not? He was a guy who ran over people to get what he wanted. He assumed I'd go along with his desires. I might have made a show of disagreeing in the past, but I'd always gone along. I swished around the little wine left in my glass.

I reminded myself what it would be like to work for him. No, he couldn't pay me enough to do that, lucrative job or not. "Warren, don't you trust Richard to close this deal? He needs it to get out from under his little embezzlement problem. I'm not the one stopping him. I can't help it if I'm not all in. Putting a spin on facts and telling a big fat lie are not the same. Sorry, no sale." I walked out, leaving him to pay the bill. I resisted the impulse to turn around and see the expression on his face. I told myself he was surprised, but that might have been wishful thinking.

* * *

On Thursday night, I turned off my cell phone and laptop. No one would be able to reach me while I watched a movie on cable. I picked a good British mystery, so I'd be eager to watch all the way to the end. I was afraid someone like Sam or Richard might actually come over, but no one rang my bell.

Friday was my sick day, although I didn't bother to call in. Richard knew what to expect. The management team would be busy with UndauntedAI's executives. I had planned to spend the entire day at home, but by lunchtime I was restless. I couldn't stop thinking about Rip.

I turned on my laptop and looked up the website for the temple Rip and I had visited. I knew they had Friday night services, so calling the rabbi might be futile. He'd be refining his sermon and ignoring calls. I was preparing to leave a voicemail when he surprised me by answering his extension.

"Rabbi, I hope I'm not disturbing you."

"Not a problem. Letting people disturb me is part of my job."

"My name is Sylvie Manhardt. I was at your service several weeks ago with my friend. He's Jewish. I'm not, and . . ."

"And that's a problem?"

"He's going back to school to become a rabbi, and to marry him, I'd have to convert. Can I talk with you about what's involved?"

"I can make some time for you on Sunday, say 10:00 at the temple?"

I thought I had settled the issue of conversion in my own mind and couldn't account for why I made that phone call. Perhaps my solitary confinement to avoid what was happening at the office had allowed thoughts to surface I didn't know I had.

■ ■ ■

Rabbi Jacobson looked more wrinkled and grayer than he had when I saw him from a distance behind the lectern Rip called the "bima." He wore khakis and a golf shirt, so I thanked him for making time for me on what I imagined was his day off. His study was lined with books on two sides. The other walls displayed art in the style of Marc Chagall, and on his desk were family photos.

He invited me to sit on his sofa and settled into an easy chair across from me. "Tell me, Sylvie, do you want to convert to Judaism?"

"That's why I'm here."

"No, you told me you were considering it because of your boyfriend, not that you had a desire to convert. I'm asking because it's a big undertaking, and it could be difficult to follow through if you're not entirely committed. Are you prepared to learn Jewish theology, rituals, customs, and culture? Will you attend services? You're probably looking at a year's work, although it varies from rabbi to rabbi. You'd be able to choose your own rabbi to work with."

I was silent for a moment, taken aback by the dedication required. How to respond? His kind expression made it easier to allow my mixed-up thoughts and feelings out, although I feared I sounded incoherent. "I'm not sure of anything right now, not even sure I believe in God, let alone a set of religious teachings. In business, well in my business anyway, I feel as though right and wrong, ethical and unethical, are shrouded in gray. There is no God, only stockholders. Choosing a religion seems so beside the point. They all teach some version of the golden rule, don't they?"

"Ah, Sylvie. You're enough of a questioner to be a Jew, but, you know, surrendering to faith has value too. I could argue that Judaism would help you find your way through all that gray. I'm afraid you'd need to believe or at least hope for that before taking on the rigors of conversion. Otherwise, where would your motivation come from? You shouldn't change your religion because someone else wants you to. I can't help you make your decision. I will say, though, that you don't seem ready to make one. Give yourself some time. Your friend won't become a rabbi overnight."

■ ■ ■

No one called me—not Rip, Eileen, or anyone from work. When I drove into the office on Monday, I wondered if Richard had locked my door. Had I been exiled without anyone remembering to tell me?

I walked down to Sam's office, unsure of the greeting I'd receive. He looked up from his laptop but said nothing.

"Sam, I know you're pissed at me, but how did it go Friday? Are we on speaking terms?"

"Is your conscience clear?" he asked, his tone unmistakably sarcastic. "Hope you're over your stomach flu."

"I'm sorry. I did what I had to do. I hope you got what you wanted."

He leaned back in his chair. "Richard got what he wanted, and that's because he made sure you were there by video, addressing the vast opportunities in front of AI*future* this year."

"I don't understand. Shit, not another deepfake video?" I dropped down into the chair in front of Sam's desk.

"You shouldn't be surprised. The stakes were too high for Richard to let you create doubt in the minds of the UndauntedAI execs. Richard recruited the person who had the experience and could produce a video quickly."

"Warren? Who screwed *AIfuture* on his way out the door? I suppose no one on our executive team blew the whistle."

Sam shrugged. "What difference does it make now that you're obsessed with truthfulness? Not enjoying the moral high ground?"

I was furious and frustrated enough to spit, to scream. I wanted to punch him. How could he act as though none of this mattered, as though I didn't matter? "So, it's true, Sam. Everyone has a price, even you. We're all highly principled until the stakes are so high we give in to temptation."

Sam just looked away.

Sick to my stomach, I ran to the ladies' room and locked myself in a stall, but the feeling passed. So much for artificial intelligence, the technology whose promise I had believed in. Downside risk didn't begin to describe its potential for evil. I would have flushed AI if I could have.

■ ■ ■

On the way home, I stopped at my favorite liquor store to purchase a bottle of Cabernet. I was thinking of drinking the whole thing myself, upset stomach be damned, but given my underwhelming capacity for alcohol, the emergency room seemed an even more depressing place to spend the night than my apartment. Perhaps I'd invite Mary Jo in to share the bottle with me.

A half hour later, Mary Jo was at my door in her white parka. She fanned her face and removed her jacket. "Time to put this away till next winter." I couldn't imagine her without it. She reminded me of Marvel superheroes, each of whom was able to save the day in a unique outfit.

Mary Jo was curious about what was happening with Carlos since I'd last seen her. I poured each of us a generous glass of wine, filling her in on the events of our visit to Cat Rock Park. "We never got past the parking lot before he came at us like a lunatic."

"He is a lunatic, Sylvie, but scarier. I hope he's in jail."

"My ex-husband bailed him out."

"But he's a criminal."

"I know. Carlos claimed it was an accident. I know it sounds crazy. I'm not going to bore you with that long story." Mary Jo was taking one sip of wine to each of my gulps.

She pointed to my empty glass. "You might want to slow down, hon, or you'll find yourself sleeping under the coffee table." She stood up and carried her glass to the kitchen. "Have to get my chicken in the oven."

"Don't worry. I'll be fine, just a lot going on in my life right now."

Mary Jo hesitated for a moment at the door. "I wasn't going to mention this, because I assumed that Carlos character had gone back to Florida. It's just that sometimes, when I look out my window at night, I think I see someone who looks like him down the block near your house. Probably my overactive imagination since everyone looks the same in winter coats."

My stomach cramped. "Thanks for letting me know. I'll be on the lookout, although I don't think he'd risk loitering near my house with a court date coming up."

CHAPTER 36

I hadn't called Rip because I didn't know what to say. Not only was he was leaving for New York, he had asked me to marry him without actually asking me. His speech about becoming a rabbi reminded me of the flowcharts I'd learned to draw in my basic programming course: an if/then analysis, followed by more branching if/thens, until the lines showing possibilities overwhelmed the page.

He wouldn't go so far as to ask me to convert, but if he were to ask me, and if I wanted to marry him, then I'd have to convert, but only if he actually became a rabbi. It was dizzying. We hadn't spoken since I left his apartment. Berating him for leaving town without warning had worked. He'd responded to the police investigating the accident that had killed Dinger and broken Eileen's leg.

At the end of the week, he called to say goodbye and offer some of his books before he closed up the cartons. I agreed to stop over before he left, although I already knew I wouldn't take home his books or any other reminders of him. Too painful. On impulse, I stopped at a bakery and bought a loaf of fresh challah. It seemed like the kind of thing you would bring a rabbi.

I was shocked when I saw his apartment, although it's always a jolt to see a space bereft of its furnishings and household accessories. Everything soft was gone: Rip's reading chair, his old rugs, and the jacket and running pants that were perpetually draped over one or another of his kitchen chairs. The apartment had lost its identity, and in that moment, I felt as empty as his space.

The loaf of challah seemed ridiculous when there was no place to eat it, but he smiled when he saw it and tore off a piece for each of us. Its fragrance filled my nostrils, although I had little appetite.

"Someday in the future, Sylvie, there will be robots much smarter than the ones that use your company's software and roll around warehouses picking up boxes. Maybe we'll each have a personal robot to perfectly complement our lives. We'll have a companion programmed to do everything that pleases us, and it will never find its goals in conflict with our own. Humans are messy. What's worse, or maybe better, people change. I've changed." He tossed the challah on one of his cartons.

I tried without success to hold back my tears. Rip held me, his cheek warm against my hair. I could have stayed there forever. If he had asked me to convert to the church of green aliens, I'd have done it, but he didn't. He released me, his eyes as wet as mine. Somehow, I managed to wish him good luck and get myself out the door. When I climbed into my car, I covered my face with my hands and sobbed.

■ ■ ■

As much as I hated to cloud Eileen's day with my mournfulness, I craved her presence, even if it was only as a disembodied voice from Florida. Just hearing her say hello was a comfort. I told her about Rip's departure.

"I'm so sorry, Syl. I have to confess, I didn't think you guys were that serious."

"It's weird how subjective our sense of time is. It seems to zoom by or crawl, even though we know it moves at an unalterable pace. What could be more impassive than the face of a clock? Yet Carlos's wild drive through the Cat Rock parking lot made everything in my life speed up. It precipitated Rip's trip to New York to apply for rabbinic studies and his declaration that he wanted to marry me, even though he couldn't. The thought of losing him made me realize how much I want to keep him, even though I can't."

"A good massage would help you let go of some of that emotion. You're spinning like a top."

"Unfortunately, my massage therapist has left the state. Maybe I'll climb into a wine bottle instead."

"Much as I appreciate your loyalty, there are other massage therapists I can recommend."

I couldn't imagine a massage would make me feel any better, but Eileen was insistent, so I called her friend, Caitlin, the next day. Eileen must have given her a heads-up because Caitlin said she'd had a cancellation and could take me immediately.

Her massage practice was in Newtonville, not far from my apartment. I rang the bell at her stately blue Victorian and was welcomed into a high-ceilinged front hall. Caitlin, a tall, muscular woman with meaty hands that suited her choice of profession, directed me to a small room off her kitchen, probably a maid's quarters long ago.

I apologized for the urgency. "Eileen's idea, not mine."

She assured me it wasn't a problem.

Once I was on the massage table, trying to relax while listening to spa music, Caitlin remarked on my tight neck and back. "You're one big knot. I don't know if an hour will be enough."

It was. I relaxed so much I began to cry. I was embarrassed and apologized, remembering how my mother had cried when Eileen gave her a massage in Miami. But my mother had a good excuse. She'd been dying of cancer. I'd be living with my woes.

■ ■ ■

The evening was mild for early spring, the air warm enough to carry the scent of thawed soil. I breathed it in and felt the tiniest hint of optimism like the shoots of crocuses barely visible outside my house. My kitchen was a mess. I hadn't had enough drive to clean up my breakfast dishes for two days nor the dinner dishes from the night before. The counter was covered with Cheerios from a distracted pour.

Cleaning would be therapeutic. *This is called pulling yourself together.* When the dishwasher was loaded and all the scraps and crumbs deposited in the sink disposal, I ran the water and turned on the motor.

Something was wrong, a sharp pain in my back. What had Caitlin . . . ? So cold. I couldn't turn. Carlos was behind me pushing and turning a knife in my flesh, his voice guttural in my ear.

"This is what back stabbers get."

I couldn't stop screaming and heard banging on my door. Then the pain came again, agonizing pain. Screaming, banging, falling, silence.

CHAPTER 37

Where am I? I tried to sit up but couldn't. I could see now. This was a hospital room, but why was a policeman at the door? This was a dream, a scene from a TV program. A young man in scrubs smiled and said, "Ah, there you are, finally."

"Here I am, yes, but why?"

"Because you had a good surgeon. In addition to a stab wound, you had mild brain trauma. You've been in a medically induced coma for two weeks."

Brain trauma. I reached up and felt the bandage on my head. Two weeks. *Fucking Carlos!* I tried to sit up, but the nurse restrained me. He seemed bigger and stronger than the policeman peeking in at me from the door. The room seemed to grow darker and darker until it disappeared.

The next time I woke up, Mary Jo Carter was sitting at my bedside. Outside the window was nothing but darkness. "Sylvie, nice to see you with your eyes open." She patted my hand. "How are you feeling? You scared the hell out of me."

"Mary Jo, you were there? The banging?"

"I knew it wasn't my imagination that I saw that maniac, Carlos, lurking in the neighborhood. I was dog sitting my niece's beagle and walked him down your way that evening, close enough to hear you screaming. You got a set of lungs on you, sister. That beagle started howling and pulled his leash right out of my hand. Took off after Carlos when he came out the side of your unit. Bit him on the leg. Poor dog got stabbed, but he's okay. Someone called 911. Thank God the ambulance came right away, because I was freaking out. They got in through the sliding doors on the side where Carlos got in.

"We found you lying on the floor bleeding," Mary Jo continued after a brief pause. "You must have fallen backward and hit your head on the kitchen table—scared the shit out of me. The police followed Carlos's blood trail, but it disappeared. He probably cut through to Valley Lane and got into his car. Don't worry, they'll find him."

If I could have gotten out of bed, I would have hugged Mary Jo. I clutched her hand. "If it hadn't been for you, I'd be dead! Where do I start? 'Thank you' is inadequate."

"Hey, you're okay now, and that's payback enough. Try not to dwell on it. What's important is that you're going to be fine." A doctor appeared in my doorway, chart in hand. He was so tall I thought he'd need to duck to come through.

Mary Jo gathered her things to leave. I grabbed her hand again. "Wait, I don't have my cell phone or laptop. Can you call Eileen for me and notify my office that I'll be out indefinitely?" I told her my cell phone password.

"Eileen and I have already spoken. She would have flown in, but no one was allowed to visit till now. As for your office, they probably read about you in the papers. I'll try to get into your apartment if it's not still cordoned off like a crime scene."

■ ■ ■

The doctor informed me that the knife wound had lacerated my kidney. "When you lost consciousness, you fell on the corner of a table. Lucky for you, your traumatic brain injury is mild. You need to be patient, though. You're not going to just bounce back from this."

"When can I go home?"

"Everyone asks that. Let's see how you progress from here, not only with healing, but rehab. The neurologist will also need to weigh in. Don't worry. Now that you're awake, you'll get all the information you need, but you should be thinking months before you go home, not days or weeks."

Months! I didn't want to sleep, but exhaustion carried me away.

I soon learned that my stab wound was the least of my problems; healing was proceeding well. What was most disheartening was discovering that the symptoms of even a mild brain injury would be with me for an indeterminate length of time.

Headaches, sensitivity to light, dizziness, nausea, depression, and even cognitive impairment were on the long list of possible symptoms that sent me into a tailspin. Was my depression situational, or was it a symptom of my condition? I was already experiencing headaches and light sensitivity. I feared my tears alone were enough to cause dehydration, and I was grateful for the visit from a hospital psychiatrist.

Time moved fast working in a technology business, in part because the digital world was always changing. Competitors cranked up the pressure, so there was no standing still, only getting ahead or falling behind. When it came to healing, time moved slowly, requiring patience and a whole new frame of reference. Instead of being happy because I had succeeded in my career, I needed to be happy I hadn't died, a considerably lower bar.

A tall, rangy police detective, Sergeant Henry, came to see me and provided an update on their search for Carlos. It was a short visit, since the police couldn't find him. When I moved to rehab, I would no longer have a guard outside my door, but security at the Gale Institute was tight, and only those on my list of permitted visitors would be able to see me. No one would be allowed upstairs. A nurse would bring me to a secure location for my visits.

■ ■ ■

Eileen and Miguel flew in to see me at the rehab institute. They tried hugging me at the same time, which made me laugh and cry.

"If I knew you both were coming, I would have put on makeup and a cool outfit."

"I had to bring Miguel because he keeps threatening to go after Carlos with a shotgun. I need to keep an eye on him."

"Not true." Miguel was indignant. "No one knows where Carlos has gone. Besides, Sylvie, you're beautiful without any makeup . . ."

"And without any clothes?" I asked.

He blushed.

"That's okay, Miguel. Around here you only get complimented on how hard you're working, not how good you look, so thank you for that." I was so happy to spend time with them I hated to deliver bad news. "This is painful to say, but I'm not going to be able to make the wedding. It's already April, and though it's possible I'll be out of here by June, I've been told not to make travel plans that soon."

Eileen and Miguel looked at each other. Miguel spoke first. "We know. We've educated ourselves on traumatic brain injury. That's why we've moved the wedding back to September 7."

I began shaking my head. Eileen put her hand on mine. "I'm not getting married without my matron of honor standing beside me. I know you. You're deadline driven. You'll be ready by then or we'll send a private medical jet to get you. Oh, yes, and a handsome doctor for company."

In truth no one knew for sure how long my recovery would take. I wondered if Eileen and Miguel knew five months was pushing it, at least for a full recovery. No point in saying that now. I wasn't going to let them delay the wedding a second time.

"Would you like me to get in touch with Rip for you? Does he even know what happened?"

"Thanks, but I could do that myself now. I have my phone and laptop. I haven't called him because I don't want him to turn up here out of guilt or a sense of obligation. I know he'd come in a heartbeat, but it's best to let it alone for now. He's busy with school anyway."

Eileen crossed her arms and scowled but said nothing.

CHAPTER 38

I wondered if Rip remembered my evaluation at BodySculpt when I told him I felt like "thirty-four going on ninety." Given my recent experience with the precariousness of life, I won't ever make that joke again. Stressed or relaxed, exhausted or rested, being alive was a gift. Death could come at any moment, even standing at your kitchen sink. I understood how "life is precious" got to be a cliché. It's used excessively because it's apt.

The only names on my list of acceptable visitors were Mary Jo, her husband Leon, Eileen, and Miguel. I didn't want to see anyone from work. AI*future* seemed like a boat cut loose from the shore, receding into the distance and disappearing from view. I wasn't having memory problems. I just couldn't bring myself to care about the fate of one technology company up against the enormity of what had happened and was continuing to happen to me.

I worked my ass off in rehab, and though I hated puns, I had to say that all of me, ass included, was thinner. At the end of July, I was ready for discharge. My plan was to hire someone to help at home with chores I wasn't quite up to yet, but Eileen and Miguel were having none of that, at least initially. They flew into town and took over, setting themselves up in my guest bedroom.

My house seemed like a palace after rehab. It was spotless, none of my doing, with the kitchen cabinets stocked. The refrigerator appeared to belong to some other very domestic person with higher standards than mine. The salad drawer had no ancient bits of celery stuck to the bottom nor pesky pieces of escaped onion peel. There were, however, fancy cheeses and dips. A bottle of Prosecco sat beside caviar and crème fraîche.

Mary Jo and Leon came by at 5:00. She had come to visit me four times at the Gale Institute, and I was still overwhelmed with gratitude whenever I saw her. I gave her a bear hug, hard to do, given her greater height and bulk.

"Look at you," she said, pulling away. "You're a mere wisp of a thing. We'll have to do something about that, starting tonight."

Mary Jo had met Eileen when we went to court. She'd talked with her several times by phone while I'd been in the hospital and rehab, but she'd only met Miguel in person yesterday when she delivered the Prosecco. A couple of glasses made us all into the best of friends. No one mentioned my new alarm system or the security guard posted outside the house. I went to bed that night feeling grateful and lucky. If I didn't feel 100 percent safe, I knew it was a groundless fear, at least while I was in my home with friends under the same roof.

* * *

Over the following days, I waded through the pile of mail that had been held for me at the post office. When I went into rehab, I authorized Mary Jo to bring some of it to me at the Gale Institute. I wanted to handle only what urgently required my signature. Everything else went into a carton in the corner of my living room.

The only legal matter I really cared about was stepping down from the position I shared with Miguel as trustee for Luis's estate. I would need a Florida lawyer for that, but I didn't think the issue could be settled while Carlos was still at large. Luis would not have been pleased, but I was done pleasing people, especially posthumously.

Carlos still haunted me in my nightmares but less frequently. Miguel tried to reassure me. "I know my brother. He's too smart to stay in the area now that he's wanted for attempted murder. He's probably in Mexico by now."

"Geez," said Eileen. "Someone ought to warn the women of Mexico."

Eileen and Miguel had been saints, making sure I could recuperate in peace with no demands on my time and no need to leave my house. I wanted them to return to Miami. In spite of Eileen's casual attitude about leaving the details of her ceremony and reception in the hands of her wedding planner, I knew she wanted to be involved, so I insisted I was fine and no longer worried about Carlos. He'd be caught sooner or later, probably far away from Boston and its suburbs.

I'm not sure if it was my salesmanship that worked or just Eileen's desire to get back to Florida, but she and Miguel prepared to board their flight two days later.

"Who's going to eat all that food you packed into my refrigerator?"

"Sorry," Miguel said, gesturing helplessly. "No way to get it through airport security."

The first day after they left, I tried to tell myself I was enjoying the peacefulness of my empty apartment, but, in truth, I missed them. I had a home health aide who came for a few hours a day, although I was sure I could manage without her. Eileen and Miguel refused to hear of that, so cleaning help and support services continued. I had committed to being at their wedding, so I was diligent about my physical and occupational therapy.

Despite the months I'd spent recovering from Carlos's attack, during which time AI*future*'s merger activities had seemed remote, I'd become curious. Like a book you stop reading but then wonder how it ended, *AIfuture* and its fate drew me back to the internet. I had a yen to find out how the acquisition had turned out for the people I knew.

Between Google and online technology publications, I was able to put together most of the missing elements. UndauntedAI took the bait, and its acquisition of AI*future* was almost complete. Richard would no longer be CEO, but given that he wasn't in jail, I assumed he'd land on his feet at some other company. That was how it always worked. Sam was taking over as UndauntedAI's chief sales executive, working out of their Westborough headquarters.

It would have made Sam's wife, Susan, happy to have him back in the United States, but they were divorced, so too little too late. I looked up the management team at Distributon and found that Kate was no longer there. I wondered if her drinking had anything to do with her departure, but, of course, that kind of information existed only on the rumor mill.

I was delighted to find an invitation in my carton of mail asking me to attend an engagement party for Rona and Fannette. The date was long past, but Rona's email address was at the bottom. I sent a note of congratulations and apologized for my late response. I told her I'd love to treat them to lunch as soon as I was fully recovered.

When Rona wrote back, she asked if I'd heard that Warren and Maya Malik had separated. According to Rona, Maya was disappointed and disillusioned. Warren had been so absorbed in his new business venture he'd ignored Maya's needs as well as their infant's. Maya had been weakened by the difficult birth, and the baby was a preemie.

I remembered Maya at the AI*future* Christmas party—youthful, pregnant, and radiant. She'd looked adoringly at Warren, declaring he'd make a wonderful father. Poor disillusioned Maya. Poor baby.

■ ■ ■

Deciding what to do with the rest of my life hadn't been top of mind while I was fighting my way back from my injuries. Regaining my health was my single-minded objective. The decision could no longer be delayed. What my goals were was a question I should have asked myself a long time ago. I took heart from what Rip had done. He'd had the courage to face the mistakes of the past and choose a different direction, even though that direction didn't necessarily include me. My original goal years before had been to please Ashton. After the divorce my goal had been to piss off Ashton. I made a pact with myself to purge him from my thoughts. I would start by purging him from my identity. Time to go back to my maiden name.

During the time I was in rehab, several recruiters had left me voicemails about job opportunities. I went back and paid closer attention. Every message was about a sales executive position at an AI company. As much as I loved selling, I couldn't see myself going back to it. I'd seen the dark side of AI and been burned by it. There must be a way to advocate for the benign uses and obstruct the harmful ones.

I googled business ethics and AI, and an entire new world opened for me. I found articles dealing with the risks and complexities AI created for software developers, companies buying the technology, and end users. I discovered AI was part of the curriculum at institutions that offered courses online and in-person, both undergraduate and graduate. There were even certificates and degrees related to the broad scope of business ethics, some with a focus on media companies and fast-changing technology.

There were opportunities for me in this field, perhaps in one of the consulting firms that advised companies on how to organize and manage their businesses so ethics became integral to each discipline. I was excited by articles I found in business publications such as *Forbes*, *Fortune*, and the *Harvard Business Review*. Not till I closed the lid of my laptop to make dinner did I remember that there was still a reason I was afraid to leave my house.

When I looked out the window, the security guard was there as always. It wasn't the same guard, since there had been a succession of them, each looking as though they'd been football players in a past life, even the women. I realized that whether they appeared ready for hand-to-hand fighting or not, a gun was the great equalizer. I couldn't hide here forever, though. I wanted my life back.

I texted Miguel to let him know I felt secure with my new alarm system. It had so many sophisticated features, I could call in the National Guard if necessary. I thanked him for his generosity and let him know I would no longer require the company's services. For one thing, I was getting a guard dog.

I don't know where that idea came from, but the more I thought about a dog, the more I thought about Dinger. He was so sweet, the antithesis of a guard dog, but I hadn't been specific in my text to Miguel, leaving him, I hoped, to imagine my acquiring a pit bull or Rottweiler.

Remembering Dinger made me wish I had a dog, although I wondered if it was really Rip I missed. A dog would be only a proxy but a good one. I looked online for goldens and was disappointed to see how few there were until I realized most of the rescues were mixed breed. Getting a dog was a crazy, impulsive idea anyway, since I didn't know when or where I'd be working, but I had a hard time convincing myself to give up on it.

I spent the rest of the week continuing my research on AI ethics, sending emails to consulting firms, professors, and the authors of articles. I couldn't remember being excited about embarking on a new career path since . . . well, forever. I sent off applications to several programs and settled in to wait.

CHAPTER 39

As the weeks went by, the vigorous green buds poking up through the soil grew into mature plants and flowers, turning the landscape into the color of renewal. The sun's spring warmth that drew me outside overplayed its hand in July and August, chasing me into my air-conditioned living room.

Looking forward to the September 7 wedding had helped motivate me in my exercise program. I might not have been in optimal shape, but I had my neurologist's permission to travel to Florida. "Not a good time to take up surfing," he admonished. Once I had his okay, I took my mauve gown in for tailoring, Ubering both ways. I was thinner than when Eileen picked it out for me, but the seamstress assured me that taking it in would be quick. She was glad she didn't need to let it out.

Packing for Miami posed challenges. Not only had I lost weight during my hospital stay and rehab, I hadn't been shopping for clothes since the attack. Carlos was probably far away, a fugitive from the law, but not knowing where he'd gone kept me hypervigilant. Whenever I saw someone who resembled him, I shuddered. It was an involuntary reaction, I knew, but it diminished my desire to browse the stores.

A cold snap arrived with September and heightened my sense of anticipation, which stayed with me until my Uber pulled up at the crowded terminal. Suddenly nervous, I scurried through the airport, cleared security, and waited close by the gate to board. Once we were above the clouds—and Carlos—I closed my eyes and slept.

■ ■ ■

My first morning in Miami, I awoke refreshed, feeling as though I'd left most of the terrifying events of my life back in Boston. By the time I joined Eileen on the patio, where she pressed a mimosa into my hands, I was fully unwound.

I could see her frowning as she checked out my bathing suit, swimming on me without benefit of water. "Seriously thin, Syl. Look, I know you're still not 100 percent. When Miguel and I were with you in Needham, I made a joke out of how deadline-driven you were. I was hoping that would motivate you to be ready in time for the wedding. I hope you don't think I really meant to push you."

"Don't feel guilty. I wanted to be here. If anyone got pushed, it was my doctor. I think he said yes so I'd stop harassing him." The sun penetrating my bones and the scent of salt water were as therapeutic as a lavender oil massage. The sound of ocean waves approaching and retreating while the royal palms above us waved in the breeze created a rhythm more conducive to relaxing than anything I'd heard in a spa. It didn't take long for me to doze off.

Eileen awakened me an hour later. "Tan is beautiful; burnt like toast is not. C'mon, we have stuff to do."

What could we have to do, I wondered, *if the wedding planner had handled everything*. "Hey." I grabbed her arm. "There is no wedding planner, is there. You made that up so I wouldn't fuss about you and Miguel taking care of me."

Eileen's mouth turned down in mock sadness. "My bad. Actually, there was, and she did a bunch of stuff for us, but I let her go. She liked to talk politics, and we didn't agree on anything."

"Did she want you to walk down the aisle with a MAGA hat?" I hoped Eileen was serious that the woman accomplished "a bunch of stuff," because I knew nothing about planning a wedding. My mother had run the show when I'd married Ashton.

We visited the church where the ceremony would be held with its stunning murals, carvings, and windows. A trip to the florist felt like a year's worth of aromatherapy. The owner had created a sample centerpiece for the tables using Eileen's requests for her bridal bouquet as a template. He also showed us the boutonnieres he would provide for Miguel and his best man.

There would be no bridal party, since Eileen knew so few people in Miami, and Miguel had so many friends, he didn't know which ones to choose. I was glad he had one particularly close friend, Enrique Sanchez, because under normal circumstances, Carlos would have been at Miguel's side as best man. Enrique, deeply tanned and well-built, was delighted to be asked, a fact he reaffirmed with a sweet smile when I was introduced. I wondered if Carlos even knew about the wedding—probably not if he had indeed crossed the border into Mexico.

When Eileen went for her final fitting, I used the time to consult a lawyer, a specialist in trusts, about transferring my trusteeship to Miguel. He agreed to obtain the will and other necessary estate documents so he could begin the process of changing control over Carlos's inheritance.

When I walked out the door of his building, despite the humidity weighting the air, I felt lighter and freer. I thought about Eileen's holistic potions, some of which were guaranteed to remove toxins from your system. Who knew seeing a lawyer could be just as effective?

* * *

When there was only one day till the wedding, Eileen went from calm and efficient to scatter-brained and anxious. I stopped her from taking a sleeping pill the night before and confiscated the pills.

"Don't you dare. I don't want to be searching for you in the middle of the night while you're sleepwalking the length of Miami Beach. A couple of these and you'll be a zombie tomorrow."

"What if they don't like me—all the Cubans who are coming—I mean, I'm not what anyone would pick for Miguel."

"Are you nuts? Only Miguel gets to pick for Miguel, and his judgment is superb."

Miguel stood by the open front door, letting in the damp breeze and grinning at us. "We invited zombies? We can have 'Thriller' as our wedding song."

He embraced Eileen, who tried to push him away. "You're not supposed to see me till the wedding."

"But I know what you look like."

"Still, it's bad luck."

"Okay, okay, I'm going." He kissed her before she could stop him and headed for the door humming "Thriller."

"Eileen, that bad-luck thing goes back to when marriages were arranged. The family had to be sure the groom wouldn't bail when he saw the girl he was getting shackled to. It's a superstition." Despite her grumbling, I could see she was calmer after Miguel's quick visit.

■ ■ ■

The morning of the wedding was cooler and less humid, the weather gods smiling down on the deserving bride. We took leisurely baths and had our hair and nails done. I would have enjoyed a walk, but Eileen wanted to rehearse the vows she had written.

I dressed in the late afternoon, adding pink South Sea

pearls left to me by Margaret. I hadn't wanted her jewels, but she was so fond of Eileen she would have been pleased to see how beautiful they looked with my mauve gown.

Eileen could have been a model stepping out of *Brides* magazine, only twice as beautiful.

"I hope Miguel knows how lucky he is."

Eileen squirmed. I thought it was the compliment that made her uncomfortable. "Syl, I have to tell you something before we leave, but please don't be mad at me. I invited Rip. I found his cell number in your phone. You really should change your password from your birthday."

"Eileen! I can't believe . . . he won't come anyway. He's in New York."

"He's here. C'mon, our ride is outside. We have to go."

The white limousine that arrived to take us to the church had an elegant white satin interior. I hadn't traveled in such luxury for my own wedding. The chauffeur helped me out first so I could lift Eileen's train. The church was filled with flowers, including bouquets at the end of every pew. The scent of roses from Luis's beloved garden mingled with that of tropical blooms. Guests were already assembled in the pews, although I didn't see Rip.

Miguel and Eileen had opted for a rite of marriage ceremony instead of a full mass. I figured that was a good thing. I could just imagine Eileen joking with the priest when she was handed the wine during communion. I doubted he'd be amused if she toasted "L'chaim."

When the music began, I walked slowly down the aisle as I'd been advised. I was buoyed by the admiring glances that greeted me and turned to smile when I reached the alter and took my position.

As the notes of the "Wedding March" rang out, Eileen floated toward me on the arm of Alberto Aceba, Luis's friend and family lawyer. He was just as I remembered him from the reading of

Luis's will. Eileen towered over him, but he wore a wide smile and a very white tuxedo. Eileen moved into her position beside me, and after I adjusted her train, I took her bouquet.

Our eyes turned to the sacristy at the side of the altar, anticipating Miguel's and Enrique's entrance. Instead, we heard raised voices. Eileen stiffened beside me. Miguel was upset with someone, but it couldn't be Enrique. The next voice, loud and agitated, belonged to Carlos. I froze.

"Look at you, pretending to be some kind of white knight while I'm the black sheep of the family. You helped that viper, Sylvie, convince Luis I was a rapist. You greedy bastard—"

Eileen's face blanched. Alarmed guests in the front pews turned to tell others what was happening. The hum in the church grew louder.

Just as the priest started for the sacristy, the sound of a gunshot stopped him. Guests rushed for the aisles. Someone must have called 911, because the swelling sound of sirens quickly followed. I wanted to help Eileen, who was trying to get to Miguel, dragging and twisting her train. Instead, I passed out.

When I regained consciousness, Rip was kneeling beside me in the empty church, his face bruised, his tuxedo and shirt bloody. He was holding a wet paper towel on my forehead. An equally disheveled Miguel had his arm around Eileen as they stood off to the side conferring with the priest.

I sat up, alarmed. "Where's Carlos?"

Rip supported me as I struggled to stand. "You're safe. The police have him."

Eileen rushed over to me, clutching tissues in one hand. "Are you sure you're strong enough to be standing?"

"I'm fine now. Really."

"Do you think you can stand beside me? The priest is going to marry us."

"Now?" I looked out at the empty pews. They were still

adorned with flowers, although some lay in the aisle, dislodged by fleeing guests. "Where's Enrique?"

"He's in the hospital with a flesh wound, but he's okay. Carlos shot him before Rip could wrest the gun away. That's where we're headed next, so I need you to come over to the altar while the priest performs the ceremony."

Eileen was babbling, which made it hard to assimilate the abbreviated information she was giving me, but there was no denying her. She grabbed Rip's arm and instructed him to stand beside Miguel.

Miguel responded to Rip's quizzical expression. "I know this is unusual, but I appreciate your participating in our ceremony. Enrique would be happy to have you take his place."

We arranged ourselves at the altar before the priest. The ring was still in Enrique's pocket, so Miguel improvised, pulling a flower from Eileen's bouquet and twisting the stem into a botanical version. Their vows made me cry, and if the tears were only because of my emotional state, it didn't matter, because when the two embraced and kissed, I felt pure joy.

No one was there to throw rice, but despite everything that had gone wrong, they'd pulled it off.

As we left the church, Miguel said, "I thought that bit about 'does anyone know a reason why these two shouldn't wed?' was a formality."

Eileen turned to him. "I told you it was bad luck to see the bride before the wedding."

■ ■ ■

"You look like a dream, Sylvie. God, I've missed you." In the marble-floored hotel lobby, Rip sat close to me on a rattan loveseat tucked away beside a potted palm.

"I wish I could repay the compliment." I ran a finger down Rip's bruised cheek, but even my gentle touch made him wince. "What happened in the sacristy? Why were you there?"

"I arrived late at the hotel, which made me late to the church. I had to park my rental car on the edge of the lot. That was when I saw that maniac who killed Dinger going in the side door of the building. I followed him, or rather I followed the sound of fighting. He was going berserk, yelling at Miguel. Enrique was trying to shield him, but that lunatic pulled a gun, and instead of shooting Miguel, he hit Enrique. I jumped Carlos, catching him by surprise, and knocked the gun away. Unfortunately, Carlos got off a few good punches, but I beat him up pretty good and tied his hands with my bow tie. Glad I didn't wear a clip-on." He grinned. "I don't know if I could have kept him pinned down, but he heard the sirens and just lay there, spent or resigned or I don't know what. Miguel and I tried to help Enrique. Thank God the police arrived when they did."

The hand I'd been holding over my mouth dropped to my lap. "You could have been killed!"

"I wasn't thinking. I just reacted. And what about you? Why didn't you tell me Carlos tried to kill you? Why didn't you let me know you spent weeks in the hospital and months in rehab? I didn't know any of that until Eileen called me about the wedding."

I apologized and stumbled around trying to explain that because of how we left things, I didn't want him to feel obligated, plus he was in school. Rip exhaled in frustration.

I hadn't sorted out my reasons for keeping him in the dark, so it was no surprise I wasn't credible. If Rip were no more than a friend, I would have told him, although I realized that made no sense. I should have let him decide for himself whether to come. Maybe I'd been punishing him for going to New York. "I wasn't sure you'd want to see me again."

He shook his head. "How could you think that?" He pulled me toward him and held me. I had no answer, so I just stayed in his arms, grateful to have him for as long as it lasted.

* * *

Before Eileen and Miguel left for their honeymoon, they begged me to stay in Miami. Despite the luxurious accommodations and tropical sunshine, I wanted to go home. For the first time in perhaps forever, I was looking forward to embarking on a new journey. Not my mother's plan for my life, not Ashton's, but my own. If it weren't for the pain of seeing Rip and losing him again, I would have been positively cheerful.

Despite Rip's original arrangements, he couldn't return immediately to New York. The local papers called him a hero and pursued him until he agreed to do some interviews. When he finally departed, I left for Boston, wondering if I'd ever see him again.

CHAPTER 40

I named her Rapha because it means "healer" in Hebrew. She was a golden retriever puppy, a rescue from an unwanted litter; not a purebred, of course, but I figured I didn't have a pedigree either. She'd been giving me plenty of exercise, which had allowed me to see more of Mary Jo Carter and meet some of my other neighbors. The walks were as good for me physically as they were for my psyche.

Rapha and I went to a puppy training class at a local pet store. Practice at home was obligatory. I circled the property at Old Mill often, reinforcing Rapha's lessons on leash walking without pulling. I was afraid when she got to be Dinger's size, any squirrel crossing her path would lead both of us on a high-speed chase. I was careful not to wrap her leash around any part of my body or clothing.

Having a puppy seemed like a lot more work than having a baby, pure speculation of course, although Rapha proved a fast learner and so worth the effort of training her. The only real surprise was finding out how fast puppies grew. Actually, the surprise was how fast Rapha grew. According to the vet, she was off the charts and becoming a woman to contend with. He called her an amazon. I wondered if there were a Saint Bernard in her lineage.

As wonderful as Rapha was, she couldn't help me with my nightmares about Carlos. They'd returned after I came home from Miami. I hated the idea that after making so much progress in anticipation of the wedding, I was regressing, but I knew Carlos's attack at the church was responsible for my setback.

■ ■ ■

I searched out a therapist. Dr. McGregor was a tall, angular woman with auburn hair pulled into a bun. She wasn't plain, yet she wore little makeup in our sessions, and she dressed in slacks and pastel sweaters, as though she wanted to keep me from being distracted by her appearance. Her office was in her home. It looked like a den with bookshelves and earth-tone upholstered furniture, an easy place to relax and converse. Only the desk in the corner and a large file cabinet gave the room a more functional look.

Dr. McGregor was remarkably patient and didn't push me, even though I had trouble opening up at first. I stuck to the surface like a water bug. Perhaps it was her probing questions or my own needs that made me go deeper, but once I took the plunge, my words flowed. At the end of each session, she would say, "We're going to have to leave it there," and inevitably, I was disappointed. Can't say I blamed her. If she hadn't stopped me, I would have stayed way more than fifty minutes, maybe all day.

I told her I was a people pleaser, a character flaw I needed to overcome.

"Oh, I don't know." She stroked her chin. "Would you want to be the opposite, a woman who pissed off everyone?"

I hated when she asked hard questions, not that the answer was difficult. She was reminding me of the complexities within myself, within all of us, that required sorting out and accommodating. I needed to find a balance.

I wondered if Carlos had ever tried to find a balance. Without stress, he was a charmer, but under pressure, even self-inflicted, he went from anger to rape and from stalking to attempted murder. In my rational brain, I knew his descent was not my fault. How to marshal my emotions was the problem.

When I asked Dr. McGregor if it was wrong for me to feel guilty, she said, "You're not responsible for Carlos's decompensating. I can't diagnose him from a distance, but he has serious problems that should have been addressed years ago. Regardless, only he is responsible for his choices."

Eventually we got to Rip, and once I started, I couldn't stop talking about him. She asked me what I knew about Judaism. "I know I'm not going to convert."

"Not what I asked you."

Of course, I knew little, except what I'd observed at the one service I'd attended and what I'd learned from Rip. I might not ever see Rip again, but if I did, maybe I'd understand him better if I knew why he felt drawn back into his faith.

Rabbi Jacobson remembered me when I called him. I explained I had been on Google looking for a good introduction to Judaism, but there were too many. He laughed. "Too many Jewish opinions on one subject. What a surprise." He suggested a good overview and urged me to call him with questions. "Don't worry. I won't recruit you."

■ ■ ■

A month later, I was curled up on my couch in a bathrobe and socks, the ones they gave me at the hospital with grippers on the bottom so I wouldn't slip. I was halfway through the book recommended by Rabbi Jacobson. Rapha lay at my feet, stretched out like a shag rug, a honey-colored mass of fur. Perhaps I needed a bigger apartment. The rain that had been falling off and on all day was now accompanied by a crescendo of thunder and lightning.

The sound and light show distracted me from my book. I began to count the seconds between lightning bolts and thunderclaps to divide by five and calculate when the storm would be directly overhead, an old habit I'd picked up in eighth grade science.

Before the next bolt arrived, I heard my doorbell ring. The FedEx deliveryman often showed up in the late afternoon and rang as a courtesy to alert me to my package. *Poor guy must be drenched by now.* Rain pelted the windows. He rang again. *Ugh, must be something I have to sign for, something from the lawyer.*

I padded over to the door, squinted through the peep hole, and flung the door open. Rip was soaked, but I didn't give that a thought before falling into his arms. We held on to each other and stumbled inside.

"Aren't you going to ask me why I'm here?"

"No, I don't care."

He took off his jacket and flung it over the back of a kitchen chair, where it continued to drip on the tile floor. He guided me into a chair and pulled one up for himself. "I need to tell you anyway. After the wedding, when I got back to New York, I was haunted by how close I'd come to losing you. I didn't know about Carlos's attack because I was far away, and no one knew how to reach me."

I touched his hand. "I thought you and I were over as a couple. Eileen didn't tell me till right before she walked down the aisle that she had invited you, but I didn't see you in the church. When I heard that gun go off, I thought Carlos had come to kill me. I thought I'd never see you again, and—"

"Sylvie, don't." He took my hands in his. "I'm here. You're fine. I think we stopped talking about our relationship too soon. That's my fault. I'm sorry I left for New York so abruptly. I'm not sure how you feel about the future after everything you've been through. I'm guessing it's changed you. How could it not? Studying to become a rabbi has given me a lot of time for thinking. I've realized I need to be less judgmental, which is what you told me in many ways. I didn't listen."

I touched my fingers to his lips. "Don't. Some of what you said was right."

"I've also come around to believing it's okay for people in love to compromise without feeling like they're selling out. Sort of like figuring out an optimizing algorithm."

I couldn't hold back a groan. "The first compromise, before there's any talk about the future, has to be no more algorithms, no more lines of best fit. Life is too complicated for math."

"Done."

"And I'm going back to school." I told him about the courses I'd enrolled in and my hopes for a new career. "I'll still be involved with AI but in a different way. I may have to travel or even move."

"I don't know how long that will take you, but I have years of school ahead of me too. With artificial intelligence impacting every aspect of our lives, people will need comfort and guidance. What are the implications of AI for religion? One important thing I've just learned has nothing to do with AI. In Reform Judaism, a rabbi can marry someone who's not Jewish. He just has to wait until after he's ordained." Rip looked hopeful.

"Is this another obliquely worded proposal? Are you asking me to wait for you?" I wondered if I'd always be searching for the right balance between selling out and being intransigent. It couldn't be an intellectual exercise, or any humanoid equipped with artificial intelligence could figure it out. Robots couldn't love, only pretend. "I don't know what to say."

Rapha was noisily lapping the puddles beneath Rip's jacket. He knelt and stroked her head. "Rapha, what should she say?" He looked up at me. "She told me you should say 'yes.'"

ACKNOWLEDGMENTS

I'm fortunate in having a supportive husband and family in my work as a writer. Since I've already had a career, I feel lucky to have an opportunity for a second one. Maria Black's weekly writing group has also played a major role in my life as I developed *The Deepfake*. Writing can be a solitary activity, and having advice and support along the way makes all the difference.

In addition to Maria, I'm indebted to the other members of our group: Terry Wise, Molly Boxer, Lydia Littlefield, and Julie McCarthy. All of them have made helpful suggestions, and in some cases, kept me from going down ratholes. My good friend Virginia Spencer, an astute reader, also did me the favor of going through the manuscript, as did my husband, Bruce, and my daughter, Heidi Miller.

I'd like to thank the editors, designers, and staff at She Writes Press, especially Brooke Warner and Shannon Green for their invaluable advice and guidance.

ABOUT THE AUTHOR

Originally from Mount Vernon, New York, Joan Cohen received her BA from Cornell University and her MBA from New York University.

She pursued a career in sales, marketing, and executive-level management at technology companies and after retirement returned to school for an MFA in writing from Vermont College of Fine Arts. She is the author of the novel *Land of Last Chances*, published in 2019.

She has been a Massachusetts resident for many years, first living in Newton, where she raised her family, and later in Wayland. She now resides in Stockbridge, in the Berkshires, with her husband and latest canine addition.

SELECTED TITLES FROM SHE WRITES PRESS

She Writes Press is an independent publishing company founded to serve women writers everywhere. Visit us at www.shewritespress.com.

The Land of Last Chances by Joan Cohen. $16.95, 978-1-63152-600-8. When an unmarried executive discovers she's pregnant and doesn't know which of the two men in her life is the father, she realizes her professional risk management skills don't extend to her personal life. Worse yet, she may carry a rare hereditary gene for early-onset Alzheimer's. Whose needs should prevail—hers or the next generation's?

The Sleeping Lady by Bonnie Monte. $16.95, 978-1-63152-387-8. Rae Sullivan's comfortable existence as a shop owner in a small northern California town is upended when her business partner is murdered in Golden Gate Park. Frustrated with the avenues the police are pursuing, Rae embarks on her own investigation, which eventually leads her to France and puts her marriage—and her life—in jeopardy.

A Marriage in Four Seasons: A Novel by Kathryn K. Abdul-Baki. $16.95, 978-1-63152-427-1. When New York couple Joy and Richard experience a devastating stillbirth, the must navigate the repercussions of their loss—including infidelity, divorce, and an illegitimate child—before finally reconciling.

What's Not True by Valerie Taylor. $16.95, 978-1-64742-157-1. Just as a soon-to-be divorced woman commits to reviving both her career and love life, a conniving woman from her husband's past forces her to protect and defend what is legally and rightfully hers.

Wishful Thinking by Kamy Wicoff. $16.95, 978-1-63152-976-4. A divorced mother of two gets an app on her phone that lets her be in more than one place at the same time, and quickly goes from zero to hero in her personal and professional life—but at what cost?

Clear Lake by Nan Fink Gefen. $16.95, 978-1-93831-440-7. When psychotherapist Rebecca Lev's father dies under suspicious circumstances, she becomes obsessed with discovering what happened to him.